D0015460

The Swallows' Flight

Also by Hilary McKay

Saffy's Angel
Indigo's Star
Permanent Rose
Caddy Ever After
Forever Rose
Caddy's World
Wishing for Tomorrow
Binny for Short
Binny in Secret
Binny Bewitched
The Skylarks' War
Straw into Gold
The Time of Green Magic

McKay, Hilary,
The swallows' flight /
[2021]

cu   11/09/21

The Swallows' Flight

HILARY MCKAY

Margaret K. McElderry Books
New York London Toronto Sydney New Delhi

MARGARET K. McELDERRY BOOKS
An imprint of Simon & Schuster Children's Publishing Division
1230 Avenue of the Americas, New York, New York 10020
This book is a work of fiction. Any references to historical events, real people, or real places are used fictitiously. Other names, characters, places, and events are products of the author's imagination, and any resemblance to actual events or places or persons, living or dead, is entirely coincidental.
Text © 2021 by Hilary McKay
Originally published in Great Britain in 2021 by Pan Macmillan
Jacket illustration © 2021 by Dung Ho Hanh
Jacket design by Karyn Lee © 2021 by Simon & Schuster, Inc.
All rights reserved, including the right of reproduction in whole or in part in any form.
MARGARET K. McELDERRY BOOKS is a trademark of Simon & Schuster, Inc.
For information about special discounts for bulk purchases, please contact Simon & Schuster Special Sales at 1-866-506-1949 or business@simonandschuster.com.
The Simon & Schuster Speakers Bureau can bring authors to your live event. For more information or to book an event, contact the Simon & Schuster Speakers Bureau at 1-866-248-3049 or visit our website at www.simonspeakers.com.
Interior design by Karyn Lee
The text for this book was set in Celeste OT.
Manufactured in the United States of America 0921 FFG
First U.S. edition 2021
2 4 6 8 10 9 7 5 3 1
Library of Congress Cataloging-in-Publication Data
Names: McKay, Hilary, author. Title: The swallows' flight / Hilary McKay.
Description: New York : Margaret K. McElderry Books, [2021] | "Originally published in Great Britain in 2021 by Pan Macmillan." | Audience: Ages 8–12. | Audience: Grades 4–6. | Summary: The lives of two sets of best friends, Kate and Ruby in England and Erik and Hans in Germany, as well as a stray dog in London are brought together in unexpected ways during World War II. Identifiers: LCCN 2021013549 (print) | LCCN 2021013550 (ebook) | ISBN 9781665900911 (hardcover) | ISBN 9781665900935 (ebook) Subjects: CYAC: Friendship—Fiction. | Family life—Fiction. | Dogs—Fiction. | World War, 1939–1945—Fiction. | Great Britain History—George VI, 1936–1952—Fiction. | Germany—History—1933–1945—Fiction. Classification: LCC PZ7.M4786574 Sw 2021 (print) | LCC PZ7.M4786574 (ebook) | DDC [Fic]—dc23. LC record available at https://lccn.loc.gov/2021013549. LC ebook record available at https://lccn.loc.gov/2021013550

For Venetia Gosling, who started this story with
a memory from her own family,
and for Molly Ker Hawn, my very lovely agent.
You have both been utterly wonderful.

ONE

Erik and Hans

Berlin, 1931

One summer, when he was ten years old, Erik became famous for buying dead flies.

"Really!" said Hans, who was in the same class at school and had just moved into the apartment below. "You're always becoming famous for something embarrassing!"

"I know," admitted Erik, because it did seem a bit that way. The falling off the bridge on the school expedition to the river; his hospital for dolls—he'd fixed one small girl's doll and the news had got round, "Erik can mend dolls!" and suddenly he'd found himself with a bedroom full of prim china faces not necessarily attached to their bodies.

And now he was buying dead flies.

The reason Erik needed flies was a family of little birds. Their nest had fallen; the fragile shell of dry mud had crumbled and split from the wall and two fledglings had been lost, but three had survived. Erik's *kleine Schwalben*, his little swallows.

He'd tried finding enough flies for them alone, but without having wings himself, it seemed impossible. He'd taken a teaspoon to every rosebush within walking distance, scraping off greenfly. Both the baker and the butcher had asked him very forcefully to get out and mind his manners when he'd offered, as politely as he could, to remove the wildlife buzzing in their windows. He'd haunted the rubbish bins at the back of the apartment building. Even so, he couldn't manage to keep up with the little birds' hunger, and so he'd recruited his classmates. They naturally said they were not going to spend their spare time collecting flies for nothing, and demanded to be paid.

Erik had paid first in fruit drops, from the box he'd had for his birthday, and next with an assortment of rather chipped marbles, and after that with cigarette cards: scenes of old Berlin, Flags of the World, and his precious Exotic Birds and Animals. He had a few French cards too, mostly pictures of famous film-star girls.

"Girls!" said Hans, scornfully, when he came with his flies to trade. Hans had a sister named Lisa. She was one year younger than Hans, but she was taller than he was, and she bossed him about. Lisa had a hundred friends, or so it seemed to Hans. "I've enough girls at home."

"Well then, choose a flag," suggested Erik, "or an armadillo or a camel or something."

Hans said he didn't care about flags, and that the camel and the armadillo had unfriendly faces. In the end he chose a girl after all, one with great waves of hair, and a very small top hat tilted over one eye, not at all like his sister or any of her friends. In return he gave Erik an envelope full of bluebottles, mosquitoes, and other small flies. The mosquitoes were squashed and so no use, but the rest were all right. Erik, for about the tenth time that day, explained why squashed were no good, with all the juice wasted.

"You do know everybody is talking about you, don't you?" said Hans.

"Are they?"

"Saying you are crazy!"

"Oh, well, yes."

"What other cards do you have to trade?"

"I don't really, Hans," said Erik.

He did have an album of fairy-tale cards, collected for him by his mother, long before. He couldn't trade those, because she was still fond of them. Now and then, on winter evenings, she would turn the pages and murmur, "Yes, I remember," when she came to the seven swans, or the tin soldier, or whatever. Erik also hoped that he might keep his five Dogs of the World: the German shepherd, the husky, the St. Bernard with the little barrel on its collar, the English sheepdog with the smiling face, and the small French poodle. He had owned them for as long as he could remember, given them names and dreamed them stories. They were old friends, and yet . . .

He'd known these swallows since they were eggs: every summer a nest was built above his bedroom window; already the parent birds were building there again. And now Erik had these three.

He kept them in his bedroom, in a box by the open window, snuggled together in his winter hat, which would never be the same again. Hans came to watch his latest delivery of flies disappear.

"More than an hour's work gone in seconds," he remarked. "However do these ridiculous birds manage in the wild?"

"Easy," said Erik. "They can fly. What I really need is a butterfly net and a very small plane."

"What you need is my uncle Karl," said Hans.

"Why?"

"He can fly. And he's nuts, like you. I'll tell him about you, next time I see him. Have you given them names?"

Erik laughed and shook his head, so Hans named them on the spot: Cirrus, Nimbus, and Cumulus.

"Cumulus is the fat one," he said. "He's my favorite. I shall go and catch his supper right now."

After that, Hans stopped charging for his flies, and he was a great help to Erik because the little birds were constantly hungry. They were growing so fast that every few hours they seemed to change. Real colors replacing the down. Their pin-feathers coming through on their wings. All three of them stronger every day, stretching out a wing, jostling for the next beak-full of food.

"How did you learn to care for them?" asked Hans, and Erik explained that two years before, it had happened just the same, a nest had fallen and he had scooped up a nestling and fed it on baby food. Bread and milk. And it had died. He wouldn't make that mistake again, though, he said. Flies, that was what his swallows needed, from four in the morning until darkness at night, flies by the dozen, flies by the hundred, not caught in airy swoops around the rooftops like the parent swallows did, but delivered by a train of helpers with matchboxes, cocoa tins, or sometimes just clenched fists. Up and down the building stairs, driving the occupants mad.

"Wash your hands!" his mother ordered the children, with every new delivery, and sent them to the kitchen sink and made sure they did it properly. The soap wore out and people got so tired of washing they stood under the windows and yelled instead, "Erik! I brought more flies!"

⤳ 𝒳 ⤳

"How much longer?" asked his mother, and Erik said perhaps a week or a little more.

"A week or a little more!" she groaned, and suggested egg yolk, minced sausage, and canary seed soaked in water. Erik shook his head. He dared not risk it.

"Well, well," said his mother. "I suppose you must do what you can."

Erik did, although it wasn't easy. To part with the German shepherd, who he'd named Otto, after his father, who had died before he was born. With dear brave Brandy, the St. Bernard, hero of so many imaginary snowbound adventures. Comet, the blue-eyed, curly-tailed, moonlight-colored husky. Tessa, the smiling sheepdog. "Take care of her," said Erik, as he handed Tessa to her new owner, and there was an aching beneath his ribs that was beginning to feel familiar even though he still had Belle, the little French poodle.

"She's pretty," said Lisa, who had come to see what all the fuss was about. "One day I will have a dog like that, with a pom-pom tail and a pink ribbon in her hair."

Lisa, although nearly always indignant or angry, was also pretty in a furious kind of way, and Erik gave her Belle, even though Hans disapproved.

"She got exactly what she wanted then," he grumbled, when Lisa, clutching Belle, had run away downstairs again.

"Good," said Erik.

On the fourteenth day after Erik found them, his three swallows flew from his open window, straight from his hand into a bird-filled apricot evening sky, joining dozens of others circling the roofs and eaves and skyways of the city.

Never, ever had Erik known such illuminated joy, such a lift of bliss that it felt as if he could have flown with them.

"Well," said Hans, who had come to say goodbye to Cumulus and the others. "That's three more birds in the sky."

"Yes," agreed Erik, hanging out of the window to watch. "Imagine being a swallow. Racing about like that!"

"You'd have to eat flies, though," pointed out Hans. "What do you think they taste like?"

"Pretzels and lobsters," said Erik, so matter-of-factly that Hans started shouting and flinging his arms about and exclaiming, "Erik? You didn't! Hey, tell me you didn't! You can't have! Are you crazy? Are you joking?" Then he stopped jumping about and came up close to look into Erik's face. "You are joking," he said. "Aren't you?"

"Yes."

Hans pushed his shoulder affectionately. Erik pushed him back. They both, at the same moment, realized how much they liked each other. Hans remembered how Erik had leaned over the bridge and leaned over the bridge and leaned over the bridge, and said, "Oh, dear," and vanished with hardly a splash. Erik remembered how quickly Hans had pulled off his jacket to wrap him up when they fished him out again.

"Nutter," said Hans, catching Erik in a casual headlock.

"Nutter yourself," said Erik, wriggling out backward and dumping Hans flat on the floor.

"I wouldn't be surprised if they *did* taste like pretzels and lobsters," said Hans, thinking about it, stretched out on his back. "Perhaps you're not so crazy after all. Perhaps one day you will be head keeper at the Berlin Zoo."

"Perhaps," said Erik hopefully, once more gazing out of

the window. "Do you know, Hans, those little birds will go to Africa."

"Oh, here you go again!" said Hans. "Africa! I was wrong, you really are a nut. . . . Hey! Erik!"

Erik's brown curly head was suddenly nodding. He wobbled where he stood, leaning against the comfortable wooden window frame. Only four hours' sleep every night for two weeks and three insatiable babies all day, and now night was coming in over the rooftops.

Hans leaped and grabbed him just before he toppled out of the open window.

"Thank you, Hans," said Erik.

TWO

Ruby

Plymouth, Devon, 1927

R uby was her name, and even that caused trouble. All the girls in the family had flower names—there were Lilies and Daisies and Roses, an Iris and a Violet, once a Marigold. It was a family tradition, unbroken since goodness knew when, until Violet, who was Ruby's mother, said, "Ruby."

"Ruby?" asked a whole bunch of flowery relations, gathered in the room above the newsagent's shop. "Ruby?"

"I like rubies," said Violet, "better than diamonds or pearls. I always wanted a ruby."

"You can't pretend Ruby's a flower name," said bossy Aunt Rose.

"I wasn't," said Violet, in a mind-your-own-business voice.

"It's flashy," said Aunt Lily, who had no tact. "It'll draw attention."

"Attention?" repeated Violet, in a tone of such unexploded fury that Aunt Lily took a step back. Even as she retreated, though, she couldn't help glancing toward the baby sleeping in the wicker basket, and then, one after another, everyone else in the room glanced too.

Ruby's face was splattered with what looked like dark brown paint. Birthmarks; a large one, like a paintbrush had swiped below her left eye, and showers of smaller ones patterning both sides of her face. They were the first thing anyone saw, and nobody could say a word to Violet about them that didn't make her angry.

The family discussed it in murmurs when Violet was out of the room. There had been, according to Violet's mother, other babies born in the family with marks just the same. A boy was remembered, fifty years before.

"They said his might fade," Ruby's grandmother remembered.

"And did they?" demanded Rose.

"He died when he was six or seven. They hadn't faded then."

"Better not tell Violet," whispered Iris.

"You can't tell Violet anything," said Rose.

"I know," agreed Lily, nodding. "Ruby! What kind of a—"

"Shush!" hissed everyone, but too late.

"What are you shushing?" asked Violet, appearing suddenly in the doorway.

A twitching silence followed while people tried to remember what they'd said.

"It's about the baby, isn't it?"

"We were just talking about her name," said Iris soothingly. "I was thinking that there's Clover, and I once heard of a Lavender."

"Clover is a cow's name and Lavender's for bath salts," said Violet witheringly. "Anyway," she added, picking up the sleeping baby and rocking her on her shoulder, "you can all stop fussing because she's going to have a flower name too. Her dad picked it out."

Violet paused.

"Go on, then," said Rose.

"Amaryllis."

"Amaryllis?" repeated the whole bunch, Iris, Rose, and Lily.

"*Amaryllis?* What in heaven's an amaryllis?"

"I've never *heard* of an amaryllis," said Ruby's grandmother.

Neither had Violet. The name had been in a library book about gardening. There hadn't been a picture, just a list of "Rewarding Rarities" at the end of a chapter and the lovely word among them: *amaryllis*, which rang like a chime and a charm. Ruby's father had read it aloud and it had caught Violet's heart.

"Ruby Amaryllis," she said proudly. "Her dad's looked it up and everything. He says it's a flower like a lily, but better."

"It's even fancier than Ruby!" said all the horrified relations.

"Good," said Violet.

It hadn't stopped there. The christening had been as extravagant as the new baby's name. Violet had sewn white silk into a christening gown, and her best friend Clarry had brought from Oxford a shawl of snowflakes in soft white lace. Clarry was to be Ruby's godmother, and she arrived for the christening with other presents too: a rattle with silver bells, and a whole collection of parcels for Ruby's eight-year-old brother, Will.

Will was already sick of the whole business, the fuss, the new clothes he was required to wear, and the bone-deep knowledge that he would never again be loved as exclusively and completely as he had been loved before the arrival of the ugly, wailing baby. Therefore he unwrapped his flashlight, his book called *The Pirate's Parrot*, his jar of sweets, and his box of colored marbles with very bad grace, and when prompted to say thank you, said, "They're just to shut me up."

To Will's disappointment, Clarry didn't immediately turn on him in indignation. Instead, she said cheerfully that maybe he would like them later, and nodded in agreement when he said he supposed they'd do for trading.

All the grown-ups seemed to be amused by him. They talked to him about trains and school and soccer, as if he cared. He longed to ask if the brown marks made it more likely that the baby would die soon, but he didn't dare in case they guessed his darkest thoughts. His life was ruined, and no one understood. He tried to make himself sick in church but failed.

Ruby Amaryllis grew up in the three little rooms over the newsagent's shop, with her mother and father and Will, who she always treated warily, half ready to run. Plymouth was a naval town, with huge dockyards on the river that had their own train station. Ruby's father was a porter there, riding backward and forward on his bicycle every day. He said when Will was old enough, he should get a job there too.

"Not me!" Will used to exclaim scornfully, whenever this boring idea was suggested. "I'm going to do something a lot more exciting than that!"

Will was like his mother; tall, with creamy skin and gray-green eyes. There was no understanding between him and Ruby. She still caused trouble. She was a pest. At school they said, "What's the matter with your sister's face?" and he said, "I don't know. It's horrible."

"You're going red," they said, and he would set about them with his fists and get in trouble with the teachers.

Ruby thought Will was much worse than a pest. Ruby thought Will was awful, and had done ever since she was five. There was a scullery behind the shop, and that was where she'd been the day that she'd heard his voice, husky and solemn, asking, "Can I help?"

He had been busy in the backyard with the boy from the house next door. She heard him again. "Can I do one too?"

The scullery door was nearly always a little open, in order to let out the perpetual damp. Ruby had pushed it wider, to look.

They were drowning kittens in a bucket.

"Stop it! Stop it!" Ruby had screeched, exploding out, and launching herself at Will. "Stop it!" and she'd kicked his shins, head-butted his stomach, grabbed his hair, and done her absolute best to drag him to the bucket and drown him, too.

Will had not fought back. Instead, he'd held her off at arm's length, shouted to his friend, "Save the black and I'll make our mum have it," and then carted her indoors and tried to explain.

"You have to drown them," he said. "There'd be millions of kittens, else. They don't know nothing. They just go to sleep in the water. I promise."

"I hate you and I'm telling Mum!" wailed Ruby.

"Telling Mum what?" demanded Violet from behind.

"She found me and Danny sorting out them kittens," explained Will.

"They were DROWNING them in a BUCKET," roared Ruby, and Violet said, "Well, it's a shame you had to see that." (*Taking Ruby's side as usual,* thought her brother.) "You and Danny should have been more careful, Will."

"We were being careful," said Will indignantly. "We shut their cat Sukey in Dan's house with the kitten that they're keeping for themselves, and then we did the other five in our yard so Sukey couldn't see. We couldn't have been more careful. We warmed the water, and everything. And I've told Danny to save the black for us . . ."

"Will!"

". . . because Ruby's so upset."

"He asked," exploded Ruby, "if he could help! 'Can I do one?' he said. I heard him! He's a murderer!"

"Only to learn how," said Will.

"Learn how!" shouted Ruby.

"I've had enough of this!" said Will resentfully. "Are we having the black or had I better go back and tell Danny—"

"NO NO NO!" screamed Ruby, and Violet groaned and said it had better be a boy kitten, that was all, and it was, and when he was old enough, he came to live with them and was Ruby's cat, Sooty. For weeks after that Ruby didn't know if she was grateful to Will, for saving Sooty, or hated him for what had happened to the rest. She couldn't forget his voice asking, "Can I do one too?"

Ruby's dad was not told anything about the whole awful event. Violet ordered that. "It would just make him miserable," she said. "He's a good dad to the pair of you, and he hates how you quarrel."

Will and Ruby didn't argue about that. They knew it was true. And they knew he was a good dad, hardworking and generous, handing over all his earnings to Violet except for a few shillings every Friday. The shillings were usually spent on presents to bring home. Oranges, or a flower in a pot for Violet, another small bell to hang on Sooty's collar, sometimes a book for them all to share. He was never, ever cross. He was a gentle man.

Violet was the opposite. She was the boss in the family. The three rooms over the shop were rent free because Violet worked there. She was a hard worker, and because of her, the money stretched like magic so that there were warm suppers every night, schoolbooks and birthday cakes, Christmas stockings and days at the fair, coal for the fire in the living room and the tub in the scullery, where they had their baths on Saturdays and Wednesdays.

Violet made the three rooms into a comfortable home. The living room had a table in the window and a sofa made of tea chests and cushions. There was a shelf of books, a little range for cooking, and a cupboard for the plates and saucepans. Will had his own room to sleep in, and Ruby had a curtained-off corner of her parents' room. When she was six and went to school and could be trusted with a candle, her parents promised they would whitewash the attic and she could sleep up there, with a view over the rooftops and across to the dockyards.

Ruby turned six, and this happened. Also, she went to school.

For those first years of her life, Ruby hadn't known there was anything different about her face. The three rooms above the shop were mirror free, and no one ever mentioned it. Not any of the flowery-named relations, nor even Will. Somehow, Violet stopped them all.

That was why, on the first day that Ruby started school, when fifty children, maybe more, looked at her face and demanded, "What's those marks?" she honestly didn't know what they were talking about.

She didn't find out till she got home.

Sooty, now a half-grown cat, came with Ruby to the dark little scullery and watched as she climbed onto the tub to reach down for the small speckled mirror that her father used for shaving.

That was when she saw her reflection; saw it properly, for the first time. In truth, the marks were not as shocking as they once had been. They had not grown larger as Ruby grew; they no longer entirely dominated her face. But still, they were bad enough.

Ruby stared and stared.

At school the next day a girl asked, "What would happen to your face if you washed it?"

"I do wash it," Ruby said bleakly, still stunned from the scullery mirror.

"Washed it hard?" persisted the girl.

It was true, Ruby didn't wash it hard, and neither did her mother. They didn't work at it, like her dad did with the nailbrush, grinding the station grime out of the cracks in his hands until the water in the basin went scummy and gray. That was hard washing, the way he would scrub and scrub.

And in the end, his hands would be clean.

After school on that second day, Ruby got the bar of soap from its soap dish on the scullery shelf, and the family washcloth from its hook, and she scrubbed her face very hard indeed. Her cheeks became hot, and very clean, but her reflection in the mirror didn't change. Will came in while she was busy, with Danny trailing behind.

Will burst out laughing and said she might as well scrub Sooty white while she was at it, but Danny said solemnly, "It's the water."

"What?" demanded Ruby, spinning round.

"You need special water."

"What special water?"

"We have special white water at our house," said Danny. "If you use the right brush, it scrubs anything white."

"There's no such thing as special white water," said Ruby stubbornly, and Danny said, "Want me to prove it?"

"How?"

"Give us Sooty!" said Danny, and suddenly bent and scooped him up and shoved him under his jacket. Then he was gone, with Will running after him, and Ruby shrieking, "You dare scrub Sooty! You dare!"

"I'll only do one foot," called Danny over his shoulder, and in an incredibly short time was back, with a brown earthenware jug, and Will, clutching a small scrubbing brush and exploding with mirth in the background.

Danny had something squirming under his jacket.

"Look!" he said, unfastening buttons, and out tumbled Sooty, furious and fighting.

With one wet paw, snow white.

"Special water," said Danny, showing Ruby the jug.

"And the right brush," added Will.

"You painted him!" said Ruby, and she picked up Sooty (still indignant from the jacket) and looked carefully at his wet front paw.

It wasn't painted, though. It was truly white. Pure white fur with pink skin underneath.

"See," said Danny.

Ruby looked at him, and at Will. She squinted at her reflection in the little freckled mirror. She looked at Sooty.

"Give me the special water," she said at last.

"Give you?"

"Yes."

"Manners."

"Please," conceded Ruby. "Give me please."

"It costs," said Danny. "Shilling a jug."

"I haven't got a shilling," said Ruby, looking at them both with hate.

"You've got threepence," said Will.

It was true. Ruby had got threepence. Every Saturday she had one, shiny silver from her dad.

"Hmm," said Danny. "Perhaps." Then he made Ruby fetch her threepence and say please, and also pretty-please-with-sugar-on-top, but at last he nodded to Will to hand over the scrubbing brush and gave Ruby the jug and she looked inside at the white water and said, "It's milk."

"Milk!" scoffed Danny. "Taste it and you'll drop dead."

"Dead as dead," said Will.

Then they took Ruby's silver threepence and went away and they left her with the jug and Sooty.

Sooty sniffed the jug.

"No, no," said Ruby urgently, just in case, and she poured the special white water carefully into the enamel washbasin, where it looked more than ever like milk, and Sooty sniffed even harder and patted it with his white paw.

Ruby stuck in the tip of a finger and licked it. It was very salty and unpleasant, but she didn't drop dead.

Sooty asked for a taste again.

"It's not for drinking," Ruby told him, and she picked up the scrubbing brush and dipped it in the washbasin. Then she gritted her teeth and began to scrub.

On the other side of the scullery door, Will and Danny laughed and laughed in silent, doubled-over agony.

Ruby scrubbed until she bled red blood into the white water and she couldn't see in the little mirror for the tears of pain in her eyes. Sooty, meanwhile, turned into two cats.

Two cats.

At first Ruby didn't notice, and then she did, because they were both sitting on their haunches watching her. Two sooty dark cats, one with a white paw, one entirely black.

Two of them.

Two.

"Two cats?" said Ruby, and called, "Sooty, Sooty," and both Sooties came and rubbed their heads on her hands and she was entirely bewildered and cried, "How?"

On the other side of the scullery door, Will and Danny gasped in pain, beset with laughter, and Ruby heard them.

Then Ruby's mother arrived. She saw the boys, staggering around, still howling with mirth. She saw the jug and brush, which had both been hurled. She saw smashed brown pottery on the floor.

"Ruby AMARYLLIS!" shouted Violet, and grabbed her so she had to stop kicking the boys with her new school shoes, all stained with salty milk.

Ruby's face was so swollen her left eye wouldn't open. It burned like fire. It was a week before she went back to school. First she couldn't, because her face was so sore, and then she wouldn't because her heart was so sore. By the time she did, everyone knew the story.

"My beautiful Ruby," said Ruby's father, and he polished her school shoes until they shone like new and gave her a pink balloon, a green hair ribbon, and a chocolate bar. Even so, every day of that week she was sent to bed early, not for kicking and fighting, but for being so silly.

Said Violet.

Also, every day of that week Will had dry bread and milk for supper and dry bread and milk for breakfast and dry bread and milk to take to school for his dinner and nothing else, not even butter. His father could hardly bear it. He said, "Your little sister, Will."

"Little tiger," said Will.

His father put a chocolate bar behind the clock for him, and said, "That's for when you're friends again."

"It can stay there then," said Will, and it did.

One interesting thing happened, which was that the white-pawed cat never went back home. It wouldn't. It refused to stay there. It went to live with Ruby and Sooty.

It wouldn't answer to its name. Ruby had to pick a new one for it: Paddle.

"You can tell them at school about Paddle and Sooty," said her mother encouragingly, but Ruby never told anyone at school anything.

Around her grew legends. The legend of the scrubbing of the dark marks on her face. Of the stolen cat. Of her strange name. There wasn't another Ruby in the school, never mind an Amaryllis. The marks on her face would not paint out, not with Violet's face cream and powder, nor with flour mixed up to paste.

Once Ruby found a fallen bunch of cherry blossom, tumbled

in the street. Carefully, she licked the pale pink petals, stuck them on, and peered into the little freckled mirror. It almost worked: there, for a few moments, was a girl she had never seen. Green eyes, astonished. Dark curls and dark eyebrows. A missing front tooth.

"Look!" cried Ruby to her mother, but the cherry petals would not stay. They curled with the warmth of her skin and fell.

"Are they still saying things at school?" demanded Violet fiercely, and Ruby, equally fiercely, said, "I don't care if they do."

Violet cared, though. She marched to school and through the gates, which parents hardly ever passed, and gave out orders in the playground: "You leave my Ruby alone!"

So they did.

THREE

Kate

Oxford, 1928–1936

K ate was the youngest and her name was Katherine Clarissa, after Clarry, who was her aunt and her godmother, too.

"Say you'll do it, please say you will," Vanessa, Kate's mother, had pleaded. "It'll be easy. You only have to adore her."

"Only," remarked Kate's father gloomily, looking down at his newest daughter, half lost in the shabby billows of the family christening dress, and he joggled her a little, to see if she would smile.

She didn't. She was a skinny, purplish person with an ancient, unhappy frown. Nevertheless, Clarry laughed at her brother and said, "Don't be silly, Peter. I'll have no trouble adoring her at all."

"As if anybody could!" exclaimed Vanessa, and added that Kate could be a friend to Clarry's other goddaughter, Ruby, in Plymouth.

"They can write to each other," agreed Clarry.

"I don't know about the one in Plymouth," said Kate's father, "but this one here doesn't strike me as the literary type."

"You're wrong, you know," said Clarry. "She has a very intelligent face."

Peter said that it was a common mistake to confuse baldness

with brains, but good old Clarry anyway, and Vanessa said, "Yes, definitely, it's awful trying to find godparents for six, Clarry, you've no idea, people just run. We'd have nobbled you ages ago, but you were always off gallivanting with Rupert at the critical moment."

"Oh, well, you've nobbled me now," said Clarry cheerfully.

Kate was the last of the Penrose children, who had begun with Janey, who was brainy, swiftly followed by untidy, merry Bea. Bea wore glasses that she lost so often she tied them on a string, and ran a farm on her bedroom windowsill: carrot tops growing in saucers, two mice in a box, and a flowerpot of earth where she planted apple pips.

Janey and Bea were a team, and Simon and Tod (whose real name was Rupert), the good-looking musical twins, were another. After Simon and Tod came noisy, impulsive Charlie. And then there was Kate, who was not brainy or untidy or merry or good-looking or musical or noisy or impulsive. Kate was shy and breathless and had to be looked after and have orange juice with cod liver oil because she caught illnesses so easily. This meant she missed a lot of school and in winter was wrapped in extra warm layers, in foggy weather kept indoors, and on rainy days was steered around puddles and had umbrellas held over her head. Even in summer, Kate sneezed and sneezed with hay fever, although she lived on a street in Oxford where there wasn't any hay for miles.

Kate's parents kept her carefully close, within arm's reach if they were out and about, beside them in the car if they were driving. They did this so as to be handy if she needed help. People always did help Kate. "Pass it over," they would say, if she dried knives and forks too slowly in the kitchen, or struggled to undo a knot, or turn a key, or sharpen a pencil. In the mornings someone (usually Bea) would plait her hair into two mouse-colored tails, in the evenings someone else (usually Janey) would whizz her through her homework. Her shoes were always magically polished and her bed magically made.

Except for her illnesses, Kate's life was entirely safe. Bea fell flat on her face roller-skating, smashing her glasses and chipping a large corner off a new front tooth. Janey broke her arm when her bike skidded sideways racing Tod and Simon across the market street cobbles. Charlie, practicing being a burglar, climbed a long way up a drainpipe before it detached slowly from the wall. Simon and Tod found and repaired an ancient leaky punt, which frequently disintegrated mid-river and sent them home dripping and shivering.

But nothing ever happened to Kate except kindness and illness.

"Is she like Beth in *Little Women*?" Bea once worried to Janey, but Janey said no, Beth only got ill because she visited sick people to take them muffins and firewood and other useful things. Completely the opposite to Kate, who was ill naturally, without helping anyone. Janey explained this, and Bea nodded, reassured.

Although it did make Kate sound a little bit useless.

"I expect she's brilliant at something we haven't discovered yet," said Bea, and Janey said probably, yes.

Kate was actually very good at being nearly invisible. A number of people hardly noticed she existed, and one of these was Rupert, the Rupert after whom Tod was named. To everyone except Kate, Rupert was a sort of unofficial uncle.

"Why aren't you a real uncle?" Charlie asked him.

"Because I'm not a relation."

"Not even a bit?"

"Not at all."

"But did you used to be?"

"I used to think I was," admitted Rupert. "But then I went to India and found out that I wasn't."

"How?"

"Oh," said Rupert, "it's hard to explain. No, it's not. It's easy. I found out that my father wasn't my father after all. And that meant my grandparents weren't the people I thought they were. No one was who I thought they were. It explained a lot."

"What?"

"Like why my parents dumped me on my not-really grand-parents in Cornwall when I was three. And why the not-really grandparents dumped me at boarding school when I was seven. That sort of thing."

"Were you very sad?" asked Bea, and she touched his sleeve sympathetically.

"Not at all. I'd guessed already. I just needed to know the truth."

"We would never dump you," said Bea, and Charlie agreed, "You're safe now, promise."

"Stuck," said Janey.

"Trapped," said Tod.

"You don't dump us, we won't dump you," agreed Simon, and Rupert solemnly shook hands with all of them, except Kate, who was as usual, invisible, and said, "Deal."

But none of this was really necessary, because Rupert was part of the family anyway, mobbed every time he came through the door, hauled off to look at the drainpipe, taken for trips in the leaky punt, and advised, for the hundredth time, that he'd better marry Clarry.

"True," said Rupert. "But easier said than done."

"Why?"

"Bit busy, both of us."

"It would only take an afternoon!"

Rupert laughed, and said, "Look at the time, I must be off. Bye, you Penroses. Be good."

"You're always going!" Charlie complained, and it was true, he was. Rupert doubled their pocket money, made them laugh, provided boxes of fireworks on November the fifth, but more than anything, he vanished.

"Where are you going this time?" demanded Janey.

"London, of course," said Rupert. "Work in the morning."

"What sort of work?"

"I'm a servant," Rupert told her solemnly. "Civil. And uncivil, sometimes. In Westminster and Whitehall. I listen to people. I listen and say, 'Do you think so?' and they pay me."

"Just for that?" demanded Bea incredulously.

"Yes," he said.

"They can't pay you much," said Janey. "Not for that and nothing else."

"True," agreed Rupert, "but every little bit helps. One day I'll take you with me, and show you."

After he'd gone, they looked at each other and said, "He won't," but they were wrong.

He began with Janey and Bea, taking them on the train to London, showing them the long corridors and dusty courtyards of

Westminster, the cupboards in walls with mousetraps inside, and what was in the middle of the clock tower of Big Ben.

"Stairs," reported Janey.

"Stairs and a cat," said Bea.

"I didn't see a cat," said Janey. "Are you sure that you did, Bea? You do see things that aren't there sometimes."

"I saw the cat," said Clarry, who happened to be visiting. "I stroked it too. It followed us right to the top of the staircase."

"You and Rupert?"

"Yes. Very early one morning. An inky black cat, like a shadow with golden eyes."

"That was the one," agreed Bea, who had loved the whole adventure, but the cat most of all.

After that, Rupert would often swoop over to Oxford for a handful of Penroses and cart them away to see the sights. In Westminster he would park them on the green leather seats of the Commons or the red leather seats of the Lords, where Janey and Bea roosted like swallows, listening intently. In contrast to their brothers, who read comics, wrote unparliamentary poetry in their heads, exploded into painful silent giggles, and in Charlie's case, bounced with indignation and had to be carted away like a bundle. Quite often on those trips, a Penrose would hear, "Ah, Rupert, if you have a minute . . . ," and then, after much more than a minute, fidgeting hours it seemed sometimes, "Do you think so? Oh."

At school, no one believed Janey when she told them where she'd been and what she'd seen. "Mousetraps?" they asked, and those who had imagined Big Ben to be like a giant grandfather clock, "Steps inside? Cats?"

"One cat, anyway," said Janey, but even one cat was too much for most of them, so Janey stopped talking about their trips to London with Rupert, although it was hard to keep quiet when he gave her and Bea one of the Trafalgar Square lions for their own, to share.

When the twins heard of this, they demanded a lion too.

"The rest belong to other people," said baffling Rupert, and took Tod and Simon to South Kensington and gave them the Minerals Gallery in the Natural History Museum instead. "Just you two," he said. "Not Charlie. It's not a place for Charlie to be charging about. All that glass. And meteors. Asking for trouble."

The twins agreed, and they didn't tell Charlie, but he found out anyway and was outraged and demanded to be given the polar bear instead. It was an enormous yellow beast with a narrow, furious gaze and shoulders like monuments, and Charlie admired it very much. But Rupert was unhelpful. He said the bear was not his to give away, and if he was, he'd keep him for himself. However, to cheer Charlie up he took him swimming in the Serpentine, which was excitingly full of ducks and paper bags and other things, floating and submerged. One of these caught Charlie by his foot and he screeched and screeched, remembering too clearly underwater monsters he had seen in the museum and assumed to be extinct.

"There are no ichthyosaurs in the Serpentine," said Rupert sternly, and dived and retrieved an old umbrella and clambered out with it onto the bank, showing all his awful purple scars as if he didn't care. It was a black umbrella and Rupert opened it and closed it and said, "I wonder if I knew the man who owned it," in such a thoughtful, alarming way that even unquenchable Charlie was silent.

"Well," said Rupert, shooting out the umbrella's slimy folds and examining the pointy bit, "you have to admit, it's odd."

"Why?"

"No concealed sword. No hidden camera. No wind damage, so it's not been used for parachuting."

"Parachuting?"

"Didn't you hear? Nothing like that. Perfectly good umbrella."

"Can I keep it?"

"No, of course not," said Rupert, and hung it by its greenish-yellow handle from the back of a bench, and then he made Charlie trot about to warm up and afterward they went to tea in a Lyons tea shop. There they ordered Welsh rarebit, which wasn't even on the menu and only appeared because Rupert said, "Oh, do you think so?" to the waitress girl when she said it wasn't possible. These must have been magic words, because seconds later she was taking down instructions about grated cheese and a little mustard (French, of course) and a beaten egg and beer. It was so good that Charlie ate three platefuls and turned down ice cream in favor of a fourth.

"How old are you?" demanded Rupert, who was drinking tea with lemon slices and not eating anything at all.

"Eleven," said Charlie, "nearly."

"Not just you. All of you."

"Janey's seventeen, nearly. Bea's sixteen, nearly. Simon and Tod are twelve but it's nearly their birthday—"

"We'd better get a move on," said Rupert. "Come on!"

"But—" protested Charlie, who still hadn't finished.

"You can bring that last piece with you!" said Rupert, left an enormous tip, half a crown, and hurried him home.

↳ ✗ ↲

Charlie was the last Penrose who Rupert took to London. Kate, with her nearly invisibleness, never got to go. After Charlie, Rupert disappeared.

"Where's he gone this time?" Charlie wondered. Clarry, who was spending the evening getting on with her school marking and keeping an eye on him and Kate while the rest of the family were out, looked up from her work and said vaguely, "Traveling."

"Traveling," murmured Kate. She was being unwell again, wrapped up in a blanket of patchwork roses, writing in her diary.

The fact that Kate kept a diary always amused her family. What could she possibly find to put in it? they wondered. If they'd been the sort of people who read diaries uninvited, they'd soon have discovered the answer. Kate's diary was all about other people. All the trips to London had been noted: the black cat inside Big Ben, and the lions in Trafalgar Square, with miniature drawings of both. A recipe for Welsh rarebit was carefully recorded. Other things too. The mystery of Bea's missing mice. A new patch on the punt.

Now Kate wrote, *Clarry's here but Rupert's traveling.*

"Traveling," said Charlie enviously. "Lucky, lucky Rupert."

Charlie's homework was going very slowly that evening. He'd eaten a handful of biscuits, two apples, and a lump of cheese, doodled his name in red and blue ink, drawn round his eraser and turned the outline into an elephant, decided how he'd spend a hundred pounds if he had a hundred pounds, and still it wasn't done. Kate was useless. She'd tested him on his Latin, checked the words in the dictionary, and marked every answer wrong.

"I asked you to test my Latin, not my spelling," Charlie said. "Spelling didn't matter in Latin days. Ancient Romers hardly ever wrote things down."

"Absolutely untrue," remarked Clarry.

"I wish Rupert had taken me with him. Where's he gone?"

"All sorts of places: Germany, France, Russia."

"Russia?" repeated Kate, and thought of Russian tales of bears, and witches with iron teeth, and great frozen rivers that creaked and shattered into icy torrents and swept travelers away. She shivered, and Clarry noticed.

"Don't worry," she said, smiling at her. "Rupert has nine lives, like a cat."

Charlie, remembering the banks of the Serpentine, said, "Yes, but he's probably used most of them. You should see his scars! His back looks like someone tried to chop him up, and one of his legs has a hole in it."

"A hole?" asked Kate, in a frightened voice.

"As big as . . . as big as an apple. Half an apple, anyway! It's not red or bloody or anything. It's just a hole. It's great. I bet he'd show you if you wanted."

Kate asked, because she couldn't help it, "How did he get a hole in his leg?"

"In the war, of course," said Charlie.

"I didn't know he was in a war."

"'Course he was," said Charlie. "Same as Mum's brother Simon who was killed."

"Killed? Killed?"

"How can you not know anything, Kate?"

"I knew he died, but I didn't know he was killed. I thought it was when he was a boy."

"He was seventeen, not quite eighteen," said Clarry. "So you're right, he was a boy."

"Oh," said Kate, and she didn't say any more, just wrote unhappily and coughed a bit, until Charlie flung away his homework books and said he wished there was a war now, so he could have some fun.

Then Kate shouted, "CHARLIE!"

It was the first time she had ever shouted in her life. It made her cough a lot more, but it shut Charlie up.

FOUR

Dog

Scrapyard, East London, exact date unknown

T here was a dog who lived in a scrapyard. It had lived there so long that it had become part of the landscape, like the rust stains on the ground, the lace edge of broken bottles that topped the scrapyard walls, and the rattle of the gates in the wind.

All the good things about dogs were not true of this dog. It loved no one, and trusted no one. It wasn't loyal or merry. It didn't have wise brown eyes, or a hopefully wagging tail; in fact, half of its tail was missing. Also its fur was coarse and grayish and matted behind its ears. Its legs were long and knobbly at the joints, and they ended in paws with thick black nails, chewed down to iron stumps.

The dog made its living by its bark, which was harsh, like stone dragged on stone. Also by its lunge at the end of its chain. The chain was the dog's home.

By day the chain held the dog, but at night its ears fluttered, and its paws flexed and twitched.

By night the dog ran in its dreams.

FIVE

Erik and Hans

Berlin, 1936

Ever since the three swallows, Erik and Hans had been best friends. They had very much in common: the same school, and the same apartment block (although Hans's home was much bigger). Both their fathers had fought in the 1914–1918 war. The consequences to their families were with them still. Erik's father had been gassed and had never properly recovered. He had died when he was still quite young, two months before Erik was born. Hans's father was never really healthy either, and his left leg was missing below his knee. Now he walked stiffly on his wooden half leg, and worked in the post office, which was good because he could sit down nearly all day. Hans's mother didn't work at all, but Erik's mother did.

Erik's mother worked all the time. Every morning she swept and scrubbed the entrance hall and staircases of their building, and of the one next door as well. In the late afternoons she cleaned the local elementary school. When Erik was little, too young to be left alone, she used to take him with her. Erik had played in the empty classrooms, and helped dust the chalkboards, and every day he'd climbed with his mother the shadowy narrow staircase that opened from their own landing to the two miniature attic rooms belonging to his mother's old lady: Fräulein Trisk. Fräulein Trisk lived all alone, tiny, white-haired, and permanently annoyed. Her movements were annoyed, and her eyes were annoyed, and every now and then, she would burst into miniature eruptions of spluttering annoyedness, like the sound of cold water drops in a hot frying pan.

"Tck! Tck! Tck!" scolded Fräulein Trisk. It took nothing to set her off: a bird shadow passing the window, a call in the street far below, the smallest noise from Erik, one little sniff, and she would explode, like a dolls' house firecracker.

No person ever visited Fräulein Trisk. No letter with her name on ever arrived in the wire letterbox behind the door. No one, not even from Hans's family, ever asked, "How is Fräulein Trisk these days?" Very probably Hans's family never knew she was there. By the time they moved into their apartment, she had long since stopped going out. It was Erik's mother who fetched her shopping, cooked her soups, and apple tarts, and on Saturday mornings in wintertime, went early to light her very small fire. While his mother was busy, Erik would sit on a wooden chair by the window where Fräulein Trisk had her green fern. It was the only bright thing in the room; everything else was faded with age, just as Fräulein Trisk herself was faded. Time went very slowly on those visits for five-year-old Erik, trying not to fidget, wishing he dared stroke a fern leaf, secretly huffing on his chilblained fingers when he thought Fräulein Trisk might not notice.

She didn't seem to notice, but she must have done, because one day she handed him a parcel, wrapped in crinkled brown paper, with a green woollen bow, and when Erik untied the bow and opened it, he found to his utter astonishment that she had knitted him some mittens. Green woollen mittens.

Erik was so pleased that he hugged her.

"Tck! Tck! Tck!" exclaimed Fräulein Trisk, like a horrified small wren. "Make sure you don't lose them!"

"I never will," promised Erik, who was young enough still to believe in never.

All that winter Erik had worn his green mittens, every time he visited. Then something awful happened. Somewhere, between the school and the streets and sweeping stairs, the mittens were lost.

"Lost!" exclaimed Fräulein Trisk, when honest Erik had made the mistake of telling her, and she walked to the window and stood looking out over the green fern and made many, many furious firecracker sounds.

It was disastrous. After that she always mentioned the mittens in a way that made Erik feel bad. Sometimes the whole visit would pass and he would think this time she had forgotten at last and then she would say, "Those mittens, you are still searching?" or "I used very good wool for your green mittens," or, worst of all, "I could knit some more, but what would be the use?" Always something like that, and the firework scolding more fierce than ever. Erik would feel terrible and sit even more carefully and worriedly on the chair by the fern, and afterward go home and search yet another time. But at last he was old enough to go to school, and after that he hardly saw Fräulein Trisk, unless he craned his head back very far to look up at the window from the street. Sometimes she would be there, gazing out.

Erik's mother still helped her, though, and every June she

would make Fräulein Trisk a very small birthday cake. "Poor old lady, with no one to make a cake for her," she would say to Erik. One year she sent him to the confectioner's to buy a sugar rose to decorate the top. Erik carried it carefully, so as not to break a fragile petal, and it occurred to him as he walked that his mother never had a birthday cake with roses on it herself.

"I have you," she said, when he pointed this out. "Better than a sugar rose."

For years afterward, now and then, she would call him her sugar rose to make him laugh. "Good night, sleep tight, my sugar rose," she would say. After he and Hans became friends, Erik begged, "Never let Hans hear you say that, please!"

"Never let Hans hear me call you my sugar rose?" asked Erik's mother, not in a whisper, and the window open too.

"No," said Erik.

"Hans's mother told me that when he was little, she used to call him Dumpling Boy," said Erik's mother. "Because of his soft round dumpling cheeks."

"Not anymore," said Erik.

"Not anymore," agreed his mother, and although she was usually a very cheerful person, she sounded sad, and Erik was worried and asked, "What's the matter?"

"You're growing up," she said.

"Isn't that good?" asked Erik.

"Of course," she said, and added, "And you are probably right. No more sugar roses."

"Well," said Erik, who was absolutely incapable of making anyone miserable on purpose, even for the very good reason of not being called a sugar rose. "Well, think how Hans and the boys at school would laugh if they heard you call me that! But, perhaps, in private, you could do it in an emergency. How about that?"

It made her smile, as he had hoped it would, and she hugged him and said, "Thank you. Well then, I will only call you a sugar rose in times of great emergency."

And so it was agreed.

Erik's mother was right. He and Hans were growing up. The seasons raced by. Every summer there were swallows. Every winter there was snow. In between there was school, where Erik worked hard because he liked it, and Hans worked hard because he wasn't going to let Erik beat him.

One spring, in 1935, there was a great surprise. A new baby in the family for Lisa and Hans.

"Another girl," said Hans, rolling his eyes in pretend dismay.

Baby Frieda reminded Erik of his little birds: constantly needing to be fed, exhausting and astonishing. He mentioned this to Hans.

"Oh, good," said Hans. "Maybe in a few weeks she'll stop squawking and fly out of the window."

"She doesn't squawk much," said Erik.

"Not as much as Lisa," agreed Hans. Lisa, now thirteen, had lately become even more of a nuisance than before. Not only was she bossier than ever, but she had taken to marching to music and doing gymnastics at inconvenient times on the sitting room floor. When her family complained, she argued that they were unpatriotic.

"I am doing it for Herr Hitler, our chancellor," she said.

"Herr Hitler, our chancellor, doesn't have to step over your legs," said her mother. "Nor does he have a baby to get to sleep, and I am sure he would have more sense than to roll up the rugs and dump them in the hall where your poor father might fall over them."

"If we had a proper balcony, I could do my exercises outside," said Lisa.

"Not half dressed like that you couldn't!" said her mother. "The poor chancellor might come by and see you prancing about in your underwear and have a heart attack."

Then Lisa became indignant and rude, and her mother became angry and shouting, and Frieda woke up and howled louder than either of them and Hans escaped upstairs to have a good, long, disgruntled grumble about his family.

"It's all Lisa's fault," he said. "That stupid club of hers has taken over her senses. 'The League of German Maidens,'" he quoted, mimicking Lisa's voice. "The Plague of German Maidens, more like. They're supposed to be going camping. The sooner the better, I say. What are you doing?"

"Show you in a minute," said Erik, busy at the kitchen table with ink and writing paper. "Lisa can't help it. Everyone is joining those clubs."

"I know," said Hans. "Marching with flags, and singing songs about the Fatherland that don't rhyme properly. Half our school, I should think."

"More," said Erik. "I suppose we should too. If you don't, they say you're useless and unpatriotic. Anyway, I wouldn't mind camping."

"Camping is one thing. Being told what to think, I don't like."

"No one can tell you what to think, Hans," said Erik cheerfully.

"All my family tell me what to think all the time, except the baby, and that's only because she can't talk."

"Mmm," said Erik, drawing a tiger.

"You're not listening properly!"

"I am," said Erik. "Lisa is going camping. Frieda can't talk. Now look at this! What do you think?"

He sat back so that Hans could look at his work. He had designed a poster. A tiger leaped across the top, a parrot decorated the bottom, and the words said:

Free!
Guided Tours of the Berlin Zoo
with Expert and Knowledgeable Students
Erik and Hans!
Stay as long as you like!
Ask a thousand questions!
All you pay is the entrance fee of your
expert and knowledgeable guides!

Berlin had a wonderful zoo. Erik had loved it ever since he could remember. He went whenever he had a chance, and it was always his birthday treat. Every year it got better: every year there were fewer bars, more outdoor spaces for the animals. There was a place where you could walk round a corner and come face-to-face with a lion. Whatever else was happening, you could go to the zoo and think that things were all right. Better than all right, wonderful.

But it cost money to visit, and that was the difficulty. Money was hard to come by. Erik sometimes earned it by delivering groceries, and sometimes waiting at the station, and running to carry bags or call cabs for travelers. In winter there was snow to shovel. However, most of what he earned went to help his mother; there was not much left for Erik.

Nevertheless, now he'd had this wonderful idea. All he had to do was find somewhere to put up his poster, and then he and Hans would stand beside it, ready for the queues of people needing their help.

"Ask a thousand questions?" said Hans. "Expert and knowledgeable? Us?"

"We'll need to study a little first," admitted Erik. "But that's no problem. There are two shelves of animal books in school."

"All right," said Hans. "When I've read the two shelves of animal books, I'll do it, and meanwhile we should put on our oldest clothes, and borrow your mother's brushes that she uses for cleaning the stairs and hall, and I will bring our snow shovel, and we'll turn up early on Saturday morning and tell them we've come to sweep the paths."

Erik said it was a very good idea except that his mother needed her brushes on Saturday mornings, so they tried it on Sunday instead. It worked, and they got in, and for two hours or so swept industriously and happily near all their favorite animals, until a zoo official in uniform came and demanded to know what they were doing. He had just reached the point of taking down their names when who should come along but their schoolteacher, Herr Schmidt.

"Names, names, you do not need their names!" said Herr Schmidt. "These are my students. I will take charge of them now." Then together with Frau Schmidt, and grandmother Schmidt and a whole tribe of little Schmidts, he escorted Erik and Hans to the turnstiles and requested a thousand-word essay from each of them. He gave them the title, right there, at the zoo: "How I Spent My Sunday Morning and Why I Will Never Do It Again."

"For tomorrow morning!" said Herr Schmidt. "And be thankful I came along!"

Erik and Hans were groaning over this task, late on Sunday afternoon, working in Hans's bedroom because Erik would rather his mother didn't know anything about the matter. Erik had finished and was helping Hans by dictating long sentences about flamingos. He had learned a lot about these birds in preparation for being an expert and knowledgeable zoo guide, and it seemed a pity to waste it.

"The flamingo's nest is cone-shaped, made of mud and fine gravel, which the birds gather with their curved beaks. Male and female birds take turns sitting on their eggs. We saw these birds this morning at the Berlin Zoo, as we swept the path near their enclosure."

"More, more!" begged Hans, counting words. "I need at least another hundred."

"We also noticed swallows," dictated Erik, counting words on his fingers as he spoke.

"I didn't," interrupted Hans.

"They were everywhere, you must have done," said Erik. "Come on, hurry up! Swallows build in colonies, many nests close together. Their nests are also made of mud, collected by the birds from the edges of puddles and pools. For example, the otters had swallows visiting their pool. These beautiful black-and-white birds arrive in Europe in the spring, after spending the winter in Africa. They feed on insects caught on the wing and are among the many interesting creatures I saw as

I worked without permission at the Berlin Zoo this morning, which I will never do again, on the instructions of my teacher, Herr Schmidt. Nine hundred and ninety-nine words . . . my esteemed teacher . . . One thousand! Done it!"

"This is very interesting, tell me more," said a voice from the doorway, and they looked up and there was Hans's uncle Karl, grinning down at them. "Sweeping the zoo without permission, eh? Both of you, am I right?"

"We were doing a good job," said Hans.

"We can hardly ever get in because of the cost," explained Erik. "And we really did sweep, and pick up paper bags and orange peels and all sorts of rubbish."

"Very enterprising," agreed Uncle Karl. "I didn't know you were so fond of animals, Hans."

"That's Erik," said Hans. "I just wanted to see if we could do it. It was my idea. Erik thought of something completely different. Look!"

He had kept Erik's poster. Now he passed it to his uncle, who read it carefully, started laughing, and said, "Expert and knowledgeable, eh?"

"Well, Erik really is an expert," said Hans. "Especially about birds."

"I remember you telling me about Erik and birds, and how he wished he could fly. Tell me about your swallows, Erik."

So Erik did, starting with the fallen nest, and ending with the flight from the window. "You should have seen them," he said. "One moment in my hand and the next, like . . . like little darts, like ribbons in the air, like arrows, can you imagine?"

"Yes," said Uncle Karl. "And what do your family think of all this cleaning-at-the-zoo affair?"

"My mother needn't know," said Erik. "She worries about things."

"And your father?"

"Oh," said Erik, rather uncomfortably because he guessed he was going to make Uncle Karl feel bad. "You perhaps don't know, but my father died before I knew him, a few years after the war."

"I'm sorry," said Uncle Karl.

"He'd breathed gas in the trenches and he caught the flu. So . . ."

"Hans's father, my brother, still suffers from that war," said Uncle Karl. "And now he worries about Hans."

"Well, he needn't," said Hans. "I'm no soldier, and neither is Erik. Erik is going to take charge of the zoo when he finishes school. And I shall have a very expensive pastry stall, just outside the gates. With little tables, and hot chocolate and lemonade and things. But then the problem will be, who will wash the cups and glasses? I'll have to think about that. Perhaps Erik could train some monkeys."

"Certainly not," said Erik. "My monkeys will be far too busy in the jungle I will make for them. I'll come and help you, though, after the visitors go home. You can pay me in hazelnut creams and iced gingerbread."

"You see," said Hans to Uncle Karl. "Our futures are secure!"

Uncle Karl looked at him as if he had a hundred unspoken thoughts in his head, but all he said was, "Meanwhile, however, I suppose the zoo is closed to you next weekend?"

"Maybe something will turn up," said Hans.

"Maybe it will," said Uncle Karl.

⤻ ⁊ ⤸

Erik and his mother were poor. No pretending otherwise.

Hans and his family were just-getting-by.

Uncle Karl was different. He was younger, he never seemed to worry about money, he had fun. He was employed by the motor works, and with his job traveled all over Germany, and he owned a car.

It was bright red, beautifully polished, with black mud-guards, and a black roof that folded back for hot weather. Hans's father, who was terribly jealous, said, "That car is wife and family to you, Karl!"

"Better!" said Uncle Karl. "Four-cylinder engine and over seventy miles an hour. No wife or family could compete!"

"And you are an old woman about it!"

"Certainly am," agreed Uncle Karl, and he produced two folded dusters from a clean linen bag, gave one each to Hans and Erik, and said, "Wipe your shoes and jump in, since the zoo is not possible just now."

It was Erik's first time in a car, and for a few minutes he sat stiff and silent, too overawed to move. Beside him, Hans was equally speechless, and when Uncle Karl asked, "Didn't you agree that maybe something would turn up today?" he could only nod and smile.

Then they turned a corner, and slowed down, because a whole lot of people were crossing the road, and at that moment everything changed. A miracle happened.

"The Schmidts!" cried Erik, and so it was, Herr Schmidt, and Frau Schmidt, and the grandmother Schmidt, and a whole line of little Schmidts, all staring at the wonderful car with Erik and Hans inside. All the little Schmidts waved very cheerfully, and Erik and Hans laughed and waved back at them, and Herr

Schmidt raised his hat and nodded in a definitely friendly way. So Erik and Hans forgave him and their faces melted into huge grins, and Uncle Karl tooted the wonderful horn that belonged to the superb red car, and they went on their way across the city.

Afterward, Erik remembered that day as being one of golden sunshine from start to finish.

Uncle Karl drove through the long streets of Berlin as if he owned them. "We are following part of the route that the Olympic torch will travel," he told them. "Less than a month now! You will need to turn out early if you want to see it pass. The whole city will be there."

"We thought we might camp out," said Hans. "So as to get a good place. If the parents will agree."

"That's the spirit," said Uncle Karl. "Of course they will agree. I will have a word or two. Three thousand runners in relay, all the way from Greece to Berlin! How could you miss it! You know how they will light the torch? Straight from the rays of the sun!"

"With a lens?" asked Erik.

"With a mirror. A great parabolic mirror. Now then, we come to the Lustgarten. See the banners!"

There had been Nazi flags all the way, red and white, with black swastikas in the center. Now, there were also great white banners displaying the many-colored Olympic rings. "Glorious Olympic flags," said Uncle Karl, smiling up at them. "Here the torch will arrive, and the next day out to the stadium."

"Lisa is going to the stadium," Erik told him.

"She is?"

"Her Plague of German Nuisances got tickets," said Hans. "I

can't imagine how, since everyone says they are like gold dust to find."

Uncle Karl's eyes twinkled across at him, but all he said was, "Is she pleased?"

"Very. Will you be going too, Uncle Karl?"

"I will. No patriotic German would miss such a spectacle if they could possibly manage otherwise. I am hoping to see the track events. I was a sprinter too, you know."

Hans spluttered, and even Erik had to turn his head away.

"Ha!" said Uncle Karl. "You may smile, but I know about these things. There's a young athlete going to be competing that I am very anxious to see."

"German?"

"American."

"American?"

"African American."

"African American?"

"Jesse Owens. You remember that name, and one day, many years from now, you can tell me . . ." He paused to glance sideways at them. His grin was wicked.

"Tell you what?" asked Hans.

"Oh," said Uncle Karl. "That I was absolutely right. Now then, we'll do a little sprinting ourselves. . . . Hold tight."

Neither Hans nor Erik had ever known such speed. Out of the city, past the end of the tramlines, and suddenly green countryside was flying by in a blur of white dust. The engine sounded like a thousand bees. Uncle Karl tooted his horn at every bend, and Hans and Erik waved and called to every plodding cart and cyclist and pedestrian they passed.

"This is wonderful!" shouted Hans. "Where are we going?"

"Airfield," said Uncle Karl. "Got a friend who says he'll show you his glider."

There was a long wooden hut. You could get beer or coffee and sausage and bread. Uncle Karl introduced them to friends all talking of aircraft and engines and little airstrips. Erik knew already that Uncle Karl could fly a plane, but now he came to realize what Hans already understood, which was that Uncle Karl had been an airman when their fathers had been soldiers. Also, that whereas their fathers' memories had been of bad times, Uncle Karl's were mostly the opposite.

"But it was a terrible war," exclaimed Erik, in astonishment.

"Yes, yes," said Uncle Karl guiltily. "But also, you know, it was fun. . . . I flew an Albatross. There's a bird for you! They used to flip very easily. . . . We have a picture somewhere here. . . ." He called across the hut, "Is there still that old album?" and then somebody began opening drawers in an ancient bureau, and after a while they called, "Here!"

Erik and Hans found themselves looking at an old photograph, an airplane on its back with its wheels in the air, and the pilot, who was Uncle Karl, hanging upside down from his straps, and unable to free himself for laughing. Looking at it, Uncle Karl began laughing again.

"It happened at the very last second," he said, mopping tears from his eyes. "Never a sweeter descent and then the wind underneath and whoops! That day! If I could pick one day to live over, one hour, it would be that one! Who'll give the boys a ride?"

Hans went first. He had second seat in a glider: it went ten times faster than he'd thought it would, and the view made his stomach clutch his spine in fear. He was so cold he became rigid. The last fifteen minutes he spent concentrating all his willpower on not being sick. He staggered back to Erik as pale as paper.

"What went wrong?" asked Erik.

"You wait, that's all," said Hans.

Perhaps because Erik had watched so many birds—the scythe-cuts of swifts, the kestrels on their sky hooks, the ribbon trails of his beloved swallows—perhaps because of these, the air seemed to him a natural place to be, from that very first flight. Coming back to ground level did not seem sensible at all. So many obstacles down there to be dodged, and the speed suddenly gone, and then clambering out onto the airfield, and the shock of discovering the way that gravity clung to your legs.

Back on the green grass, Erik took a step, then a few more, then stood uncertainly. He found himself staring at a tree and thinking vaguely how you only saw them properly from above. Then Hans came running and asked, "Are you feeling sick?"

Erik shook his head.

People were collecting round him, laughing. One of them was Uncle Karl. "Well, Erik," said Uncle Karl. "What's the verdict? Do you think you can get used to it?"

"Oh, yes," said Erik, looking at the grass, and he nodded solemnly and rubbed his eyes and said, "Oh, yes, of course, I was before."

"He means the flying, you dope, not the coming back to earth," said Hans, and there was more laughter and when Erik understood, he joined in too.

"We'll make airmen of them yet," Erik overheard Uncle Karl

say to the friend who had found the album, and, as he and Hans walked back to the hut with their arms across each other's shoulders, he heard the friend reply.

"I think we already have."

SIX

Ruby

Plymouth, Devon, 1936

The chocolate bar stayed behind the clock for weeks, and months and years. Violet moved it when she dusted, but she always put it back. The writing on the paper wrapping faded a little, but it was still there when Will left school, got cider drunk, was sick in the yard, joined the army and went away. For good, Ruby assumed, and was confounded when she came home from school only a couple of months later and found him sprawled on the sofa.

"Does Mum know you're here?" she asked.

"Yep."

"Where is she?"

"Rushed out to the shops for kippers for tea."

Kippers were his favorite, Ruby remembered. Will's favorite; her worst.

"I'd forgotten how dead this place is," he continued. "What time does Dad get back?"

"Not for ages. He's on late shift."

"I was going to drag him out to the pub with me."

"It'll be too late. He'll be tired."

"You in charge now, are you?"

"No."

"You don't seem very pleased to see me."

"I thought you'd gone to the army," she said.

"'Gone to the army,'" he mimicked. "Do you know what you sound like?"

"What?"

"Stupid."

Ruby digested this. Perhaps she did. Even so, she persisted. "When Dad was in the army, he had to fight. He fought in a war."

"Well, double-stupid, I can't do that because there isn't a war."

"What, not anywhere?"

"Nope."

"Why did you join then?"

"To get away from you," said Will. "Have you pinched my chocolate yet?"

"Of course not," said Ruby indignantly.

All the same Will got up to check behind the clock, and when he saw the chocolate bar still there, said, "That's a surprise."

"I wouldn't take it."

"You've taken everything else," said Will. "Have you been sleeping in my room?"

"No!"

"Touched my stuff?"

"No."

"I bet you looked inside the door, though."

Ruby flushed red with guilt. She had looked inside the door. She'd looked and gloated: *He's really gone.* Will saw her face, and knew she had.

"Other people's families are sorry when they go away," he said.

"I was sorry," lied Ruby.

"You don't know what that camp's like."

"Is there a camp?"

"You don't know anything," said Will. "I wish I'd never come back."

Will had come back, though, and he came again, one bitter December day with the chocolate bar still behind the clock, and the clock stopped and the fire out, and his mother sobbing, "Oh Will, oh Will, oh Will," because he was too late. His father had been knocked off his bike and hours later died in hospital, very quickly, like something already arranged.

"What was he thinking of?" cried Violet. "Straight under a bus. They said he turned right in front of it. Oh, Will, I'm so angry! And Ruby ill too, she's not half over measles. Mrs. Morgan took her yesterday so I could be at the hospital. What else could I do?"

"You couldn't do nothing else," Will said staunchly.

"I hope she's not thinking I've sent her away."

"'Course she's not," said Will, and built up the fire, and made tea and toast and answered the door with equal good manners to well-wishers and nosy parkers alike. He stayed for a week and was everything a son should be, said Violet. She was glad of him at the funeral, solemn and handsome in his uniform, giving her his arm. Everyone said he looked a credit to the family and his dad would be so proud.

Ruby, still not well enough to go out, spent that long sodden day with Mrs. Morgan. She knew her well; she was an old friend of her mother's.

Mrs. Morgan was strong and practical and kind. She said, "I

mind the day your parents married and your mum wore your aunt Clarry's pink velvet beret."

"I don't call her aunt because she's not my proper aunt," said Ruby, much too miserable to be nice. "My proper aunts hate me because of the birthmarks on my face."

"Oh, Ruby Amaryllis, what nonsense."

"They hate my name, too."

"Absolute rubbish."

"I still don't know what an amaryllis is."

"It's a flower like a lily but better," said Mrs. Morgan, and Ruby could hear her dad's voice in those words so clearly that she doubled up and sobbed.

"Their wedding was a happy day," said Mrs. Morgan, gathering Ruby in her arms and holding tight. "I gave them a horseshoe I made myself. I had five. Your mum and dad had one. Our Christopher had one. Peter, Clarry's brother, he had one when he married that Vanessa, who always made me laugh. Miss Vane, their neighbor, who married the rag-and-bone man, had one. And there's one left I'm keeping for special."

"What happens at a funeral, Mrs. Morgan?"

"There'll be flowers. I sent roses. White. There'll be a lot of flowers because he was a highly thought-of man. They'll have readings and hymns. They'll say how happy he was, which he was, and how he loved you all, which he did. And he will be laid to rest in the good earth. With the flowers over him. I'll make us a cup of tea and then we'll have a look at the hens. I've not collected the eggs."

Mrs. Morgan lived out of the city, in a cottage that you had to go to in a taxi if you were in a hurry, or on a slow bus if you weren't, because it was nine miles. Or you could ride a bicycle, like Mrs. Morgan often did, into town and back again, to do her housekeeping for Clarry's father, old Mr. Penrose. Mrs. Morgan was tough. She'd known hard times and survived them. She got Ruby through that day with words and hot soup, wood chopping for kindling, *Children's Hour* on the wireless, and sit-down-at-the-table-and-write-this-shopping-list-for-me. It was such a long list that Ruby fell asleep over it, and when she woke up, Clarry was there to collect her, saying, "Will has had to go back this afternoon, Ruby, but I've borrowed my brother's car and I'm staying for a few days to give your mum a hand. There's a lovely fire at home, and a cottage pie in the oven for supper."

"Is Mum all right?" asked Ruby.

"Yes, she is, but she'll be much better for seeing you. And I've brought you a letter from my other goddaughter, Kate."

Halfway home Ruby demanded fiercely, "Is he in heaven now?"

Clarry stopped the car, and put her fists under her chin to help her concentrate while she thought about this. Ruby watched her with great care.

"Yes," said Clarry, nodding. "Yes, I think he must be," and started the engine and drove on again.

SEVEN

Kate

Oxford, Christmas 1936

Kate's grandfather lived in Plymouth, in the narrow stone house where her father Peter and Clarry had grown up. He was as firmly fixed in it as a tortoise in its shell. He would never come to visit them, and when they made the journey to go and see him, he would ask, "How long is this for? Is it necessary?"

Every year Kate's parents invited him for Christmas, and each time he wouldn't come, until one year, instead of saying, "Er . . . perhaps not," he said, "Oh, very well. If I must."

"Hurray!" said Kate's mother, Vanessa. "He'll be happy and looked after and do all the proper Christmas things."

"All the Christmas things in Christendom wouldn't melt that heart of stone," said Kate's father. "And I bet he'll change his mind."

"We won't let him," said Vanessa, and when a postcard arrived from Plymouth, just as she was about to set off to fetch him, she put it writing side down on the mantelpiece and arranged a spray of holly on the top. Then she rushed away and the next day returned triumphant, with Grandfather beside her looking exactly like someone who had written to say that on second thought, they would very much prefer to stay at home.

Which he had.

"I'm completely unprepared for all this," he complained, as they helped him out of the car, and he looked with distaste at the holly wreath on the door and murmured damningly, "Quaint."

Kate got behind Janey for safety.

"In we go, in we go!" said her mother, her arms full of luggage that Grandfather made no attempt to carry. "Boys, bring the rest for us. Charlie, be careful!"

Charlie had picked up his grandfather's briefcase and staggered at the weight. "It feels like it's full of rocks!" he exclaimed. "What's it got in it?"

His grandfather turned and looked at him.

"Sorry," said Charlie meekly.

Vanessa remained cheerful. "Now," she said, "you must make yourself at home with us and not worry about a thing."

"Hmm," said Grandfather doubtfully, and he looked around the little hall, with the Christmas cards on the table and the banisters twisted with ivy and red paper, and said, as if to himself, "Gifts, I imagine, will be expected."

"Oh, no, no!" protested everyone, Janey, Bea, the boys, and their mother; even Kate shook her head. "No, you mustn't think . . ."

Grandfather ignored them all, looked down at Kate with his cold pale gaze, and said, "Perhaps this child can advise me."

"Me?" squeaked Kate, and began her panicky coughing. "Me? I don't think . . . I don't know . . . I . . ."

"Of course Kate and I will take you Christmas shopping, if that's what you'd like," said Vanessa, while behind her back Janey dabbed eucalyptus drops onto a handkerchief and held it out to Kate. "We can visit the lovely bookshop, and afterward get chocolates and things, almost next door."

"I suppose that would suffice," said Grandfather, and Kate stopped coughing and gave him a glance of startled interest, because *suffice* was a word she had never heard outside *The Tailor of Gloucester*. It gave her hope to hear Grandfather use it. Did he care for mice in satins and taffeta? Would he buy, with his last pennies, milk for a cat? The Tailor of Gloucester had been very, very poor. Was it fair to take Grandfather unexpectedly Christmas shopping?

As soon as she could, Kate dragged her mother aside and whispered these worries.

"Kate, he has dragon hoards of cash!" said Vanessa. "And he can't spend it all on booze. It isn't good for him. Besides, it was his idea."

"Perhaps he'll forget," said Kate, but he didn't. The next day at breakfast he asked peevishly, "What about this bookshop? Has the child remembered?"

So they went with him to Blackwell's, and although he glanced around the Christmas displays and asked, "Who buys this stuff?" he did allow them to pile onto the counter *Sweet William* for Charlie, *Cold Comfort Farm* for Bea, Arthur Ransome for Simon (who liked stories), an atlas for Tod (who didn't), a lovely blue diary with silver-edged pages for Janey, and *The Box of Delights* for Kate (which she pretended not to see).

After this, Kate's mother led the way to the sweetshop, where they found chocolate cherries for Clarry, and Kate managed to secretly buy her grandfather a gold chocolate pocket watch with her own private money. Then they took him home,

Vanessa pointing out the beauties of Oxford on the way.

"Dank," said Grandfather. "It gathers the fog. It was dank in my day, and it's dank yet and the pavements are still a disgrace."

"Did you . . . did you used to live here?" asked Kate, surprised into speech.

"Classics," Grandfather said.

"He studied here," translated her mother. "Like Daddy."

"*Not* like your father," said Grandfather. "He was a damned medic. Mind you, that Rupert was worse. Never got here at all. Wished on us by the silly woman my brother married, he was. Took everyone in but me. I had my doubts from the start. There never was the slightest family resemblance. No brains at all."

"He loves him really," whispered Kate's mother to Kate.

Grandfather snorted.

"And it's *Christmas*!" said Vanessa. "Christmas Eve! The carol service tonight, and all the boys in the choir."

"Must be a relief to get them out of the house," grunted Grandfather.

"That's not . . . ," began Vanessa. "I meant . . . Oh, never mind. Poor Peter can't make it, he's at the hospital till ten, but the rest of us have been looking forward to it for ages, haven't we, Kate?"

Kate nodded.

"The children are going to get on with decorating the tree this afternoon," continued Vanessa brightly. "And Clarry will be with us for supper."

Grandfather said he'd had a headache ever since the unspeakable coffee at breakfast time, that he must have lunch exactly at one, and that he couldn't miss his afternoon rest.

"It was terrible coffee; it was out of a bottle," Vanessa agreed. "You shall never have it again."

"I'd like to think not," said Grandfather in a voice of such melancholy that Kate looked up into his face. For one swift moment his eyes gleamed back at her with such intensity that she was astonished. Was he angry? Or was he, possibly, laughing at them?

"Poison," he said.

"What?" asked Kate, startled.

"Bottled coffee."

"Oh."

They took him home and cosseted him with soup and smoked salmon and scrambled eggs. Also tea and hot-water bottles up in his bedroom, and his briefcase left handily by his bed. Kate noticed it clinked very gently, and Charlie, loitering outside the door, heard it too.

"Like bottles," he said. "Bottles nuggling up to bottles. Hurry up, Kate! Dad bought electric lights for the Christmas tree."

Always before they'd had candles—beautiful, fragile, extraordinarily unsafe. These lights were an extravagance, and Charlie unpacked them solemnly. "They cost nearly a pound," he said. "Nineteen and six. More than the turkey."

"Charlie, you be careful with them," warned Janey.

"I am being careful," said Charlie, and wound them round his neck like a necklace and plugged them into the wall, so that his face glowed green and yellow and red and blue, all at once.

"Take them OFF," ordered Bea, and unwound him while Simon and Tod fetched battered boxes from the cupboard under the stairs. They were filled with homemade snowflakes, glass balls, pipe-cleaner reindeer, fat felt robins, and a china angel for the top of the tree. There was an argument about what was junk (most of it, said Simon), and what was family heirloom (most of it, said Bea), but in the end it all went on, and so did the colored lights. The room became a chaos of empty boxes, pine needles, molting strands of tinsel, and crumpled tissue paper. Grandfather looked round the door and said, "Good Lord," and disappeared.

"It does look awful," admitted Janey. "Let's tidy and then have a proper lights-switch-on with everybody here."

So the floor was cleared, the adults rounded up—Clarry with them, just in time—the room darkened, and Janey said, "Now, Kate."

"Me?"

"You can be switcher-on-er," said Janey. "Get down behind the tree."

"Not me," said Kate, shaking her head.

"Of course you," said Janey, hardly impatiently at all. "Scrooch down on the floor and be ready when we all say 'Now.'"

"I don't think I know how."

"You just shove," Charlie told her.

"Shove what?"

"The plug into the plug socket," said Janey. "Now then, *three* . . ."

"Does it matter which way up?" asked Kate, groping around in the dark.

"It only fits one way. You can't get it wrong."

"I trust you have checked that they are properly earthed?" inquired Grandfather.

"They worked when Charlie put them round his neck," said Simon cheerfully. "And necks don't come much earthier than Charlie's."

"Is this a countdown or not?" demanded Tod. *"Three, two . . ."*

"Gaudy gimcrack rubbish," remarked Grandfather. "Don't say I didn't warn you if the whole house goes up in smoke."

"We won't, darling," said Vanessa cheerfully, taking his arm and hugging him. "Ready, Kate? *Three, two, one . . .*"

Kate fumbled madly, found the plug, located the socket, discovered she was sitting on the lead, tugged in desperation, and cried, "Wait, wait!"

"NOW!" chorused all her relations except Grandfather.

Kate yanked at the lead, and to her relief it came suddenly loose. "Got it!" she panted, and plunged the plug into the socket.

Sharp blue fire flickered between the newly wrenched wires. The room lit up in a rainbow flash of color. *Bang!* went every colored light bulb, all of them blowing at once, and Kate leaped screaming to her feet and became terribly tangled in fir branches.

The tree toppled sideways and thudded to the floor.

Tinkle, tinkle went the thin broken glass of the fragile colored balls, and the branches seemed to sigh.

It was no use telling Kate that it wasn't her fault, because it was. Her last desperate pull on the lead had been disastrous. Even after two hours' doctoring by Clarry, the tree was not the same. The branches were bent, the nicest decorations shattered, the angel with her silver wings had landed in several pieces. Early supper in the kitchen with chicken pie and deviled eggs was supposed to be a treat, but Kate couldn't eat. She coughed miserably over her pink Jell-O, spilled her lemonade, and drooped.

"Kate, you're a bit dampening," complained Tod. "Nobody liked that angel anyway."

"I expect she'll glue back together," said Bea. "Did anyone save the bits?"

Clarry said guiltily that she knew where most of them were, and everyone tried to look as if this was good news, as if they didn't know perfectly well that the angel would spend the rest of her Christmas sifting slowly down to the bottom of the dustbin.

"Whole thing was inevitable from the start," said Grandfather, and pulled out a silver flask and gave himself some whisky as a reward for being right.

"One day I'm going to have a flask like that," said Charlie admiringly. "I know something that'll cheer you up, Kate, only I can't tell you."

All day, Charlie had been bursting with a secret. He, the second smallest choirboy, was to be the opening soloist in "Once in Royal David's City" at the carol service that night. This honor, known as being "Once In," was a privilege that no choirboy was ever given twice. Usually, people were only told at the last minute, but Charlie, who was so often late, had been given a hint about being on time and had understood at once. No one else was to know, though, and to put his family off guessing his secret, he said, "If it's me being Once In, no one's to look at me in case I laugh."

"You won't laugh," said Tod, who was safe because he'd done it the year before. "You'll be dying of fright."

"It might be any of the other boys," said Janey. "Or Simon. He's never done it."

"Not me," said Simon sadly. "Too old."

"And too dozy," said Tod.

Their mother took charge then, and demanded help with the clearing up, and in the rushing about that followed, Charlie dropped a dish of trifle much too close to Grandfather, who immediately trod in it.

"Whoops!" said Charlie, and vanished, and didn't reappear until much later, when all the work was done.

"Hello," he said, sticking his head round the kitchen door, "you've washed up supper. Good!"

"You've got a flipping cheek," said Tod. "And you'd better get moving. The choir's supposed to be there half an hour before the rest."

"Quickly, then," said Vanessa. "Off you go. Scoot! The rest of us will be along soon. Oh, Kate . . ."

Kate was coughing again. It was awful. She'd ruined the Christmas tree and now she was going to cough all through the carol service. She said, "Could I not?"

"Not go?"

"I don't mind staying on my own."

"Of course you can't stay on your own, Kate darling," said her mother, and a chorus of people chimed in to say of course not, of course not, but they would love to stop behind too.

"Er . . . ," said Grandfather. "I haven't the slightest intention of singing carols."

They paused, the whole room.

"And I trust you don't think me incapable of supervising er . . . er . . ." He looked at Kate.

"Kate," she said faintly.

"Kate," he repeated. "Yes."

"Oh," said Kate, and gazed around at her family, who were all suddenly watching her very intently indeed.

"Would you be all right?" asked Clarry, so hopefully that despite her alarm, Kate had to say of course she would. The next thing she knew, she was abandoned. The front door had slammed and the house was suddenly very silent.

"Fuss," said Grandfather, and then he looked at Kate, now blinking back tears, and demanded, "What? You wanted to go with them?"

"Yes, but I cough."

"Control it. Are you coughing now?"

"No, but—"

"Well then. For heaven's sake!"

"What?"

"Get your coat! Wait in the hall. Hurry up."

"I—"

"Before I lose patience," said her grandfather.

That was how Kate found herself scurrying after him, out of the house, and down the street and into a seat far back in a chilly corner of the lamplit church. The organ was playing. There was no sign of her family. She guessed they were near the front, but two bundled-up people came to their pew and asked, "Do you mind if we join you?"

"It would be quite intolerable," said Grandfather coldly.

Kate blushed in shame as they backed away. She wished she'd never come, yet here she was, Grandfather on one side, a large cracked tomb on the other. She began to cough.

Grandfather took from his pocket his silver flask, with its cap that unscrewed to make a cup, half filled it, and handed it to Kate. She smelled it instantly. Whisky.

"Calm down," he hissed. "Sip."

Kate shook her head and gasped desperately.

"Sip the water."

It was water. It smelled of whisky, but it was cold water. It was a miracle liquid. It saved her. She could hold up her head and wipe her streaming eyes, and there were the candles, dazzling bright, and the choir in white surplices, and the most tremendous feeling of happiness all about, because it was nearly Christmas.

The service began, and it was Simon after all who was Once In and sang the opening verse, neither too old, nor too dozy, nor dying of fright, his voice dropping the notes like the chimes of a clear bell into the golden light.

It's perfect, Kate thought.

Grandfather's eyes were half closed with boredom and his thin lips folded shut. The stone statues in their alcoves looked more alive than he did, yet three times he saved Kate, filling and passing the silver cup.

His eyes snapped open when the final blessing began. He sat tense until, at the words "now and forevermore," he nudged Kate with a very sharp elbow.

"Amen," finished the minister, and echoed the congregation, all except Grandfather, who ordered, "Now!" and under cover of the general shuffling and collecting of dropped bags and service sheets got sharply to his feet.

"Out!" snapped Grandfather, and as the organ began flinging

"In Dulci Jubilo" up to the roof arches and all along the nave, he hustled Kate into the night. "And you keep quiet about this, or they'll be bleating even more."

"Who . . . ?"

"Wretched family, flock of sheep, never a moment's peace."

"But—"

"Don't you start bleating too!"

"Aren't we going to tell them?"

"Are you an absolute fool? Faster, please."

"I thought your flask had whisky in it. Did you pour it away?"

"Pour away good whisky? Of course not, I drank it. Filled it in the kitchen while you were dithering about."

They were almost home, and they were unpursued. There was time to pause under a streetlamp and catch their breath. The lamplight pooled around them. A few snowflakes fell. Somewhere a bell chimed.

"It was lovely, wasn't it?" asked Kate timidly.

"It was absolute bilge," said Grandfather. "Supposedly intelligent adults wallowing in ridiculous fairy tales. Come on!"

They'd accidentally left the door unlocked, but they hadn't been burgled. They were back in the living room when the rest of the family appeared, marveling at the snow, teasing Simon, and most of all, congratulating Kate and Grandfather, who'd survived so well without them that everyone was too kind to mention that they'd let the fire go out.

"I saw you!" said Charlie, as soon as he and Kate had a moment together. "No one else did, though."

"Don't tell!"

Charlie held up a finger, licked it, and drew it across his throat.

"Did you mind not being Once In?"

"No," said Charlie, who'd seen Simon's face when he'd said, "Too old," and left as soon as he could, to sprint all the way to church, blurt out, "Simon wants it more than anything," and run all the way back home.

"Stockings!" said Clarry, coming in with a bundle of red and green and blue ones, made long ago by Vanessa. "And bedtime, Kate, or you'll be too tired for Christmas in the morning."

(Over by the fire Grandfather raised a sardonic eyebrow.)

"You as well, Charlie boy," agreed Peter, just home from the hospital.

"Will you come up, Clarry, when we're ready?" asked Charlie. He had a camp bed in with Kate that night, while Clarry had his room. "And stay and talk to us?"

"Perhaps," said Clarry, but she sat down quite willingly when she arrived and admired their dangling stockings.

"Tell us your best Christmas present ever," said Kate.

"That's easy," said Clarry. "One Christmas just before the war, Grandfather bought me a little silver watch. I have it still. I'll show you."

"What else?"

"Another year we had a Christmas party, with presents for everyone on the Christmas tree. And we danced and played games and sang carols."

"'Once In'?" asked Charlie.

"All the old carols."

"Who was there?"

"Oh, our neighbors, and Vanessa and her lovely brother Simon, and your father and me and Rupert."

"And did you have stockings?" asked Kate, but Clarry was lost in memories and didn't reply until Charlie said, "I wish Rupert was here now."

"Much too busy," said Clarry bravely. "Stockings? No. No one thought of stockings."

"You'll have one this year," said Charlie, who'd helped with the preparations and added a necklace of red glass beads as his own contribution. "Everyone will, except I don't know about Grandfather."

"Of course he will, I made him one."

Kate sat up with delight.

"Are you going to put it on the end of his bed?"

"No, no! He wouldn't like that. I'm going to leave it by his door."

"What's it got in it?" asked Charlie, so Clarry took a deep breath and recited: "A-green-scarf-with-tassels, a-pen-with-his-old-college-crest-on, anchovy-spread-for-toast, peppermint-cremes, cedar-wood-shaving-soap, a-cigar, and the-Christmas-*Illustrated-London-News*-rolled-up-with-a-ribbon."

Kate went to sleep reciting this list, and woke to find it was Christmas morning. In their stockings were sugar mice and chocolate pennies and Charlie had indoor fireworks. Kate found a glass globe with a reindeer and pine trees, and falling snow when she turned it upside down. Then Clarry came in with her chocolate cherries and a tiny model of the Eiffel Tower. It had a label underneath that read, *This time next week*.

"From Rupert," guessed Charlie at once.

"Clever boy!"

"And you must be going to Paris. Have you been before?"

"Not for ages, but Rupert has, lots. He lived there for a long while."

"It's a good present," said Charlie, busy carving a bar of pink-and-white coconut ice with a new pocketknife. "I saw Grandfather's stocking and I've tied a red balloon on the top for decoration."

"Very kind," said Clarry, laughing. "What's that you've dropped on the floor?"

"Only a sort of rubbish flashlight thing."

"It's not a flashlight, it's a bike lamp," said Clarry, inspecting it.

"What good's a bike lamp without a . . . ," began Charlie, and then leaped out of bed. They heard him jump the stairs in three bumps, the back door flung open, and jubilant shrieks.

Then it was breakfast time, and Grandfather appeared holding his stocking and saying in a very complaining voice, "I fell over this. Can somebody please reclaim?"

"It's for you!" said Charlie. "Open it! Open it!"

"Oh, really," said Grandfather wearily. "I don't think so." Nevertheless, he untied the red balloon, looked at it solemnly, said, "Very droll," and then unpacked the rest of his stocking with such withering remarks that Charlie became crimson with suffocated laughter. The twins picked him up, carted him to the kitchen, and dosed him with cold water poured over his head.

"Help!" squealed Charlie, and reached for the cooking brandy, put out ready for the pudding, and took a great swig, just as his mother arrived.

"Charlie!"

"It's all burny and lovely!" said Charlie, and took another gulp.

"Charlie Penrose," protested his mother, grabbing the bottle. "You will end up an old soak just like . . . just . . . just . . . Goodness, there's the telephone! Who would telephone at this hour on Christmas morning?"

"Bea says to tell you it's the hospital for Daddy," said Kate, appearing in the doorway.

"No, no, it can't be!" moaned Vanessa, but it was, and two minutes later Peter was gone, and no sooner had the door closed behind him than there was a loud bang, clearly the red balloon, and Grandfather's voice, sounding very aggrieved. Vanessa put down the brandy bottle and ran, and Charlie, who was suffering a very strong reaction after his extreme unselfishness the night before, had a few more fatal swigs, marched into the dining room, and sang with very great clarity:

"Wild shepherds washed their socks at night
And piled them on the grasses
Don't do your pants, the angel cried
Cos then I'll see your—"

Clarry, who was nearest, seized Charlie by his shoulders and hurried him out of the door. From the other side they heard:

"Good King Wenceslas went out
To the pub on Monday
Tuesday, Wednesday, Thursday too
Friday through to Sunday
All that day he said his prayers—
(That was not a fun day.)
Never mind, King Wenceslas!
You'll be back on Mo-hon-day!"

"Everyone, breakfast!" called Kate's mother, who had rushed back to the kitchen and returned with an enormous tray piled high. "Fresh tea and proper coffee! Eggs, hot sausage rolls, orange fruit salad. Clarry's dealing with Charlie. What a morning!"

"I think I would like to go home," said Grandfather.

Kate's mother let go of the breakfast tray so suddenly that it hit the table with a crash. "Go home?" she repeated.

"You did say that if I should decide not to stay, either you, or Clarry or Peter . . ."

"But it's Christmas Day," said Janey.

"Does that make a difference?" asked Grandfather, sounding so genuinely surprised that for a moment Vanessa's patience slipped and she said, "There are all these children in the house, a turkey in the oven that's been there since six this morning, presents under the Christmas tree, two elderly neighbors coming to dinner, and Peter's at the hospital because there was an accident at the railway crossing. . . ."

"Coffee, Grandfather?" asked Janey. "Kate, I've taken the top off an egg for you. . . ."

"We three kings of Oxford St. Giles." Charlie's voice, choirboy bright, came floating down the stairs.

"One with pimples, another with—"

"Not that one!" exclaimed Tod and Simon, and went racing out of the room together.

"They learn them in the choir," explained Bea placidly to her grandfather. "They can't help it. It's traditional."

"All sorts of lovely traditions," said Kate's mother, who was recovering with hot coffee. "Of course I'll take you back, Grandfather darling, if you absolutely insist, but . . . Kate!"

Kate was awash, silent tears pouring down her face at the thought of Christmas over before it had hardly started.

"Look at Kate!" said Janey, and Grandfather looked and said, "Really. Not again. Control yourself! Here!"

In the surprised silence that followed he splashed water into a tumbler and pushed it toward Kate, who gulped it down and said, "Thank you, Grandfather. Please don't go."

"One damned drama after another," said Grandfather. "I suppose I can wait another day. What's going on upstairs?"

"Charlie's being put to bed to sleep it off," said Vanessa, and as she spoke, they heard Clarry's voice as she left him. "Sleep tight, sweet Charlie. May flights of angels sober you up in time for dinner. . . . Hello, everyone, sorry I'm late. Yes, please, coffee!"

"Family life," said Grandfather, getting out his flask, which plainly wasn't filled with water anymore. "No, thank you!"

Then he poured himself a whisky, picked up the whole plate of sausage rolls, said, "If you can spare me," and stalked out of the room.

Only Kate saw, but as he passed, he glanced at her and winked.

A great rush of affection swept over Kate. She ran after Grandfather, calling, "Wait!" and when he turned to look at her, she very carefully, her face solemn with concentration, winked back.

EIGHT

Dog

Scrapyard, East London, 1937

The scrapyard dog belonged to the family that lived in the crumbly brick building, half warehouse, half dwelling place, at the back of the yard. There was a girl and a shrill-voiced old woman, and three or four loud-laughing, rough-booted men, who came and went. The girl was mostly invisible, but sometimes the door would open quietly and narrowly, and she would seep out of the gap to lose herself in the chaotic misery of the yard. There was a huge, broken winch that had once unloaded cargoes from the holds of ships. The girl would hunch down there, so near to the dog that he could smell her old clothes smell. Mostly she was motionless, glaring at the house, blank-faced and sniveling. Other times she would look around, at the broken-glass-topped walls, and the sky that hung just above the chimney pots, and the iridescent colors that spilled oil made in the puddles. Now and then she stirred a puddle with her toe, gazing as the patterns broke. All the time the dog watched her, in case she should suddenly lash out. Every time she moved, he flinched, although she never brought the yard broom, his greatest enemy of all.

"Hello, dog."

She was looking at him.

"Dog?"

It was absolutely terrifying, being watched like that.

"Hello, dog."

The door was pulled open then, and the old woman screeched down the yard, "Don't you make a pet of that dog!"

"Shut up," muttered the girl.

"You make a pet of that dog and it'll go soft!"

"Old bat," the girl said quietly.

"What did you say?"

"Wash your ears!" yelled the girl, so loudly she tumbled off the winch, and the old woman grabbed the broom and came scurrying down the yard.

"Waah! Waah! Waah!" barked the dog, over and over, flinging himself forward, choking on his chain, hysterical with fear. *"Waah! Waah! Waah! Waah!"*

Not gone soft at all.

NINE

Erik and Hans

Berlin, 1937

The war that Hans's father and Uncle Karl had fought in, the war that had ruined Erik's father's health so he died before Erik ever knew him, had ended with defeat for Germany, late in 1918. The next year, a treaty had been drawn up by the winning nations. It was called the Treaty of Versailles. Germany had been blamed more than any other country, and made to pay for the damage the war had caused. They had to pay with land, and with gold, and they had to agree to having a smaller army, and a much smaller navy, and no air force at all.

Erik and Hans grew up hearing opinions of the Treaty of Versailles. It was a sort of national ache that nobody could forget. Hans's father, once started on the subject, could go on for hours and hours. He said the youth of Germany should rise up in indignation about the Treaty of Versailles. He especially said this on Sundays, when Lisa and her mother were in the kitchen and Hans was the only youth of Germany about. Hans used to groan because he had heard it so many times before. One Sunday, Hans's father was saying it yet again, and Hans was groaning, yet again, when Uncle Karl arrived.

"The youth of Germany," said Uncle Karl, clapping Hans on

his shoulder, "should fetch their friend and come with me to the airfield . . ."

"Oh, thank goodness!" shouted Hans, and bolted for the door.

". . . if their father will allow," finished Uncle Karl, laughing.

"Yes, yes, take him along!" said Hans's father. "Better up in the sky than down in the mud." He was thinking—he never forgot—of the war he'd fought himself.

Quite regularly now, Uncle Karl took the boys to the airfield, and they also often went on their own. They made the journey by bike; Hans on his and Erik on Lisa's, swapping on the way back because Lisa's bike was slower and Hans was always fair.

"Everyone starts with learning to make the coffee," Uncle Karl had warned them, but neither of them minded making the coffee, nor washing up the mugs. The teasing was good-natured: "Poor boys. They have to do something now they're blacklisted by the zoo."

They didn't just learn to make the coffee. They learned map reading, and planning a route, which seemed like it should be simple and turned out to be anything but. They polished windshields, rubbed down old paint and added new, and lubricated wheels. They hauled on ropes and ran down hills to launch the little one-man sailplanes. They argued over altimeters and compasses. They found out that propellers must be balanced, and cables checked and winches greased. They went on flights with dual controls and men who sat back with folded arms and said, "You take her for a bit."

That was how it began. It was an adventure and a sort of

escape. Now in Berlin, *Heil Hitler* salutes were everywhere, and huge red-and-white flags with black swastikas were appearing all over the city.

At school, Herr Schmidt had a new responsibility and a new organization to run. It was called the Hitler Youth.

"Everyone enrolled now?" he asked his students, and everyone had, even Erik and Hans, but when it came to the long, tedious, after-school meetings, they were seldom there. This had been easy enough to get away with when they first signed up, but now things were changing.

"Boys," Herr Schmidt told them privately. "Come on. No more excuses. Gets you fit. Outside in summer. Lots to learn. Besides, bright boys like you might want to go on to university. Completely impossible if you don't join in. Even a decent apprenticeship, for that matter, would be ruled out."

Ever since the day in Uncle Karl's car when he had smiled at them and raised his hat, Herr Schmidt had been a friend, so Erik and Hans told him very cheerfully about the pastry stall and the zoo.

"This is the new Germany," said Herr Schmidt. "Open your eyes. The fairy tales are over."

He suddenly sounded terribly sad.

"Please don't worry, Herr Schmidt," said Erik.

"Don't worry!" repeated Herr Schmidt, no longer sad, but indignant. "It's you who should worry! You should have been much more involved long ago. You'll be leaving school soon. It looks very bad. Reflects on your families, too. Your father will want to keep that job at the post office, Hans. I am telling you this for your own good."

They looked at him and believed him.

"For your own good, Hans. For your own good, Erik. *Heil Hitler*," said Herr Schmidt.

When someone said that to you, you were supposed to say it back.

"*Heil Hitler*," said Hans.

"*Heil Hitler*," said Erik.

And that was that, but it could have been worse because now the airfield was doubly wonderful. And doubly patriotic. Helping at an airfield unquestionably trumped marching about with the Hitler Youth. Even Herr Schmidt agreed.

Erik was the first to take the controls and land a glider. Hans did it a week later. They went to the zoo to celebrate, and the zoo was looking magnificent. Recently Germany had passed the strictest animal protection laws in the world. Lion cubs were hoped for.

Yet even the zoo was not free from the swastika flags. Paper ones made for children could be bought at the kiosk near the entrance. Erik saw a small boy poke one through the bars of a monkey cage. A very tiny monkey reached out a miniature hand and took it, and then, with thoughtful round eyes, and nimble brown fingers, shredded the flag into wisps and fragments and let them fall to the ground.

Erik looked at the monkey with love, and murmured, "Good monkey."

Hans said, "We need more monkeys like that."

Both of them spoke carefully, making sure nobody was about who could hear. They did this hardly realizing they were doing it. Their world had changed, and they had changed with it.

One day Erik suddenly remembered Fräulein Trisk, who he hadn't thought of or seen for years.

"Poor old lady," said his mother. "Well, I always thought she would be better off staying with her niece in the country."

"Oh," said Erik guiltily, thinking that he really ought to have said goodbye, but still, it was all a long time ago and anyway she would probably have got annoyed and spluttered her firecracker splutters. "You used to bake her a birthday cake and light her stove on Saturdays," he remembered.

"Sundays," said his mother, not looking at him.

Erik opened his mouth, and then shut it without speaking. He thought, *Fräulein Trisk*, and realized for the first time that it was a Jewish surname. He didn't say anything to his mother because she was plumping cushions. They had six cushions. Erik's mother picked them up in pairs, one in each hand, and clapped them together, leaning out of the window.

Smack! went the cushions.

The rug was already hanging over the windowsill, shaken clean and upside down. The furniture was all pushed into a corner. Erik's mother flung the cushions in a heap, swept the floor like a whirlwind, dusted the shelf, swiped the table, rubbed the photograph of Erik's father with a corner of her apron, put her hands on her hips, and looked at Erik. He was taller than her now.

"Sundays," she said.

"Are you sure?" asked Erik.

"Of course I'm sure! I should know! Who else could know but me?" she cried.

"Only me," said Erik.

⌐ ⫴ ⌐

There were no Jewish students left in school. Often you saw signs on shops: NO JEWS. The signs had disappeared for a few months when the Olympic Games had been held in the city, but soon after they were back. Hans said that people were divided into three groups about the signs. There were those who were glad to see them. Those who were not glad to see them. And those who pretended they didn't see them at all.

Erik repeated this to his mother.

"Yes, yes, Hans is probably right," she said. "Such a fuss about nothing, though. There are plenty of good shops the Jewish people can use. It's not so important."

"Not important!" exclaimed Erik.

"Listen, Erik. Men have shops that women would never go to, right? And women have shops where men would blush to enter the door. And children have toy shops and book readers have bookshops and there are rich people's shops in Charlottenburg where I would never dare show my nose! Never! Not a chance! The looks I would get if I did! They really might as well write, 'Apartment Cleaners Not Welcome' on the door."

"What are you saying?" asked Erik. "Are you saying it's just the same?"

"Of course it's the same!" she cried, beginning to bang cushions about again. "Of course it is. So stop always asking questions."

There were grades of glider pilot license: A1 ("One loop and three landings," Erik told Hans. "Easy."), A2 ("Two loops, six landings, circle a church tower upside down. Easier still!" Hans told Erik). "What next?"

"Next is just the same as before but you do it with your eyes shut," said Erik. "The only problem is, you have to flip pancakes on the loops."

"Flipping pancakes is all wrong," said Hans. "You should fold them over gently, with spiced apple in the middle. I shall serve them in the mornings at my stall outside the zoo."

"With cream?" asked Erik.

"Naturally."

"You're going to be very busy," observed Erik.

"I know," said Hans. "I shall probably need staff."

"Don't look at me," said Erik. "No one can manage a whole zoo and pancakes too."

"My dear Erik," said Hans, "I plan to recruit pretty girls in white aprons, not shambling zookeepers with birds' nests in their hats."

"After national service," said Erik.

"After national service," said Hans.

National service was compulsory in Germany now, as soon as you left school.

Whenever it could be managed, Erik and Hans still visited the zoo. Their blacklisting was long forgotten, even by Herr Schmidt. And the zoo was more fascinating than ever. An Indian elephant had given birth, and a new gorilla had arrived. He looked much smaller than Bobby, the gorilla Erik remembered from his childhood, but then, sometimes, the whole zoo looked smaller.

But no less beloved.

The new Siberian tiger was the latest exotic arrival. Unusually for the Berlin Zoo, the Siberian tiger had a cage—there was no attempt to contain it with moats and ditches and glass.

Once Erik saw it charge, from stillness to a terrifying anger, shoulder first at the bars of its prison.

It was an astonishing, shocking animal, not only because it was twice the size of the other big cats, but also because it would meet a human gaze. The Siberian tiger hated people. It would lock gaze, eye to eye, in a glare of such menace and power that it would be hard to move away.

Hard to move at all, Erik found. When he first went to see it, he stayed all afternoon. Hans found him there, looking miserable, and they didn't leave till closing. They had been in a fight with some other boys that morning, and the marks were very visible, even though they'd won. Hans was still smoldering.

"We should have dropped them in the river," he said. "Nazi bullies."

Erik felt the bridge of his nose, very gently, between thumb and fingertip. "I think it might be broken," he said. "What are we going to tell them at home?"

"We'll say we had an argument!" said Hans.

"You and me?"

"Yes."

Erik laughed so much the tiger was startled. It was good to laugh again.

It was not long afterward, on the last day of school, that Erik noticed something in the attic window, high above the street. It was a fern, bright green. He was so surprised he stood still for a moment, and Hans asked, "What is it?" and followed his gaze.

"Absolutely nothing," said Erik, but when he got in, he mentioned the fern to his mother. She gave him a glance that not only shut him up, but made him decide he'd never look up at that window again. All the same, he couldn't help saying, "I thought . . ."

"Erik," said his mother. "What did I say to you when you came back here a few weeks ago, your jacket all ripped and your face like a half-fried frankfurter, trying to tell me you'd been fighting Hans?"

"Nothing," said Erik.

TEN

Ruby

Plymouth, Devon, 1937–1938

For as long as Ruby could remember, every time Clarry came to Plymouth to visit her father, old Mr. Penrose, she would hurry across town afterward to see Ruby and her mother. Then, no matter how dismal the day, everything would be transformed. If the shop was busy, Clarry would take over the till, or the shelves, or the sorting and numbering of the newspapers for the delivery boy. However, when things were quiet, Ruby's mother would turn the OPEN sign on the door to CLOSED. "Shopping?" she would ask hopefully, and all three would rush into town.

Violet was a great shopper. She and Clarry especially liked looking at hats. Ruby loved the pet shop with its perpetual supply of kittens in the window, but it didn't really matter what they did. They could be perfectly happy in Woolworth's choosing hair slides for Ruby, or buying a cake at the baker's, or a bunch of blue cornflowers from a market stall. It was the being together that they loved. Violet and Clarry would chatter and laugh, and Ruby would hop along beside them, her splattered, vivacious face sparkling with brightness. Afterward, always a little late, they would scurry to the train station, and she and Violet would wave *goodbye,*

goodbye and Clarry would call back, "Next time! Soon!"

"When did you first know her?" Ruby asked once, and her mother replied, "We've been friends since we were girls."

After Ruby's father died, things changed a little. Violet didn't seem as interested in shopping anymore. But Clarry came just the same, sometimes to eat toast and help tidy the shop, now and then to say, "Let's get a tram down to the seafront, I should like to sniff the sea." All the time, they chatted. Will's most recent letter would be shared, and the latest news about Kate, Clarry's other goddaughter, who still coughed too much and wheezed too much and missed too much school, but was getting better. Ruby always liked to hear about Kate. They'd never met, but she felt there was a sort of connection between them. Kate had written when Ruby's father died, and sometimes after that she would send a message via Clarry.

"You should reply," said Violet.

"I do reply," said Ruby, "I always say to Clarry to tell her thank you."

"Not the same as writing."

"Kate doesn't write much," pointed out Ruby. "Mostly she draws."

That was true.

> Dear Ruby,
> Clarry said you like cats.
> Here are some cats.
> Love, Kate

The rest of the page, and all round the edges, was covered in little pictures of cats, stretching, sleeping, twisting round to lick their shoulders, sharing a saucer of milk, prowling a rooftop under the moon.

Each little sketch was carefully detailed. The cats had whiskers and silky shadows, there were tiles on the roof and stars in the sky. Ruby was so clearly pleased that when her mother hugged Clarry goodbye, she whispered urgently in her ear, "Try and bring Kate one day," and the next time Clarry visited, she did.

They arrived one rainy teatime. Ruby opened the door to find Clarry smiling underneath a dripping umbrella with a skinny, coughing girl lurking just behind.

"What a lovely surprise!" called Violet, hurrying to meet them, but she didn't deceive Ruby, who with her usual fear of strangers hissed, "If I'd known she was coming, I'd have run."

"Behave!" hissed her mother back. "Don't spoil it!" and to give her a chance to get over her indignation, sent her out for raspberry jam to go with the bag of tea cakes that Clarry had produced. By the time Ruby returned, Kate had already begun toasting, obviously left to get on with it while Clarry and Violet sat at the table by the window and said, "Tell me everything, tell me truly how you are," and, "Oh, I've missed you," and things like that.

Kate looked relieved when Ruby appeared, and offered her the toasting fork.

"I fetched the jam," said Ruby mutinously.

"I only thought you might be able to do it better," said Kate. "We brought butter, too, but I don't know whether to put it on."

"Why'd you bring butter? Did you think we were poor?"

"I think it was supposed to be a treat," Kate murmured, blushing so nervously that all at once, Ruby was ashamed of her bad temper and said, "It is a treat. I love tea cakes. You toast, I'll butter. Mum made gingerbread this morning too. Now I know why."

Tea was cheerful. Sooty and Paddle were included. They had cat biscuits and milk and were endearingly polite, crunching with blissful half closed eyes, or gazing longingly at the milk jug and gently patting Ruby with a wistful, asking paw. Afterward Ruby took Kate on a tour of the newspaper shop downstairs, Will's blessedly empty bedroom, and her own snow-white attic with the patchwork quilt and the window onto the rooftops. Both cats followed after them, and when they arrived in Ruby's attic, Kate produced a pencil and a notebook from her pocket and drew them, very small.

"Draw them big," said Ruby.

"I can only draw small," said Kate. "I put pictures in my diary to help me remember things."

"Is that your diary?"

"No. It's just a book I practice in."

"Will you draw being here when you get home?" asked Ruby.

Kate looked startled, but replied hesitantly, "I might try."

"The raspberry jam? The cats having tea?"

"Oh, yes." Kate nodded, smiling.

"Clarry's umbrella when it wouldn't close?"

"That might be really hard."

"Me?" Ruby turned her face away as she asked. What if Kate said yes? What if Kate said no?

"I don't know," said Kate.

"Don't know?"

"I'm not very good at faces. I never get the noses right."

This answer was so unexpected that Ruby's eyes opened wide, but she couldn't help smiling as Kate tried to explain about noses; so sausage-shaped and yet so triangular, and the problem of the two holes in them, all right on animals but awful on humans.

"You have to be careful with noses," said Kate. "Because they're not like eyes and hands and mouths. They never change shape."

"You've thought about it a lot," said Ruby, and Kate said yes she had, so seriously that Ruby started laughing.

"Noses matter," said Kate, and Ruby laughed even more and then quite suddenly found herself being handed the notebook. There she was. Hair tangled, eyes crinkled, her laughing three-cornered mouth, and her nose a triumph, recognizably her own and not sausagey at all.

But no birthmarks. No dark, destroying birthmarks.

Only shaded shadows where her birthmarks should be.

Over the years, Ruby's mirror-avoiding had become complete. Even so, she had often wondered what she looked like to strangers. Now she was outraged.

"Are you sorry for me or something?" she demanded.

"Why?" asked Kate, astonished.

"You can't trick me!"

All at once Ruby grabbed Kate's pencil and bent double over the notebook, scribbling over the shadowed marks until they became dark and huge and dominating.

"There!" she said.

Kate was so dismayed, she protested, "They're not a bit like that."

"I know what my face is."

"But—"

"I'm not stupid."

Kate spoke all in a breathless rush, before Ruby interrupted again. "You've made that mark on your cheek as big as your ear and it's really smaller than . . . than"—she looked around for help and spotted Paddle—"than a paw print! And those others are quite little—"

"Little!" exclaimed Ruby.

"Compared . . ."

"You wouldn't say that if they were on your face!"

"I wou-wou—" Kate was halted by coughing, but when she began again continued doggedly, "Wouldn't mind."

"What a lie!"

"I think—"

"You think you're so clever, that's what you think," said Ruby furiously.

"No, I don't," said Kate, and subsided, concentrating on breathing. When she spoke again, she said, "That was the best nose I ever did, and you've spoiled it."

"I'll get rid of it then," said Ruby, and spoiled it completely by tearing the drawing out of the notebook, screwing it up, running down the attic stairs, and throwing it into the fire.

"What was that?" demanded Violet suspiciously.

"Nothing."

Violet gave her a very *That isn't true and I know it* look as Kate trailed in, avoiding eye contact with everyone but the cats, and Clarry became very brisk, saying, "We must absolutely rush or we'll miss the train. Loveliest afternoon for weeks, Violet! Thank you. Bye-bye, Ruby! Come on, Kate!" and vanished.

After Clarry and Kate had gone, there was an emptiness.

There was often an emptiness. In the past, the three rooms above the shop had made a home, but however hard Ruby's mother tried, without Ruby's father, it wasn't a home anymore. It was a place where Violet and Ruby waited.

Will came back quite often. He would arrive without warning, and (thought Ruby) take over everything. Her mother would rush into an orgy of cooking. Puddings and buns would appear that were never seen on ordinary days. Bananas, too, and eggs at breakfast, and delicious baked beans in tins. Meals would suddenly last twice as long, with extra talk as well as extra food, and Violet jumping up and down to the stove, and Will in their father's chair feeding Sooty and Paddle with cheese and fragments of bacon rind. Both cats seemed to have forgotten Will's kitten-drowning past; to Ruby's dismay, they welcomed him and jumped onto his knee.

Then, as suddenly as he'd appeared, Will would vanish. Violet and Ruby would return to bread-and-jam breakfasts and bread-and-soup suppers and there would be no spare cheese for the cats.

"He'll be here again before we know it," Violet would say, to comfort herself, and Ruby would hope that she was wrong. Then they would both go back to waiting.

They waited for the sadness to fade. For time to pass. For school days to end. For aunts with flowery names to arrive (and then, as soon as they had done, for them to hurry up and go). They waited for customers and cashing-up time, and night, when at least you could be miserable in peace, and morning, when you could get up again at last.

One day, when Ruby's loneliness had reached an unendurable level, she wrote a two-word message to Kate:

Sorry,
Ruby.

And immediately Kate replied,

It doesn't matter, Kate.

These notes went in with Clarry's and Violet's letters to each other, carefully sealed from adult eyes.

Draw a picture of yourself, wrote Ruby next.

Kate sent back a picture of herself with a towel over her head, inhaling eucalyptus from a jug of hot water.

To help me breathe, she wrote.

There was nothing to be seen of Kate in the picture, just the jug and the towel and a whiff of steam. It made Ruby laugh, and she took it down to the shop to show her mother, and she laughed too.

"What's the joke?" asked a customer, coming in at that moment, and Violet answered carelessly, "Ruby was just showing me a picture of her friend."

Somewhere inside Ruby then, a little glow began, like a candle flame, wavering into life.

"She's not my friend," she protested, as usual argumentative and defensive, but the candle flame didn't go out.

Will noticed it when he came home.

On school days, Ruby was always back before her mother was free from the shop. She'd spend the time doing what she could to help, especially the things her father would once have done: shoe polishing and coal-bucket filling, and chopping broken greengrocer pallets into kindling for the fire.

One evening Ruby was on her hands and knees in the kitchen, laying a fire with her newly chopped wood, when a voice behind her said, "That's my job," and it was Will.

Ruby jumped so hard she dropped her match and wasted it. When she reached for another, Will got the box first.

"Out of the way!" he said.

"No, thank you."

"You've got it built too far forward. You'll fill the room with smoke."

"No, I won't."

"Budge!"

"No."

"You'd better!" said Will, who still had the matches, and then, in a completely different voice, "Hey, what's the matter with that cat?"

He had moved to the window, and was staring out as if alarmed. Ruby hurried to look as well, and of course it was a trick. Will was down at the fire in a moment, dismantling her arrangement of rolled paper, wood, and coal, and rebuilding it his own way. It lit with one match, flaring into brightness as if it was on his side, and he said, "That's how to do it. Who chopped the wood?"

"I did."

"Too thick. You want to make it thinner. Lights faster and wastes less. Anyway, hello."

"Hello," said Ruby crossly.

"How you doing, then?"

"All right."

"Managing without me?"

"Of course."

"I've been thinking. Soon as I can, I'm going to chuck in the army. Oh, thanks. I see. Great."

What he had seen was Ruby's eyes open wide with dismay.

"Charming," said Will.

"I didn't say anything," protested Ruby.

"You didn't need to," said Will, and continued to stare at her curiously.

"Stop it," she said, and turned her face away.

"Mum would be pleased if I came home for good," said Will, now beginning to feed his fire with a very extravagant amount of Ruby's carefully chopped kindling. "Someone else earning. I could get work easy, share the cost of keeping you."

"I don't cost hardly anything," said Ruby, very hurt. "And I help with the newspapers and mind the shop often. And when I finish school, I can get a job too."

"How do you get on at school?" Will asked.

"Good," lied Ruby.

"Top of the class, like I was?"

Ruby didn't reply.

"You've got friends and that too?"

"Of course," said Ruby through gritted teeth. "I've got hundreds."

"Hundreds," repeated Will solemnly, nodding.

Ruby ignored him, stepped over his legs, tipped potatoes out of a brown paper bag onto the draining board, and began rinsing them under the tap.

"I'm starting supper," she said.

"Hundreds," said Will again. "Are you going to peel those spuds?"

"No, I'm doing them in the oven. In their jackets. Mum said earlier."

"Before she knew I was coming?"

"I've put an extra one for you."

"One?"

"Two then," said Ruby, splashing another potato under the tap, and then pushing past Will to put them in the little iron oven at the side of the kitchen range.

"I like mash," said Will, and took them out again. "Mash, with sausages. I'll peel them."

"You don't know how! And we haven't any sausages."

Will smirked at her and nodded toward the table, where she saw not only a paper-wrapped parcel of sausages, but also a tin of beans and a very small box of chocolates. "Remembered you liked beans," he said. "The chocolates are for Mum." And he began peeling potatoes very deftly, much faster than Ruby could have done, having had practice in the army, where he did it by the bucketful, spud-bashing being a punishment for minor crimes like messy gear, turning out late, and talking back to the sergeant major.

"You're doing all my things," complained Ruby.

"*You're* doing all *my* things," he retorted. "Tell me about these hundred friends."

"No."

"A few names? Where they live? So's I can get to know them when I move back home?"

"Mind your own business!"

"Oh?" said Will, chopping potatoes at lightning speed and sliding them into a saucepan. "Can't remember?"

"Shut up."

"Not even one?"

"Kate," snapped Ruby. "That's one. Kate."

"Never heard of her," said Will, swishing down the draining board, bundling the potato peelings onto the back of his blazing fire, drying his hands, and grinning so annoyingly that Ruby, against her better judgement, pulled a book from her school bag and pushed it into his hands.

"What's this then?" he asked.

"Look!" commanded Ruby. "Look inside!"

Will obediently opened the book.

"See!" said Ruby, pointing, and he read the words written there, *To Ruby, with love from Kate.*

"I told you so," said Ruby. "Kate. She sent it for my birthday."

Will turned the book in his hand and looked at the title: *Wild Animals I Have Known.* "Bet you haven't read it," he said.

"I have," said Ruby. "As soon as I got it."

"I'll borrow it then," said Will, standing up as if to leave. "That all right?"

"No!"

"No?"

"No. Give it back!" said Ruby, grabbing.

"Give it back?" asked Will mockingly, with the book held high above Ruby's head. "Why? You've read it. You told me so, just a minute ago."

"Not all of it."

"Not what you said! Shouldn't tell lies, Ruby. Ruby *Amaryllis*. Whatever that even means."

"It's a—" began Ruby, but he interrupted.

"I don't want to know. There's your book, then. Have it."

It was spoiled. Somehow he'd spoiled it. And he was angry, and what would he do next?

He looked behind the clock.

"Why do you *do* that?" she cried, suddenly as hurt as if he'd slapped her. "Why do you always do that? Why don't you just take it? Dad meant it for you!"

"You've forgotten what he said when he put it there," said Will. "I haven't."

He slammed furiously out of the door. Ruby also fled, up to her attic, through the window and onto the slippery sloping tiles, where she sat hugging her knees until the cold and the salt wind drove her back inside again.

After this latest visit of Will's, Ruby wrote to Kate:

> Dear Kate,
> My brother Will has gone back to the army.
> Good.
> But the war hasn't started yet.
> So he keeps coming home.
> Bad. Bad. Bad. Bad. Bad.

ELEVEN

Kate

Oxford, Autumn 1938

All that year the threat of war had been grumbling like the distant rumble of a thunderstorm far away. Even Kate heard the echoes.

At school people talked, sometimes not very sensibly.

"My mum's started saving things," said her friend Hatty, who was often confused.

"What things?"

"Light bulbs and baby wool."

"Light bulbs and baby wool?"

"For in case there's a war," said Hatty.

"Your mum," said someone, "just doesn't want to have a baby in the dark."

"But she isn't having a baby."

"That's all you know!"

Hatty went home and demanded the truth and came back not confused at all. "I'm going to be a sister!" she announced. "A sister! What's it like?"

"Depends on the baby," said everyone-who-was-already-a-sister, but Kate said, "It's nice."

"Yes, but you're not a big sister."

"I think it's still all right," said Kate. She was very relieved to hear it was a baby that was being prepared for instead of a war, and for a few days she forgot to worry and concentrated instead on helping Hatty choose baby names, even though Hatty said, "Oh, *no*, Kate," to every suggestion.

But then had come Ruby's latest letter, with its alarming fourth line:

But the war hasn't started yet.

Yet.

That *yet* made Kate's heart bump with fear. It sounded so certain. Ruby's brother was in the army. Ruby lived in a newspaper shop; she must hear all the news. Ruby was clever. Who could tell what Ruby knew?

At home the adults were also worrying.

Vanessa said, "Peter, we'll have to try to talk to your father. If the worse comes to the worst, he shouldn't be on his own. I know after that Christmas he said never again, and so did you, but was it really so bad?"

"You have a wonderful tolerance for people who are drunk by lunchtime and set fire to their beds," said Kate's father.

"He wasn't very drunk and the bed only smoldered. It could have been much worse."

"Madwoman." Peter got up and limped round the table to hug her. He was back in time for supper for once. For weeks he had been getting home later and later.

"We hardly see you," Kate's mother complained.

"I'm sorry."

"Are lots of people ill?" Kate asked him.

"Not at all, don't you worry, Kate."

"It was Kate's birthday yesterday," said Vanessa. "You entirely forgot it. She's allowed to wonder why."

"Gosh, oh, gosh, Kate!" exclaimed Peter. "I'm sorry. Did we remember presents? Did you have a cake?"

"I had lovely presents. You bought me a bracelet. Silver beads. It was a chocolate cake with pink candles and I blew them out in one go."

"All ten? Well done. Have you made a wish?"

"I'm saving it for in case."

"Very prudent."

"Why are you so busy at the hospital if there aren't lots of people being ill?"

"I've been doing extra teaching, new tricks to very old dogs. Or very old doctors. There's lots of new stuff in the hospital world that the older staff haven't bothered to learn."

"Why haven't they?"

"I suppose they thought it wasn't worth it if they were going to be retiring."

"Aren't they now?"

"They probably are, but just in case we need them . . ."

Peter suddenly noticed that behind Kate's back, Vanessa was making *Shut up* signs. He hastily changed the subject. "Can I see the bracelet I bought you?"

"I'm wearing it. Dad, now I'm ten, would you tell me if something awful was going to happen?"

"If you are thinking of your grandfather coming to stay, your mum's the one to talk to," said Peter, laughing. "But as far as I know, that idea's not going well."

"I thought I was getting somewhere a couple of days ago," said Vanessa, and it was Kate's turn to laugh, because she'd been there when her mother had telephoned Grandfather and said, "Darling, we must make some sensible plans for the future, and I thought it might be good to talk now."

Afterward, Kate had written about what had happened in her diary.

> Grandfather said, "Quite right," in such a pleased voice that Mum turned round and gave a thumbs-up sign to all of us. Because we were all listening. Then Grandfather said, "The only logical thing to do at this moment in time is to cash in all your shares and long-term bonds. Put aside enough to cover household expenses for the next five years. Invest the rest in gold."
>
> "Gold?" said Mum, in a voice like she might faint.
>
> "Let me know if you have any problems," Grandfather said, and put down the telephone.

Kate had enjoyed writing that diary entry, and beneath it she'd drawn three bulging sacks, with gold spilling out of their tops. For weeks afterward, even after Mr. Chamberlain, the prime minister, had told them on the wireless about his agreement with Hitler—"Peace with honor. Peace for our time"— Kate had turned back to look at Grandfather's sacks of gold. They made her smile, and somehow, magically, the smiling quieted the distant thunder of war.

TWELVE

Dog

Scrapyard, East London, 1938

Everything in the dog's world had its own strong smell. Traffic smells rolled in from the road, sometimes engines, sometimes horses. There was the food smell of the fish shop in the evenings, and the cold fog smell from the nearby River Thames. There was the smell of the scrapyard girl.

"Hello, dog," said the scrapyard girl, hoarse with winter, as she swept away the puddles that flooded his tea-chest kennel.

In summer, when he panted on his patch of sunbaked concrete, he heard it again.

"Hello, dog," she whispered, and found a square of old tarpaulin and rigged him up some shade.

Not without consequences, of course.

"You make a pet of that dog and it'll get what for."

What for was the yard broom raised high and brought down. What for was screeching. What for was boots. A pet dog wasn't needed. A burglar alarm was.

The dog was still quite a good burglar alarm. Footsteps in the yard, a rattle at the gate in the night, and he would be yammering and snarling and lunging on his chain.

Only not quite so swiftly as in the past. Nowadays the dog would hesitate for a moment. He would check for the smell of old clothes. He would listen for, "Hello, dog."

This was noticed at the scrapyard.

"Gone soft," they said with disappointment.

They raised the broom more often, and shouted louder, and although he was not the same savage animal he once had been, it worked enough to tide things over, more or less.

THIRTEEN

Erik and Hans

Berlin, 1938

The January evening before Erik and Hans were to go off for national service, their families, Erik's mother and Hans's parents and Frieda and Lisa, all went out for supper together. Lisa nearly didn't come because she couldn't get her plaits right. She tried and tried to look like the girls in the posters for the League of German Maidens, but when she parted her hair on one side like they did, one plait became very much thinner than the other, and yet when she parted it in the middle, she looked (she said) like a frumpy old witch.

"Never mind, we are used to you looking like a frumpy old witch," said Hans, which made things worse. Even after her hair was arranged, she was cross because she had lost her red-and-black swastika badge, and when it was found, it had been trodden on and was impossible to wear. But supper cheered her up, and she got powdered sugar all down her front and her hair came loose and on the way home it started snowing. Lisa had always loved snow, and she quite suddenly gave Erik her coat to hold and did a cartwheel there in the street, with the snowflakes swarming in the light of the streetlamps and the boys laughing and Frieda trying to copy her, and her parents saying, "Well!"

"Well, what?" asked Lisa, and did two more, very quickly, and came up red-faced and panting, saying, "At least I learned something useful at that boring stupid league."

"I thought you liked it," said Erik.

"I'm tired of it now," said Lisa. Then she went and did more cartwheels until her father sternly ordered her to stop.

"Next year you will be doing national service too," Erik reminded her when she flounced back to snatch her coat.

"More people bossing me around!" said Lisa.

"If they can," said Erik, laughing, and much later he remembered Lisa that evening, with hair all over her face and her eyes very bright, and the first snow of winter swirling down like white feathers.

The night ended back at Hans's family's apartment, in a panic. Erik had already packed for their early start the next morning. All his things were ready in a huge gray duffel bag with a drawstring top that had once been his father's. He'd left it in the shared hall, to be out of the way, and Frieda had spotted it.

"Hans doesn't have a great big bag like that," she observed.

"Hans has a new one," explained Erik. "Mine is very old."

"Older than me?"

"How old are you?" asked Erik.

"Nearly three," said Frieda.

"Much older than you," said Erik solemnly.

"And much bigger than me," said Frieda, measuring herself beside it, and it was.

"Hans's bag is full of important things," said Frieda. "He told me. So I mustn't touch it. Is yours full of important things?"

"No," said Erik, laughing, so when nobody was looking,

Frieda pulled out all the unimportant things that Erik had packed: his clothes, his rolled-up blankets, his canteen, and his book of European birds. She pushed them all under the cupboard, climbed inside the bag herself, and closed the top.

They found her by the giggling, after they had ransacked every room and rushed up and down the street outside, calling in the snow. Erik had to pack everything all over again.

"Get used to packing kit bags," Hans's father advised.

National service was almost a joke. Erik and Hans hardly had time to unpack their bags and remember how much they detested marching round a parade ground, before their flying record was discovered. As soon as it was known, they found themselves accepted into flight training. Next they were adding up their flying distances, until they reached three thousand kilometers in the air.

Three thousand kilometers was the turning point, the difference between students and potential Luftwaffe pilots. It came easily to Erik.

When Erik was flying, his senses filled with the sound of engines, the smell of the plane, the speed and height. Often, immersed in sky, he forgot there was an earth beneath him.

For those few months of hard, intense training, Erik was so absorbed he hardly remembered the outside world at all. When he wasn't flying, he was studying navigation, photography, mechanics. He hung over aerial photographs, and plans and maps. He developed a wonderful sense of direction; he never got lost.

Hans did.

They had to pass a solo flight. It was set out in a triangle, six hundred kilometers in total, with a precision landing on a target at the end. It would be a milestone in their training; afterward they would move on to a new airfield and larger planes, and in between they would have forty-eight hours' leave.

Erik managed without problems, landing on target several minutes early with fuel still in his tank and hardly a bounce. Hans was ten minutes late, half an hour late, seventy minutes late.

At first Erik stood alone, watching for his friend. As time went on, he was joined by more and more people. Hans was popular, and now long overdue. It wasn't just fellow students. The mechanics started looking up. The cooks peered out from the canteen. The old soldier who kept the grass short with two ancient donkeys and a clattering mower hobbled over to join the crowd. There were at least twenty people waiting when Hans came in at last, battling the evening wind to land like a log dropped out of a window.

Hans climbed out very shakily and bowed to the applause and said to Erik, who was the first to reach him, "I was hoping no one would notice."

"I'm sure nobody did," said Erik, who was so pleased to see Hans safe that he couldn't stop grinning. "These people staring at the sky, I think they were just admiring the clouds."

"You think so, do you?" asked Hans. "I tell you what, Erik, I hated that. It was scary. And I bet I've lost my leave."

Hans was right. His leave was canceled, and he had to do the test over again. Erik went home without him. It was November 1938, the first time for nearly a year that he'd been back in Berlin. He stepped out of the train at the station and noticed the difference at once.

When he'd left, there'd been a simmering tension in the city. The red-and-black flags. The JEWS FORBIDDEN. It had been uncomfortable, militant, shaming. But in a strange way it had also been possible to avert your eyes because things had changed so gradually, for so many years. They'd been part of his growing up.

This time, it was different. Now Berlin was alarming. There was violence loose in the city squares and menace prowled the streets. In the air was the sour smell that comes after burning. Everywhere, there was broken glass, swept into heaps like dirty snow. Erik looked in disbelief at great piles of it outside the shattered shops and businesses of the Jewish people who had once believed the city to be their home.

"Last week," said his mother. "You must have heard. They're calling it Kristallnacht."

She had met him at the station, pale-faced, clutching his arm. She said, "All over Germany, but they say Berlin was the worst. Keep walking. Don't stop and look. Your face shows too much. How can you not have known?"

"I knew. Of course, we all did. I didn't understand."

"They have disappeared. All but gone. Probably for the best, of course . . ." She looked around uneasily, and Erik realized that she was talking to protect them both from any passing stranger who might be listening to their conversation. "Look at you in your uniform!" she exclaimed. "Taller each time I see you! How is Hans?"

"Very well. A new girl every week. I have thousands of messages, and tobacco for his father, and chocolate for his mother and Lisa, and a sugar pig for Frieda. This is an outrage."

"Yes, perhaps. Lisa is away."

"No!" exclaimed Erik, so loudly that people turned to look. "Hans doesn't know that. Lisa was at school when we saw her last."

"Don't be so loud, Erik! Of course she has to do her national service, like all the rest of them. Hans must have forgotten. It's better for her parents that she's occupied. She always was a difficult girl. Come inside, it will be better inside. Did you need to bring that big bag for just a few hours?"

"It's full of presents," said Erik, a little blankly. "And Hans said to pack Frieda and bring her back for a visit . . . for a joke."

"Oh, yes, a joke," said his mother, and smiled as if she had forgotten until then about jokes, and looked uncertainly at him, and quickly away again.

"What is it?" Erik asked, and when she didn't reply, to cover the awkwardness he felt, he said, "Shall I you show you what we found for Frieda?" and pulled out a package, wrapped in brown paper. Inside was a bright red blanket, with brown felt bears stitched in the corners. The bears had bells around their necks, on green ribbons. At any other time it would have delighted his mother. She would have examined the bears and shaken the tiny bells and said how perfect for a little girl, and how clever they had been to find it. Now she hardly looked.

"Yes," she said. "Very nice. It will be warm."

"Every bear is different," said Erik, watching her with increasing alarm.

"Erik," burst out his mother. "I do what I can, but she's so frightened of you. She is so terribly, terribly frightened of you."

"Frieda?" asked Erik, in absolute astonishment.

"Not Frieda."

It's easy to forget about someone, when you don't see them

for years, nor hear them. When nobody mentions them, and you have traveled on to a different world.

"Of course, this is not how we manage day to day," his mother murmured, as she led him up the narrow, forgotten stairs. "Our apartment is more practical. Warmer, and we have the little daybed, and that does very well. But today, well, you will see. . . . Go in quietly, Erik."

But Erik was already holding his breath. The door was a little open, and he pushed it very gently, and stepped inside, and it was like walking into an ancient, faded picture of the past.

The fern in the window was dried to a gray ghost of a fern. Cobwebs laced its fronds, and laced the window, too, as they would in a room where nobody lived. The wooden chair was dim with dust. Erik kneeled down in front of it, a Luftwaffe pilot in full uniform.

Shrunken against the cushions, her hands pressed against her mouth, her eyes wide with fear, Fräulein Trisk shook and shook.

"No, no," begged Erik. No one had ever been frightened of him before. No person. No creature. Not even his swallows when he first picked them up. The feeling was terrible. He said, "It's Erik, Fräulein Trisk. It's me." He couldn't help crying, although he knew it was no way to behave, and never had been either. He had been brought up by a brave woman, to be brave. So he rubbed the tears away on his hands and said, "It's still only me, Fräulein Trisk. Only Erik."

Fräulein Trisk took her hands from her face.

"You knitted me mittens."

She nodded a very small nod. She was altogether small.

"I loved them. I am sorry that I—"

"Phut!" said Fräulein Trisk. She gave a quivering smile and reached out a hand as light as a bird and touched his hair.

Then Erik's mother, who was watching from the door, gave a great sigh, and laughed out loud with relief and looked with pride at Erik and said, "Didn't I tell you he was still my little sugar rose?"

Before he left, Erik said, "When all these troubles are over, I will buy you a new fern. I promise. Green as a forest."

FOURTEEN

Ruby

Plymouth, Devon, November 1938

All sorts of people came to the newsagent's shop, and one of them was Mrs. Cohen. The Cohens' shop was just a few doors down the street from Ruby's home.

COHEN & CO. CLOCKMAKERS AND GOLDSMITHS

Those were the words written in small gold letters across the front. The letters had to be small, because the whole shop was small, right down to the half-sized doormat that customers stepped onto when they ducked through the very small door. From the door to the counter was one medium-sized step, and from the counter to the workroom was another. Very few clocks were made in that workroom, but very many battered overwound watches were mended and clockwork toys set running again. There wasn't much goldsmithing done either, but for a few pennies Mr. Cohen could repair a chain, or fix a broken locket, or reset a stone in a treasured ring. He did this work invisibly. It was Mrs. Cohen who stood behind the counter, and dusted the shelves, and arranged the display in the small curved window. Ruby always paused to look at the cuckoo clock, the silver candlesticks, and the tray of rings. She and her mother often inspected that tray, in the hope of new and extra-bright rubies.

The Cohens were a Jewish family. They went to the synagogue on Catherine Street, and it was for them that Ruby's mother ordered the *Jewish Chronicle* once a week. Ruby liked Mrs. Cohen, who actually had a ruby ring of her own. Sometimes she would take it off and let Ruby hold it. Ruby would turn it until it caught the light and blossomed into a speck of crimson fire.

"It's a pity it's not bigger," Ruby had once remarked, and Mrs. Cohen had laughed and agreed that it was indeed a pity. She and Ruby had talked about rubies and decided together that one the size of half a cherry would be perfect for a ring. Big enough to really shine, but not so large as to be knobbly, said Ruby, and Mrs. Cohen agreed, and said that anything bigger, say the size of a whole cherry, would be better used for earrings.

"Only then you would need two rubies," Ruby had pointed out.

"Or four," said Mrs. Cohen. "Cherries are best when they hang in pairs."

"How much would that cost?" Ruby wondered, thinking what a nice present such earrings would make for her mother, and Mrs. Cohen said thoughtfully that she couldn't be sure, but she imagined perhaps between ten and twenty thousand pounds if the rubies were properly matched.

This conversation made a pleasant friendliness between the two of them, and Ruby was always pleased when Mrs. Cohen came in. She never had the feeling she had with other customers that Mrs. Cohen was secretly looking at the marks on her face.

So Ruby was dismayed on the November day when Mrs. Cohen arrived, distracted and unhappy, and hurried past, ignoring her completely.

"What . . . ?" began Ruby, and then saw that Mrs. Cohen was pushing into her mother's hands the *Jewish Chronicle* that she had bought from them less than an hour before.

"Terrible things are happening!" exclaimed Mrs. Cohen. "Terrible things! You should know!"

"Mrs. Cohen!" exclaimed Violet.

"Yes," said Mrs. Cohen. "Look! Look what I just saw!" and she flattened the newspaper out on the counter for Violet to read. "We Jewish people have already heard so much bad news," she said. "So many things, but this!"

"Show me, too," said Ruby, pushing forward to look.

"No, Ruby, you go upstairs and leave me to talk to Mrs. Cohen," said Violet, but Mrs. Cohen shook her head and said, "Ruby should see too. She should know! Everyone should know!"

Violet was reading even while Mrs. Cohen spoke.

"Nobody knows and nobody cares," continued Mrs. Cohen. "I don't think anyone in this country is paying any attention at all. I had to come. I have nobody to talk to who could possibly understand. You know Mr. Cohen. He just shakes his head, shakes his head. . . ."

Violet didn't look up from her reading, but she reached out a hand toward Mrs. Cohen.

"I felt so alone," said Mrs. Cohen, and took the hand and held it tight.

This was how Ruby first heard the word *Kristallnacht*.

Kristallnacht: the night of broken glass. The bitter night of terror and persecution that Mrs. Cohen had discovered in the *Jewish Chronicle.*

"Nobody cares," she repeated. "No one is interested. Are the other papers reporting it, have you seen?"

"I don't know, Mrs. Cohen," admitted Ruby's mother. "I can't say I've noticed, but . . ."

At this Mrs. Cohen broke down and sobbed, and Violet took her other hand and held that, too, while Ruby, suddenly inspired, rushed upstairs and returned with cups of tea so floating with too many tea leaves that they had to be fished out with a spoon. Most surprisingly, the fishing out helped, and so did walking Mrs. Cohen home afterward, but even so Ruby only partly understood her distress. This changed when Violet, with her usual resourcefulness, set about comforting Mrs. Cohen in the most practical way she could devise.

"She needs to know people are paying attention," she told Ruby. "That, at least, we can show her. You can help."

They began at once. Every night, all that week, Violet spread out newspapers on the kitchen table. Then she and Ruby would scrutinize them, and very soon they found what they needed. People in Britain *were* paying attention. Carefully they cut out columns from the *Manchester Guardian*, the *Times* and *Daily Mail*, and other papers as well. Even their own local paper, the *Devon and Exeter Gazette*, had an article.

"Right on the front page, too," said Ruby when she found it, and read out loud, "'Friday, November 11. Germany and Jews. Outrages Throughout Country . . .'"

"It's not nice to read," said her mother. "But what's happening isn't nice. It's wicked. But it hasn't gone ignored. Snip it out carefully, Ruby, and don't drop bits on the floor."

They found a report with a photograph: an image of shop fronts, knee-deep in broken glass, daubed with rough letters: *JUDE JUDE JUDE.* There were people in the picture. One of them caught Ruby's attention: a slim woman, hurrying forward and holding very tightly the hand of a small scurrying girl.

"That woman has a coat just like yours," said Ruby to her mother, and so she had; double-breasted with turned-back lapels and big buttons down the front. "It must be her good coat," said Ruby, because that was what Violet called her own winter coat. "Her good coat, but no hat."

Blond curls escaped from under the child's woolly hat, but the woman was bareheaded, her hair smoothed back from her face and gathered in a knot at the nape of her neck. Her eyes were dark and intense, looking down at the little girl.

She's pretending, thought Ruby suddenly, *pretending she hasn't noticed the broken glass. She's pretending she only cares about the girl, and she's thinking, thinking, thinking. What is she thinking?*

(She was thinking, *Hurry. I should never have offered to take care of Frieda today. I should never have come out here. I must smile. Am I smiling? Do I look like I don't care? I must persuade her to come down to us. Let the rooms grow abandoned, like no one is ever there. In case . . . No. No. Please no. I forgot, smile. Oh, God, I used to buy his school shirts from that shop. Good flannel for winter, it washed and washed. Hurry, Frieda. Smile.*)

There were other people in the picture too, standing in small groups, looking about with sidelong glances. A round-shouldered fellow, half in profile, ashamed at what he saw. A girl laughing. She wore a little cape of snuggly dark fur. *She thinks she's pretty,* thought Ruby, and unconsciously raised her hand to her face. *She* is *pretty,* admitted Ruby.

The broken glass had been very neatly swept.

"Will it really help Mrs. Cohen to see these things?" Ruby asked. "I don't see how."

"There's knowing bad things on your own," said Violet briskly, "and there's knowing them with other people. And there's a difference."

Ruby nodded, accepting that.

At the end of the week they packed up their collection of clippings and took them to the Cohens' shop. Violet handed them over, together with a reminder that her Will was in the army and was not the sort to stand for such things as were going on over there. She nodded in the direction of the sea.

"Isn't he?" asked Mrs. Cohen, her eyes angry and unhappy. "Good."

"And nor am I, Mrs. Cohen," said Violet. "For what it's worth."

"A lot," said Mrs. Cohen, nodding. "Thank you."

"And I'm not either," said Ruby, and added belligerently that if anyone smashed Mrs. Cohen's shop window and stole her rings and candlesticks, she, Ruby, would find out who they were and kill them.

"Ruby!" said her mother, but not very angrily because, miraculously, Mrs. Cohen was laughing.

"I'd be good at it," said Ruby. "I'd be perfect, because the police would say, 'It can't be her, she's just a kid.'"

"Well, you won't be called upon to do any such thing," said Ruby's mother. "Besides, anyone who interferes with our shops round here will get what for from me!"

"And what for also from me," said Mrs. Cohen, now a woman transformed.

Then she and Ruby's mother talked about how things would be if they were in charge of the country, and Ruby, listening, thought it was a pity that they weren't, they would get so much done, and so quickly. Before they left, Violet gave Mrs. Cohen a present she'd brought, a special sort of tea in a red-and-gold tin with an elephant on the lid to show it was from India. This was also a great triumph.

Ruby and Violet walked home together, feeling warm with success.

"Will there really be a war?" asked Ruby, all fired up with the thought, and her mother replied, "We've fought wars over less."

"Have we?"

"When I was a girl we did. You know that, Ruby. Your dad fought all through the last war."

"I only know it happened. I don't know anything about it much. Was it terrible?"

Violet paused.

"For some, yes, it was," she said, at last. "Yes, it was. It really was. But . . ." She hesitated again, and this time for so long that Ruby asked, "But what?"

"I worked in those days for your aunty Rose. She kept a shop that was as dead as a doornail, and I'd been stuck in it ever since I was twelve. It wasn't until Clarry walked in that I started to wake up. We bought her pink beret that day!"

The pink beret was a family wonder. Ruby's mother had worn it on her wedding day. Clarry had worn it at Ruby's christening. When Janey, aged eleven, had run away to Cornwall because she'd seen a ghost in her bedroom, she'd stolen it and taken it with her. Ruby herself had been lent it the time that Sooty had gone missing for two whole weeks.

"It cost twelve shillings!" remembered Ruby's mother now. "Twelve shillings! I was shocked. I couldn't get it out of my head at first. I lay awake and I thought, *Well, if a girl like her can get herself a hat like that, then what about me? There's more I can do than this shop!*"

"So what did you do?" asked Ruby.

"I got a job on the trams, because with the men at war there was work for girls like we'd never had before. And suddenly I was free. Out in the town all day, half the night, too, as often as not. And earning good money as well, three times what I'd had."

"It sounds fun," said Ruby.

"It was," admitted her mother. "But don't you go repeating that, because it makes me sound heartless. Which I'm not. Poor Mrs. Cohen! That Hitler's got away with too much now. It's time it stopped."

Ruby nodded in vigorous agreement.

"Our Will could keep him busy!" continued Violet. "What's the use of us having an army if we don't stand up for what's right?"

"Germany has an army too," pointed out Ruby.

"Well, I know they do, of course they do," said Violet rather crossly. She became silent, thinking perhaps of the German army, who might very well be able to keep Will busy too. Ruby was quiet as well, but every now and then, all the way home, her steps broke into a very small skip.

FIFTEEN

Kate

Oxford, 1939

In the spring of 1939, Charlie came home from school with streaming eyes and a feverish cold that his father said wasn't a cold at all.

"Measles," said Peter.

"Measles!" Vanessa groaned. "And Kate's only just got over her winter coughs."

So Kate was banished to Clarry's, where she was given the only bedroom for herself. "But where will you sleep?" she asked Clarry, slightly dismayed, and was shown how the sofa made into a bed, with its own pillow and bedclothes in a drawer underneath.

"How perfect is that?" demanded Clarry proudly, and Kate agreed it was very good indeed.

"But I could sleep here just as well," she suggested.

"You'll be much less trouble in the bedroom," said her mother, who had come to help move her in. "Then all your clutter can be out of the way."

It was true that in the rush to hurry Kate out of the house, they'd packed a tremendous amount of stuff. Far more than Clarry seemed to own. Clarry's clothes all fitted into one small-ish cupboard, and her books on one long shelf, which also held her paint box, a brown china pot of pens and pencils, a box of shells from Cornwall, and a pink pottery jug for flowers. The whole flat was so perfect that Kate thought she'd better unpack very carefully, and she was doing this when Clarry stuck her head round the door and said, "Come on, Kate! Let's do something good, since I've got you here to myself. Let's go to the cinema."

"The cinema?

"Mm."

"What to see?"

"Whatever there is," said Clarry.

It was a film about Robin Hood. It was magnificent. It made Clarry say, "I should have learned fencing," and Kate reply, "Janey and Bea do it at a club after school, but it doesn't look like that."

"Not at all?" asked Clarry.

"Much slower," said Kate. "And lots of arguing in between stabs and not the right clothes."

"No doublet and hose for Janey and Bea?"

"Undershirts and navy-blue gym shorts," said Kate so gravely that Clarry laughed out loud.

For the next two weeks, Kate went to school from Clarry's, and toiled over her homework there in the evenings. It was strange to be in a two-person home, instead of the youngest of eight. It made Kate feel surprisingly grown up. One evening they went out for supper and had spaghetti, which she'd never eaten before. Several times, after it was discovered that none of Kate's family had ever taught her to ride a bike, they had cycling lessons, round and round the empty tennis courts of the school where Clarry taught. In between, Kate discovered that she could cook. It seemed she had learned without noticing, watching her mother. Kate cooked mushrooms on toast, tomato omelets, and cheese sandwiches fried until they melted in the middle and the outsides turned golden brown.

"I was always quite careful not to learn to cook," said Clarry, "in case I ended up doing it instead of everything else I wanted to do more."

"You'd probably be safe to learn now," said Kate seriously.

"I probably would," agreed Clarry, and Kate said she'd write her out the recipes for making the omelets and things. She was busy with this one rainy Saturday afternoon when suddenly there were running footsteps on the stairs and a voice calling, "Clarry, Clarry, Clarry."

A moment later Rupert appeared in the doorway, carrying an armload of wet carnations, pink, deep red, and cream, in a cloud of misty ferns. Their scent poured from them, sweet as a rain-damp garden, and Rupert said "Clarry" one last time and looked over his flowers and saw Kate.

"Oh, hello," he said, in a not-very-pleased voice. "Is it . . . ?" He paused, and Kate could see him hunting to remember her name.

"It's Kate," said Clarry, putting an arm round her. "Vanessa's Kate, you know it is. She's staying with me and being an absolute darling while Charlie's having measles. How wonderful to see you, Rupert. Why didn't you let me know you were back?"

"Then I wouldn't be a surprise," said Rupert. "Would I, Kate?" Kate smiled speechlessly.

"Kate understands," said Rupert, kissing Clarry, ladening her with flowers and shrugging off his dark, heavy coat. Then he looked down at Kate and asked thoughtfully, "Can you sew on buttons?"

"No, she can't," said Clarry. "Sew on your own buttons, Rupert."

"Yes, I can," said Kate, deeply honored, so he handed her a large black button that had come off his coat so suddenly that the threads were still hanging loose in the holes and said "Needle?" to Clarry.

"Not me," said Clarry unhelpfully. "I go and visit Vanessa when my buttons come off."

"Clarry," said Rupert.

"Vanessa sews them on beautifully," said Clarry, sniffing her carnations.

Kate looked from face to face.

"Come with me," said Rupert to Kate, and took her down the stairs to the front door, and along the road to a shop where they bought needles, black thread, white thread, blue, green, and purple too, a thimble, a bundle of bright silks like a soft slice of rainbow, some thin pointed scissors with gold handles, a tape measure that pulled out of a round, ladybug-shaped case, and a Scottie-dog pincushion. There was a strawberry-shaped pincushion too that Kate might have had, and another like a fat little cottage, but she unhesitatingly chose the dog.

"Pins," said Rupert. "No good having a pincushion without pins."

"Oh no!" exclaimed Kate, and she held the Scottie dog protectively, as if Rupert might stick pins in him right there.

"Ah," said Rupert. "I see. No pins in the dog. Now, what else do we need?"

Kate shook her head. She couldn't imagine needing anything else for years. It seemed an astonishing amount for the repair of one black button.

"Nothing," she said.

"Wrong," said Rupert. "We need something to put it all in."

He found a basket of woven wicker with a quilted green lining. "Perfect," he said, and added it to the pile of things already on the counter. "Isn't it?"

"I don't know," said Kate uncomfortably, because the basket was plainly labeled twenty-five shillings, which seemed a tremendous amount of money—twenty-five weeks' pocket money, in fact.

Rupert looked at her through half-closed eyes and said, "You *said* you could sew on buttons."

"I can!" said Kate. "I'm sure I can!" And when they got back to Clarry's, she did, although it took her all afternoon alone in the bedroom, with the enormous coat spread out over the bed because it was so big that was the only way to manage it. As well as the original lost button, two more had come off on the way back from the shop.

"I don't know what's the matter with my buttons today," Rupert had remarked shamelessly, when the second one fell to the ground.

The thimble was very useful. Kate used it like a hammer to force the needle through the heavy cloth. The Scottie dog wasn't useful, but he was company. He wore a red tartan jacket and had shining bead eyes. Kate looked at him lovingly as she worked. She felt wonderfully happy. Through the half-open door she could hear Clarry's and Rupert's voices, catching up on all the months of news that had happened while they'd been apart. After about half an hour Rupert appeared at the doorway and said, "Are you all right there, Kate?"

Kate nodded.

"I have to tell Clarry something quite private and important now," he said. "And I know it might sound very rude to you, Kate, but I'm going to speak in French."

"It's all right," said Kate.

"You don't speak French?"

"*Seulement un peu,*" said Kate, and he burst out laughing and said, "You sound like your mum."

"Mum said the only thing she ever learned at school was French," said Kate. "And we do French together when I'm at home with my cough."

"What sort of French?"

"Fairy tales mostly."

"And are you often at home with your cough?"

"Not as much as I used to be. And you could close the door. I wouldn't mind."

"I wouldn't dream of it," said Rupert.

The conversation in French wasn't like the one in English. It was more of an argument. When Kate heard Clarry exclaim, "Rupert, *non, pas encore, non!*" she closed the door herself.

Clarry opened it a minute later and said, "I'm going out for crumpets. Or muffins or buns or whatever I can find." Her cheeks were red and her eyes unhappy and she vanished before Kate could ask, "Do you want me to come with you?"

Rupert appeared again.

"*Ça va?*" he asked.

"*Ça va bien,*" said Kate. "I didn't listen."

"I know. Well, what's the news, Kate? How's your wicked old grandfather? I heard about that Christmas! Getting you drunk in church!"

"It was only water," said Kate. "And it was supposed to be a secret."

"I won't say another word then," said Rupert solemnly. "Nor about when he set fire to his bed."

"It was Janey's bed really. She and Bea moved out into the twins' attic."

"Does that make it any better?"

"It was only a bit smoky. It was the cigar he got in his stocking. I wish there wasn't going to be a war."

"Kate?"

"If there is."

"If there is, so do I."

"Might there have to be, Rupert?"

Rupert hesitated, and then sat down on the end of the bed and said, "Perhaps there might have to be. We'll have to make the best of it, Kate."

"I don't know how."

"It's a problem," he said, nodding.

"Don't you either?"

"As a matter of fact," said Rupert, sounding suddenly very cheerful, "I've recently made up my mind that the easiest thing to do is . . . is . . ." He paused, and looked down. Kate's hand was suddenly clutching his arm.

" . . . is to be extraordinarily brave," said Rupert gently.

"Extraordinarily brave?" repeated Kate.

"It seemed obvious, once I'd thought of it."

"Yes!" said Kate. "Oh, yes!"

"I'm glad you agree."

"I do, I do!" said Kate, her face suddenly illuminated with relief to have such a simple answer. "That's what I'll do too."

"Oh, Kate."

"You'd better put the kettle on for Clarry. I've got another button to finish."

"Leave it."

Kate shook her head. Nor would she stop for tea and muffins. "Later," she said, when they told her to come, because this button sewing was the hardest thing she'd ever done. The cloth was so thick, it made her hands stiff. Her fingers were sore and terribly pricked. It took extraordinary bravery to unpick the last button that she'd fixed out of line and put it on again straight. Even so, she persisted.

"I am racked with guilt," said Rupert, when at last she staggered in to them, the coat an armload that half extinguished her, smiling in triumph, blinking with exhaustion. "Racked," he repeated. "Clarry is right. You really are a darling."

He put on the coat, and enveloped them, first Kate, then Clarry.

"I love you," said Clarry.

"I love you," echoed Kate.

"I should hope so too," said Rupert, and vanished down the stairs.

That spring and summer were full of rumors. Rumors and preparations. In factories all over the country, everything from aircraft to gas masks were hurriedly being made. People stopped wondering "What if?" and began asking "When?"

Kate, passing the kitchen door where her parents were

talking together, heard her father say that the hospital was stockpiling anesthetics, ether and chloroform, as many other drugs as possible, surgical instruments, disinfectants and dressings. They were buying a new X-ray machine. They were running out of space to store things.

Kate's mother said bleakly, not in her usual voice at all, "We never had enough rubber sheets the last time. They cracked, with all the scrubbing, and then the mattresses got smelly."

Kate knew her mother had nursed soldiers all through the last war. That wasn't what shocked her so much. It was the practical bluntness of the rubber sheets that cracked with scrubbing. The smelly mattresses.

For days, for weeks afterward, Kate would replay that conversation in her head. Every time she heard it, it was just as bad.

Meanwhile, the news from Europe became steadily worse.

In September, Germany invaded Poland.

"That's it, then," said Kate's father, and it was.

SIXTEEN

Dog

Scrapyard, East London, September 1939

When the war came, the dog was quite old, six or seven, or eight or nine. No one knew exactly, because no one had kept count, but he was a very large full-grown dog, not as much use as he once had been, because of going soft.

The war brought new worries to the scrapyard, such as air raids and food rationing. The scrapyard people looked at the large, not very useful dog.

"How are we going to feed that?" they asked. "Big dog like that, with a war on?"

All over the country, people were asking the same sort of question: What was to be done with the pets? How could they be kept safe when bombs were falling? How in the world would they be fed?

The wartime government had an answer. "Visit your vet. Before they get hungry. Before the air raids start. Do the kindest thing."

Thousands and thousands of people, tens of thousands of people, gave their pets last walks and last brushes and last favorite meals and last hugs. Then they queued outside their vets and they had them put to sleep. Going home afterward, some of them wondered.

Going home afterward was bleak.

The scrapyard people didn't have these problems. They weren't the sort to waste money on vets. They'd never troubled themselves much with kindness, either. Nevertheless, one autumn morning they came out to look at the dog.

The dog saw them looking.

"He'll have to take his chances," they said.

The dog heard the words, but they meant nothing to him. He didn't know any words in the world.

Well, two.

He knew two.

"Hello, dog."

It was not quite dawn.

The scrapyard girl was transformed. She smelled of soap. She walked lightly, as if her boots had secret wings. She carried, hugged under her arm, a small case with a paper label. Another label, just the same, was pinned on to her coat.

The scrapyard girl didn't sound the same either. Her voice was bubbling with excitement.

"Hello, dog," she said again, and she came closer to him than any person had ever done without a yard broom in their hand. She touched him.

It didn't hurt.

She crouched down beside him and held something out.

An hour or two earlier, if the dog's chain had been long enough for him to look, and if he'd known to look, he might have seen the scrapyard girl in the kitchen, heating an old knife over a gas ring. He could have watched as she burned letters onto the back of a leather luggage tag. The letters spelled the truce word that they used at school when times were difficult. They were her gift to him: a name.

The luggage tag was threaded onto a piece of cord. The girl kneeled beside the dog and slid it over his head. Now he had a label too.

It was over. The girl was standing. She was looking around in the pale dawn dimness, at the oil-stained puddles, the piles of scrap, the broken-glass-topped wall.

She looked upward at the lightening sky.

"Goodbye, dog," she said.

SEVENTEEN

Erik and Hans

Germany, Autumn 1939

After the abomination of Kristallnacht, Erik did not get home for many months. He and Hans trained in airfields far away from Berlin. Also, for the first time since they were ten years old, they were separated. It was nearly a year later, and only with much contriving and swapping of favors with friends, that they managed to arrange a short leave home together.

"Luftwaffe officers," said Hans.

Erik and Hans could say things to each other that they could say to no one else.

"I am not," said Erik, who in forty-eight hours would climb into a fighter plane to escort German bombers raiding Poland, "planning to do any damage to anyone."

"I wouldn't mind doing damage to someone," said Hans, and he pressed two fingers against his top lip in the shape of a narrow mustache.

"Stop it!" said Erik.

"Why?"

"Frieda. Lisa. Your parents."

Hans snorted with frustration, like a horse.

~ ✕ ~

Frieda was the first to greet them, racing into the hall and flinging herself into their arms, a squealing small girl pendulum swinging between them—Hans, Erik, Hans, Erik—until Hans picked her up and held her high and swooped her through the air, making Messerschmitt noises.

"Erik has brought his duffel bag," she shouted, spotting it from that height, and insisted on climbing inside again and being raced up and down the stairs on Erik's back.

"She is too heavy!" exclaimed Hans's mother, but Frieda shrieked, "I'm not, I'm not, I won't ever be too heavy."

"And much too noisy. They will hear her on the street!"

Hans's mother's protests were only out of habit. No one really minded, the excitement and brightness were so welcome. "As if we had the old days back," said Hans's father, "and children on the stairs all day."

"With cocoa tins full of flies!" added Erik's mother.

"Were the swallows back this summer?" Erik asked her, and she said, "Yes, oh yes, of course they were, and all of them asking questions about you. 'How is Erik and where is his hat?'"

"'Or did he fall out of the window?'" finished Hans. "What did you tell them?"

"I told them the sugar rose had learned to fly, and so had the dumpling boy."

Erik and Hans groaned in dismay, while everybody laughed.

In the hall, with the familiar black-and-white tiles on the floor, and the dark corner where the mop bucket lived, and the yellow light from the lamp that had never hung quite straight, and still wasn't straight, and the old smell of scrubbed stairs and polish and coffee, in that enclosed space it was hard to believe that outside the door the world had changed forever.

Later they knew.

That evening the street was full of a different noise: hammering on doors, furniture being shoved aside, orders bawled, heavy feet clattering on the tiled floors. Armed police were searching the houses, banging on shutters, pushing into homes. Hans's father had answered the door to them, with Hans's mother and Erik's mother behind him. Erik, at the first sound of alarm, had touched his mother on her shoulder, and headed up the stairs.

Frieda took one terrified look at the strangers and began to screech.

"Quiet that child!" snapped one of them, but Frieda would not be quiet.

"Where's Hans?" she howled. "Where's Erik? What are the horrible, horrible men doing here?"

"Hush, Frieda, hush!" said Hans's mother, but Erik's mother said, "They are not horrible men, Frieda. They are the police looking for hidden people."

"But we haven't got any hidden people!" wailed Frieda.

"No. But they have to look."

Erik and Hans seemed, unbelievably, not to have heard the noise, not even when Frieda screamed indignantly, "Vati! Vati! They are stealing our things!"

One of them had opened the ancient black cupboard and pulled out the hoarded bottle of brandy kept for emergencies.

"Take it, take it," said Hans's father wearily. "It doesn't matter, Frieda."

Then one of the men noticed, "There's a door behind that cupboard!" and the whole heavy piece of furniture was heaved aside. All Hans's mother's china rattled and slid and a small hand mirror with a daisy-painted back fell to the floor and shattered.

"My mirror!" shrieked Frieda, and before anyone could stop her, she had hurled herself at the nearest of the intruders, hammering with her fists. Exactly at that moment, Hans came running down the stairs, followed a minute or two later by Erik, carrying his duffel bag.

That caused a pause. Hans, tall, blond, furious, in full Luftwaffe uniform, peaked cap, polished boots, outrage on every feature. Erik behind him with his pilot's silver eagle on his breast. The sight halted the searchers, until the leader recovered and began, "Our orders—"

"Your orders?" roared Hans. "You are frightening a little child in the home of two officers of the Reich! I'll report the lot of you!"

"We were informed—"

"Names!" snapped Erik, stepping forward and pulling a notebook from his pocket. "I'll have your names and numbers. . . . Frieda! No!"

"Be very careful, my little sugar rose," said Erik's mother urgently. She glanced at Erik, but she spoke to Frieda, who had stooped for the broken glass, and immediately cut herself. Bright blood ran from her palm, her face contorted, and she took an enormous, about-to-bellow breath. Her mother pounced on her at once, clucking and exclaiming.

"I am holding you responsible," said Hans, now no longer roaring but calm and cold and furious. "Your names! One of you clear up that glass. Then my colleague and I will supervise your search. Myself down here. Erik, would you take these gentlemen to the rooms above? Frieda, very soon they will be gone. Let Mutti bathe your hand. Now!"

In a few minutes it was over, the three apartments searched, Fräulein Trisk's, clearly long abandoned, empty as a shell. Erik and his mother's, Hans's family's.

"Look under the beds!" Erik had ordered, his duffel bag still on his back. "Behind the curtains. Get this done properly. The cupboard under the second staircase. That chest!"

Downstairs, Hans was saying much the same. "Roll up the rug. Check that the floor is sound. The water closet. Frieda, lift the tablecloth!"

"That's my secret house!" protested Frieda, but Erik's mother said, "We must do what we can, Frieda," and the tablecloth was lifted to show Frieda's cushion and her doll and her china mug with the robin painted on it.

Erik came down to join them again, shepherding the searchers in front of him. The broken glass had been cleared away, he noticed, and the brandy bottle stood in the middle of the table. "Now," he said, "if you are satisfied, gentlemen . . ." He snapped open his notebook, read their names and numbers aloud, pocketed it, and looked pointedly at Frieda.

"We apologize for any distress caused to the child. We were following orders, and it was not our intention to disturb her," said the leader. "She is not hurt."

"She is hurt and frightened," said Erik. "Her parents are distressed. Her friends are angry. Is your duty here done? If so, please leave."

Even when they were gone, the rooms still felt invaded. Frieda sobbed with temper. Erik put down his duffel bag at last and sighed with weariness. Hans growled, "So this is what it's come to," and his mother looked at him with fear and said in a loud, clear voice, "They were good men obeying orders," and glanced at the door, as if they might be in the street listening even now. Hans's father said nothing, but set up a line of five glasses, opened the brandy bottle, and divided it between them.

"I'll take mine upstairs, if you will excuse me," said Erik's mother.

"I'll come with you," said Erik.

"Don't forget this," Hans reminded him, and very gently he lifted the duffel bag and held it steady while Erik looped it over his shoulder.

"Thanks," said Erik, and hurried away.

Before the night was finished, there was another happening. Erik answered the door to a gentle knock and found Hans standing outside.

"Uncle Karl has arrived," he said. "In all the trouble earlier, we forgot he might be coming. My father told him a few days ago that you and I would be here, and he said he would try to see us both. Will you come down and say hello?"

"Yes, yes, of course," said Erik. "Right now?"

"Just when you can."

"Five minutes then," said Erik, and five minutes later he was there.

Then Erik blinked in surprise, because it was as if the frantic hours of the early evening had been utterly wiped away. A transformation had taken place. Hans's mother was pouring coffee, his father was puffing his pipe, Hans was teaching Frieda to wiggle her eyebrows, and Uncle Karl, undoubtedly the one responsible for all this magic, was smiling benevolently across from the window.

"Well, well, here is the second of our young fledglings!" he exclaimed, coming forward to greet Erik, and Erik found to his absolute astonishment that he was now taller than Uncle Karl. It felt so strange and wrong that for a moment he was entirely lost for words.

Uncle Karl was the same Uncle Karl as ever. Confident, cheerful, at ease with himself and the world, dismissing problems with a wave of a hand.

"Pooh, pooh," he said, when he heard about the searching of the apartments. "Don't tell me they actually worried you! They were only doing their job."

"I cut my hand," said Frieda, holding up her bandage.

"Very interesting," said Uncle Karl. "And what's that behind your left ear? Oh, a Reichsmark. That's so nice. And behind the other one? Come, come, stand still. Another, and another, and is that one in your pocket? Wonderful. You are rich."

Frieda's face was pure delight. Her mother clapped, and Hans said, "You never found money behind my ears."

"Didn't I?" asked Uncle Karl. "Well then, let me look now," but there was nothing behind Hans's ears except two matches in a box and a stump of pencil.

"Not all people have the right sort of ears," said Uncle Karl, shaking his head sadly, and everybody laughed, Frieda most of all.

Under cover of the laughter, Uncle Karl nodded to Erik and mouthed, "A word?" and motioned him over.

"What is it?" asked Erik, too startled to hide it in his voice.

"Nothing at all to worry you. Perhaps a little drive with me when I leave? You'll come?"

Erik nodded, because who ever said no to Uncle Karl?

"Good," said Uncle Karl, and picked up the empty brandy bottle from the table, tipped the last few drops onto the back of his hand, and dabbed them up carefully, one by one, with his finger.

"They finished the bottle without me," he explained to Frieda, who was watching.

"Without me, too," said Frieda.

Uncle Karl passed her the empty bottle and said, "I was planning to enjoy it later, but you may have first sniff."

Frieda inhaled long and deep.

"Is it nice?" asked Uncle Karl.

"Very nice," said Frieda. "Thank you."

"I do what I can," said Uncle Karl, and Erik recognized his mother's phrase and felt cold fear run down his spine. He never knew quite what to think of Uncle Karl, who was everyone's friend, who a much younger Erik had once hoped might marry his mother, so that she would no longer have to scrub staircases and could ride around in the wonderful red automobile instead.

Frieda offered Uncle Karl the brandy bottle. He sniffed, and said, "Wonderful," and passed it to Erik, who held it uncertainly.

Uncle Karl gave him one of his amused, blank looks and said, "It's a game, Erik."

It was very late before Uncle Karl left, nodding to Erik, who waited until the goodbyes were all said, and the doors all closed, and then followed him into the street.

The red automobile smelled as exotic as ever, and there was still a duster for passengers' shoes. Uncle Karl laughed out loud when Erik picked it up. "Those days are long gone, I'm sorry to say," he told him. "Now then, I wanted to talk to you. I've been thinking about this since it all began. Berlin will soon be a target. I must get the family out of the city. Your mother, too, of course."

Erik said nothing. Berlin could well become a target. Their friends might leave. But his mother would stay. She would do what she could.

Then Uncle Karl said calmly, "And your grandmother."

Silence hung like a heavy curtain between them.

They were driving though the city, the buildings tall, shuttered against the night, the long streets that led to the center all empty, the great squares and monuments hung with flags, motionless, huge. If ever a city looked invincible, thought Erik, it was this one, his Berlin.

"The city will be a target," said Uncle Karl, reading his thoughts, "from the west and from the east. She will need papers, which I can arrange."

"Where could they go?" asked Erik at last.

"The Munich factory needs workers, with so many young people gone to fight. I know a place where they could live."

Erik, with the help of his father's duffel bag, had now saved his first life. He could fly a plane, a fighter plane, with heavy machine guns attached. He had twice saluted the Führer, and once momentarily looked into his eyes (pale blue, insane). But he had not yet got over the feeling that when he was grown up, he would go and work in the Berlin Zoo, with Hans and his pastry stall handily stationed at the gates.

"Munich's a long way," he said.

"I'm dropping you here," said Uncle Karl, pulling up a mile or so away from Erik's street. "Enjoy the walk. I think it will be a bright morning. Do what you can."

"Thank—"

"Don't mention it," said Uncle Karl. He started off, stopped, reversed back to Erik, and leaned across to speak.

Erik looked into his eyes (Hans's eyes; gray-green, not insane).

"*Don't* mention it!" Uncle Karl repeated, and Erik nodded, tried to smile, couldn't, nodded again, and walked away.

EIGHTEEN

Ruby

Plymouth, Devon, Autumn 1939

Once they had begun, Ruby and her mother continued searching the newspapers for information about what was happening in the outside world. They quickly discovered that the more they read, the less they seemed to know. "Where's Poland?" Ruby asked. "What's it got to do with Germany? How can there be battles in Russia? I thought it was all snow."

"Russia's east," said Violet. "Poland's . . . I don't know one thing about Poland," she admitted. "We'd better go to the library."

The library was a great help, and so was the librarian. All that spring and summer she'd found answers to their questions. Nothing ever dismayed her. When Ruby read from her latest list of things she didn't understand—"Why do Americans speak English? Why did my dad fight Germany in France? How do ships not sink when they're made of metal? What's the Treaty of Versailles and is Russia all snow?"—the librarian said calmly, "I'll show you where to look."

A film called *The Wizard of Oz* came out. Ruby and Violet went to see it. It was shown with a newsreel. Hitler, making a speech to thousands of people.

"How can anybody listen to him?" asked Ruby. "He's crazier than the Tin Man. He's crazier than the Scarecrow. He's crazier than the Wicked Witch, he's crazier than that tornado. If he behaved like that round here, they'd chuck him in the harbor to calm him down."

"That's just what we'll do if he turns up on our street," said Violet cheerfully.

"The librarian said he needs someone to stand up to him," said Ruby.

"The sooner the better," agreed Violet. "Poor Will's bored stiff."

Ruby knew that all too well. They had just had another visit. Will had stayed two days, checked behind the clock, ridiculed the library books, said of course he knew where Poland was, the Treaty of Versailles was boring, ships didn't sink because their engines kept them up, stupid, just the same as airplanes, and everyone knew that Russia was all snow.

"It isn't!" Ruby had exclaimed. "You should look at this library book, and what about sailing ships that don't have engines?"

Will had replied that she should stop trying to be so clever, sailing ships were made of wood, and had she realized that when the war came, all the kids would be sent away from Plymouth, including her?

"Good riddance," Will had finished.

Then September had arrived, Britain was at war with Germany, and to Ruby's surprise, her mother and Mrs. Cohen, instead of saying "Good, just what we wanted," had looked at each other with sober faces.

"Sooner it's begun, sooner it's done," said Violet, at last.

"I think your Will might be too young to be sent overseas," said Mrs. Cohen hopefully, but she was wrong. Suddenly Will was on his way to France. He sailed as part of the BEF, the British Expeditionary Force in Europe, laden with baggage, which included an emergency kit provided by his anxious mother. Violet had put so much thought and effort into this that by the time it was all collected together, it seemed that he truly was equipped for anything.

It held:

- Winter socks and gloves (with his name in them)
- Malted milk tablets ("It's food and a nice hot drink.")
- Four ten-shilling notes in an envelope for just-in-case
- A first aid kit containing aspirin tablets, a remedy for seasickness (supplied by Mrs. Cohen, who had never once been on a boat), some sticking plasters, and a little bottle of iodine for cuts
- Ginger biscuits
- A large pork pie

It also included a notebook full of helpful things Violet had written down, such as *Gran's birthday, Dec 2, if you have time to drop a line*, and useful reminders about foreign dogs and rabies, boiling water before drinking it, and not to forget that over there they drove on the wrong side of the road. In the back of the notebook, she had listed some French words copied from the library dictionary (*Please, thank you, I am an English boy, I have lost my way, I need a good doctor,*

I am hungry, and *No, thank you, I do not drink wine*).

Very shortly after they sailed, Will ate the pork pie and the ginger biscuits, spent the ten-shilling notes on a secondhand watch, and read the notebook in horror before dropping it safely overboard in case anyone else should see it.

He came to regret all these things; the pork pie almost immediately, the money very soon afterward, and the notebook last and most painfully, when homesickness hit him like an illness and if he could have magicked one thing into his life, it would have been his mum.

Meanwhile, at home, life was changing. Will, although wrong about Russia and snow, and engines and airplanes, was right about one thing: the kids were sent away. Ruby's school was evacuated, every pupil labeled and put on a train with their belongings in a case and a teacher in charge. They were going to Cornwall, they were told, where there wouldn't be bombs.

Or cinemas or indoor toilets, added the rumors, and there would be seagulls' eggs for breakfast, and fish bones in the beds, and the locals would call you a foreigner and the kids would beat you up.

There were a lot of tears shed on that chaotic train journey to Cornwall, but not by Ruby, who had prudently borrowed the train fare home from the shop till before she left. At Exeter, where they had to change, she found the ladies' waiting room, located the cleaners' closet, and perched herself on an upturned bucket until the brief panicking search was over and they were forced to leave her behind. Then she removed her cardboard label, tucked her school hat under her arm, and caught the afternoon train back home.

"I might have known," said Violet, but she didn't send her back.

There followed a blissful few months with no school and no bombs and no Will, either. In town they built air-raid shelters, crisscrossed the windowpanes with paper tape to stop broken glass flying, and began taking the road signs down. Ruby spent a lot of time at the library, and Violet trained to be an air-raid warden.

"I thought you'd have to be a man," said Ruby, very impressed.

Now at night, the streets were very quiet, and the houses all dark, not a chink of light that might guide a bomber to the city.

Ruby thought sometimes that the blackout worked too well. Week after week passed, and then month after month, but no bombers came. Will wrote from France that he had nothing to do, so they sent him another emergency kit: a puzzle book, a large bag of peppermints, a woolly hat (with his name in it), and his old, but nearly new, soccer shoes.

"They'll keep him going for a bit," said Violet, and she was right, they did.

NINETEEN

Kate

Oxford, 1939

By the autumn of 1939 the world had changed, and Kate's family had changed with it.

Bea was the first to take flight from the nest. She was eighteen, and had just finished school. She said, "Would you believe it! There's a Land Army, and I can join! Think of lambs in the spring! And I'll get paid! Paid! I'm going to save up for a motorbike!" Then, before her family had time to say, "Are you crazy and what about us?" she was gone. They had a postcard from a hostel where she was sent for six weeks' training:

> They let us drive tractors! Someone teach
> Kate to plait her hair. I forgot.
> Love, Bea

Janey was next. Janey was nineteen and had done a year at university. There was no reason why she shouldn't carry on studying except that she had a letter from the Foreign Office. They wanted her to come for an interview in London.

"You!" exclaimed her family. "They must have got mixed up."

"I expect they've heard she's brainy," said her father gloomily, and they had.

"It's sort of office work," said brainy Janey. "I think it might be fun."

Very soon she too was sending postcards:

> I see squirrels in the park every morning. That's all I'm allowed to tell you. Someone help Kate with her homework. I forgot. Love, Janey

Simon and Tod joined the Sea Cadets. They said it was the quickest way into the navy.

"We can enlist properly next year when we're sixteen," said Simon.

"With parental consent," said their mother. "Meanwhile you are just horrible little boys, so go and get on with your homework!"

"Poor old Mum," said Tod. "She doesn't understand there's a war on. She thinks we can carry on doing homework and messing about in a leaky punt."

"She wishes we were still choirboys," said Simon. "She can't help it. Poor old Mum."

The Sea Cadets swallowed them up. They left their punt to sink back into the River Cherwell, gave up homework, grew lean and starving, and became intensely interested in first aid. For a while their conversation was full of drowning and choking, broken bones and splints. They practiced on whoever they could catch, which was usually Charlie.

"Charlie, you've just been dragged out of the sea. Stop kicking, you're unconscious. . . ."

"No, I'm not," said Charlie, somewhat indistinctly.

"Yes you are. Shut up. You've been two hours in the water and there's something blocking your airways."

"It's a gobstopper," said Charlie, shifting a large bulge from his left cheek to his right and slurping a little.

"Spit it out, so's I can check your breathing."

"I only just put it in!" said Charlie indignantly.

"Tod, I have a noncooperative patient here with worsening conditions," reported Simon.

"No, you haven't," said Charlie, and in proof he jumped to his feet and escaped by way of the living room window.

"Let him drown," said Tod. "Right, Kate, have you still got a pulse?"

"I don't really want . . . ," began Kate, who didn't always remember that she was now extraordinarily brave.

"Make a note, Simon: patient waterlogged, but responsive."

"Noted," said Simon. "Pulse irregular and feeble. Turn her so she doesn't choke if she vomits."

"I don't feel a bit sick," said Kate.

"Conversation irrational," commented Tod, rolling her onto her side. "Shock and hypothermia. Pass me something to cover her up. The hearthrug will do."

"Too dusty. It'll start her off coughing."

"True."

"Any bones broken?" asked Simon. "What have we got? Both legs? Both arms? Any bleeding requiring compression?"

"What's compression?" Kate squeaked in alarm.

"You'll see. Tod, fetch a tea towel and fold it into a pad and hold it tight against the wound. Kate, don't wriggle."

"The tea towel tickles."

"Put up with it. Don't move till we find some splints."

"Why'd you need splints?" demanded Charlie, reappearing at the window. "How did she get broken bones in the sea? Why didn't she just get wet?"

"She was hit by flying wreckage when the ship was torpedoed, of course."

Kate sat up very quickly and asked, "Might that really happen?"

"Obviously," said Tod.

"But you say you're going into the navy!"

"And?"

"What if your ships are torpedoed?"

"Kate, how many times did that punt tip us into the Cherwell?"

"I don't know."

"Think!"

"About once a week in the summer."

"Correct. And did we ever drown?"

"No, but . . . ," protested Kate, and then their mother came in and asked, "What are you horrible sailors doing to my daughter?"

"They're saving her," said Charlie, still perched on the windowsill.

"What from?"

"Drowning and broken bones and concussion and being torpedoed and shark attack."

"Not sharks," said Simon. "There were never any sharks."

"Well, there soon will be when they smell the blood," said Charlie.

"There is no blood," said Tod. "Not anymore. We applied compression until it stopped. You missed it, rushing out of the window."

"I think we should change the subject," said Tod. "We're frightening poor old Mum."

"Poor old thing," said Simon, nodding sympathetically.

"You boys forget you're talking to a woman who has clamped more arteries than you've had sausages for supper," snapped Vanessa.

"Mum!" wailed Kate, clapping her hands over her ears.

"Mum," said Tod reproachfully, "now look what you've done. Poor old Kate."

Then, as quickly as it had started, first aid stopped. Map reading and marching and rifle skills took over. Soon training camps began, and after that the twins were hardly ever home.

Quite suddenly it seemed to Kate that there was only Charlie left. At breakfast one Saturday morning, when it was just the two of them, she asked, "You're not going to do war things too, are you, Charlie?"

"Of course I am," said Charlie, with his mouth full of toast. "I'm going to learn circus tricks. Juggling and stilt-walking and fire-eating and stuff."

"What for?" asked Kate, astonished.

"So's I can be in shows to raise money. Everyone's wanting money, haven't you noticed? Airplanes and Red Cross and evacuees and ambulances. My class at school are saving up for a lifeboat. It was my idea."

"Mum and Dad will never let you fire-eat and stilt-walk," said Kate certainly.

"They will. I've got the stilts already," said Charlie, successfully balancing a licked marmalade spoon on the end of his nose. "A boy in choir was selling them, and when I told Dad, he said, 'Excellent,' and lent me the ten bob. I'm singing in a concert, too. I've been joining everything at school. Yesterday I signed up with the drama club, and they were really pleased because I ticked the box on the joining form to say I don't mind playing girls."

"But what about me?"

"You're a girl already, and anyway, you don't go to my school. You couldn't. It's all boys."

"You know I didn't mean that! What am I supposed to do?"

She sounded so anxious that Charlie put down the marma-lade spoon and thought. What *could* Kate do? How had he known what to do? He hadn't at first, he'd been thinking and thinking, and then suddenly he'd heard of the stilts for sale and everything had fallen into place.

He tried to explain this to Kate.

"I suppose I was watching out for something useful," he said.

"It will be useful," Kate agreed. "You'll make people laugh and cheer them up as well as getting money."

Charlie was immensely pleased. So rarely did his family take him seriously. He said, "You watch out like I did, Kate, and I bet something turns up for you. Do you want to come and see me on my stilts?"

"All right."

"Will you write about them in your diary?"

"Yes."

"Can I read it after?" asked Charlie. "What else have you written about?"

"Oh." Kate thought. "Tod and Simon doing their first aid and you jumping out of the window. Bea. All the Brussels sprouts she has to pick and then having to eat them every day for dinner. Janey's squirrel that waits for her in the mornings. Ruby and her brother. Dad at the hospital so much. Clarry and Rupert. Mum when she talks about the twins turning sixteen. Grandfather's gold."

"I'd forgotten about that," said Charlie, and later when he was reading Kate's diary, he found many other things he'd forgotten. "Bea's lambs," he said, as he turned pages backward, "and when Janey used to live with us. When it wasn't just me in the choir. When we didn't have to bother about gas masks. When I swam in the Serpentine . . . It's a good job you wrote it all down, Kate. Or else it would all have been wasted."

Kate nodded.

"Bea's got her farm and Janey her squirrel place. Tod and Simon will be sailors soon. I'll be the money-getter with my stilts and everything, and you'll be the writer-downer."

"But I'd do that anyway," objected Kate. "I was going . . . I was going to try and be, because Rupert said . . . it was his idea . . . extraordinarily . . ."

Charlie waited.

". . . brave."

"I expect you'll be that, too," said Charlie kindly.

TWENTY

Dog

London, late November 1939

The dog was lost. One evening an old van had rattled to the scrapyard, and not without difficulty, he'd been loaded into the back. The journey that followed had been so painful and bewildering that he'd blanked it from his mind.

They'd traveled north and west into the city until, under the shadow of some monstrous shapes that he didn't know were trees, the van had stopped and the back had opened.

"Off you go," a voice had ordered out of the darkness, and the dog had crawled out and stood sick and trembling beside the iron railings of a shabby London square.

Then the van had gone.

Now there was no scrapyard, no tea-chest kennel, no chain, no girl, no river smell. The streets were strange. Also, for all the miles the dog had run in his dreams, in real life he'd been always chained. His muscles were wasted and his movements were unbalanced and lurching. For the first few days, this clumsiness and unease kept him to the shadows, until hunger made him desperate. Then he became bolder. He grabbed and stole and scavenged. Day after day, he wandered, in search of dustbins and scraps and the leavings of street markets. There was nothing he wouldn't eat. Nothing.

Rupert encountered him late one night in cold December. There was no moon, and it had rained and the clouds were still low. The blackout had sealed the city into the sort of deep darkness where any moment you might step off a curb, or knock into a stranger. The sort where you navigated by the smell of fallen leaves, pungent under the plane trees, the hot breath of an underground station, and the dank whiff of alleys.

Rupert had a thousand things on his mind, and he was thinking of them as he hurried along when he noticed a smell like old clothes and dustbins and ancient dead fish. A moment later something pushed him from behind. His hand touched coarse fur. He heard panting.

"Oi," he said, pausing, and the reply was a long rumble, like the sound of a distant engine.

When he started walking again, the shove came once more. When he stopped, there came the rumble.

"Waylaid," said Rupert, "by a highway dog." And he reached out his hand to the rumble and felt bones under the fur. It was weeks now, since the scrapyard.

"You poor chap," said Rupert. "You poor old chap. Wait there."

There was a pub just ahead, still open, and the comforting sound of voices came from behind its shuttered windows. Rupert went in, bought a cheese roll with very little cheese in it and a pale-looking pie from under the glass dome on the counter, and hurried out again. The pie was seized from his hand in one hot invisible lunge, and there was a choking gulp. The cheese roll went the same way.

"That's it then," said Rupert, giving the bony shoulders a rub. "Best I can do. Good luck."

He went back into the pub again, and half an hour later, when he reappeared, the dog was still there, waiting.

Rupert tried to lose him, but the dog followed. He followed all the way to the little basement flat that Rupert rented when he was in London. However, at the steep steps down to the entrance, he halted.

Just as well, thought Rupert, as he hurried to unlock the door and get inside, but the dog had not given up. In the darkness, he was very slowly negotiating his way down toward the door. Rupert heard grumbling growls come closer and closer, and then a heavy thud.

After the thud came silence, and after the silence, a long, sorry sigh.

It was the sigh that made Rupert find a plate and get out all the things he had to eat, which wasn't much, because his basement was just his place to sleep, not a home. Nevertheless, he found some smelly cheese, some biscuits, a tin of sardines, and a forgotten slice of bacon, which he toasted over the gas ring and then arranged like a garnish beside the other things. After this, he filled his largest dish with water, made himself a cup of tea without any milk, because he hadn't any milk, and opened the door.

The smell came in first, and then, very quickly after it, the dog.

The dog didn't look at Rupert. He went straight for the dishes on the floor. The food vanished in one swallow, the water in a few great slurping gulps.

"Excellent," said Rupert cheerfully, and then a most un-excellent thing happened. There was an ominous silence, some terrible sounds, and very suddenly cheese, biscuits, sardines, bacon, water, together with the pub pie and a slightly chewed roll, all reappeared in a large and hateful pile in the middle of Rupert's floor.

"No!" he cried, leaping forward, but he was too late, and helpless to prevent the whole heap being hastily eaten up again, even faster than the first time.

"Never since boarding school have I seen such a meal," said Rupert. "What's that round your neck? Will you show me?"

He reached cautiously toward the dog so he could inspect the leather tag and the three burned letters.

PAX

(*It might help,* the girl had thought.)

Pax, read Rupert.

Peace.

For years Rupert had worked for peace, argued for peace, traveled backward and forward through Europe in a quest for peace, and now here it was, slumped on his kitchen floor.

"So," said Rupert. "Pax."

The dog gave him a swift glance, like a person agreeing to a bargain.

It had been a long day. Rupert went to bed, and the dog went to bed too, on the only bit of carpet in Rupert's flat: his quite nice bedside rug. The smell that came from him penetrated Rupert's dreams so strongly that for a moment, when he woke, he didn't know where he was and remembered the earthy, stale smell of the dugouts he had slept in during the first world war.

It was quite a relief to see Pax.

There was no hot water in Rupert's basement, but there was a bath. Rupert boiled kettles and poured in soap flakes and stirred it until it was warm and bubbly, and then he rolled up his sleeves and grabbed Pax and lifted him in.

The grumbling sounds were awful, and so was the curled lip that showed a broken yellow tooth, but Rupert, remembering his dreams, said, "I faced worse than you in the trenches," and began to scrub.

The first lot of bathwater was soon the color of wartime coffee—a sort of earthy, greenish brown. The second lot was much paler. Different colors began to appear on the dog; white on his chest, and a sort of rust mixed in with the gray. Rupert rinsed him down, hauled him out, rubbed the worst of the wet out of his coat with his only bath towel, and, not knowing what else he could do with him, took him into work and parked him in a corner of his office.

For a few days, this worked fairly well. Pax mostly slept, recovering from the weeks of hunger and exhaustion. However, as he recovered, he grew restless. If Rupert left him for a while, he paced and whined, or tried to dig holes in the floor. When people came in, he growled and ducked away, even from friendly hands. It began to be that the moment he appeared in the morning, someone would say, "You're not bringing that animal in here again, are you? This is no place for dogs."

Rupert knew it was no place for dogs, that soon the whole of London would be no place for dogs. It was only a matter of time before the bombing raids would begin. The silver barrage balloons were ready (Pax hated them, as he hated all things in the sky), air-raid shelters were built, buildings piled with sandbags. Civilians had been recruited and trained: fire-fighters, air-raid wardens, ambulance drivers.

There were hardly any children about, and hardly any dogs, especially big dogs like Pax. Quite often people commented, "Blimey, what do you feed that on?"

"Horse," said Rupert. "He's horse-powered."

Now that food was rationed, horsemeat was the only thing you could buy for cats and dogs. Even that wasn't easy. The queues at the butchers were getting longer every day, and every day Rupert had less time to wait in them. In a phone call to Clarry, he mentioned that it felt like he spent every spare waking moment queuing up for dark green horse.

"Dark green?" asked Clarry.

"They've started splashing it with green dye. It's to stop people buying it to eat."

"I'm so glad I'm a vegetarian. Did you call me just to talk about horsemeat, Rupert?"

"Not just about that."

"I knew!" said Clarry, suddenly furious. "I knew as soon as the telephone rang. It's—"

"Steady on, Clarry," said Rupert hastily.

Telephone calls weren't secure. They went through a switchboard where anyone could listen. "It's what you talked about in Oxford," said Clarry. "When?"

"Very soon. Don't worry."

"Don't worry! Why can't someone else do it? There must be hundreds of people who would be ten times more use than you."

"Thank you. Mathematically devastating as usual."

"Stop it. You know you have a choice."

"Not much. Prime suspect really. Know the routines. Unattached."

"I should have married you years ago."

"Told you so."

There was a pause, while Clarry sniffed.

"Marry me when I come back."

"Yes, all right. If."

"Take back the if and I'll give you all my worldly goods."

"No, Rupert, I couldn't!" exclaimed Clarry. "Not if you mean the worldly goods that eats green horse. In this little flat, and I'm teaching all day. You'll have to give him to somebody else."

"Not easy."

"You must know someone who likes dogs."

"You'd think so, but . . . Yes, I do. Of course I do! Genius, Clarry, well done! There's the beeps! I was going to ask you . . ."

The beeps were the warning that the three-minute phone call was about to end. Rupert had just time to say, "A very small favor," and Clarry to reply, "Yes, anything," when the line went dead.

"This is wonderfully good news for you and me," said Rupert to Pax. "Clarry is going to marry me. And—this is your bit— Kate, I just suddenly remembered Kate, who is a darling, is very fond of dogs."

Kate wrote to Ruby: *I am looking after a dog called Pax till the end of the war.*

It had begun with a telephone call, overheard from the landing by Kate, answered by her father.

"What? What? Clarry, are you mad? Absolutely impractical. Typical Rupert!"

"What's typical Rupert?" asked Kate from the stairs, but Peter was still protesting down the phone.

"One daft enterprise after another!" he continued. "Swimming in the Serpentine! Carting the girls round London! Carting them *all* round London. I never could see the sense in it!"

"Perhaps," replied Clarry, "he remembered how no one ever carted us around when we were growing up."

There was silence in the hall for a moment.

"They always came back safe and joyful," said Clarry.

When Peter spoke again, his voice had changed completely. "You're right. You're absolutely right. But explain to me, why Kate?"

"Rupert seemed to think she liked dogs."

At this, Kate's fingers had closed on the Scottie-dog pincushion in her pocket, and she'd come tumbling down the stairs to demand breathlessly, "What are you talking about?"

Clarry brought him back from London on the train, wrote Kate.

The dog had hated that journey. He had been entirely distressed. If he had been free to choose, he would have been safe back in his yard on his six-foot chain.

Once again he was lost.

At the station Rupert had handed his lead to a strange woman, and, addressing her, ignoring him, said, "I'll be back before you know it. Hold out your hand, Clarry. No tears . . . It's a pink sapphire to match your pink beret. Don't worry if you lose it, I'll buy you another."

"Oh . . ."

"See? Perfect."

"Can we write?"

"No, darling Clarry. Don't be daft."

"I hate goodbyes."

"Don't say it. He probably needs defleaing. One kiss . . . There."

Then he'd vanished.

The dog had been hauled onto a train and tied up on a stack of old newspapers in the guards' car. It had been lucky the newspapers were there, because when the train lurched into movement, he'd been sick with fright. And after that, at intervals for the whole nightmare event, he'd been sick again and again. It was true that the Clarry woman had spent the journey with him, but she, for some other reason, had seemed almost equally distressed. The dog avoided her with loathing because it was she who had taken him from Rupert.

The woman had to give the guard ten shillings because he was so ill. When she got him back to Oxford, she'd washed him with rose geranium soap. The dog, who much preferred the smell of sick, had longed to bite her, but he couldn't. The memory of the yard broom swung high to wallop him in his snapping puppy days held him back. He'd curled his lip and shown her his broken yellow tooth, but she'd said, "I don't believe you," and continued with the soap.

He was damp and reeking of roses when more strangers came to stare at him. A man and a girl, who glanced and then looked away, backward and forward from the Clarry woman to his quivering self, with nowhere he could hide.

He was much bigger than I expected, Kate wrote to Ruby, and she had drawn two small sketches, a Scottie dog and Pax, for comparison.

"He's a big softy," Clarry said, and then Dad reached his hands up into the air to tug at his hair like he does when he's going crazy. We didn't know how frightened Pax was of being hit.

When Peter reached up, it was more than the dog could bear. He ran.

Down the stairs, away across the streets, causing cars to hoot, cyclists to skid, and two buckets of chrysanthemums outside the flower shop to clatter to the ground. The flower shop woman came out and began to screech.

It wasn't a long escape. He was very soon surrounded. A semicircle of people blocked his way, and he was trapped. Then the girl arrived and grabbed his leash and the man came limping up behind. He said, "I suppose we'd better take him home."

The dog didn't want to go home with them. He wanted to stay where he was there in the road until either Rupert came and rescued him, or he miraculously remembered his way back to the scrapyard. Those were the only two futures he could imagine, and so he dug in his paws and leaned backward and raised all the fur in a line down his spine and snarled.

Traffic had to go around him. Bystanders suggested a good shove with a broom, a bucket of cold water to make him jump, and fetching the police. It went on and on until the dog, who was very tired, gave up all hope of any future, lay down on the cobbles, put his head between his paws, and cried.

"Oh," said the girl, and she kneeled in the road and gathered him into her arms. Her face was against his, and her hands were in his fur, rubbing behind his ragged ears. She told him over and over that he was a good dog.

The scrapyard girl had spoken kindly to him. Rupert had

given him many friendly rubs and scratches. Neither could compare with this. For the first time in his life, the dog knew he had a heart. A proper, thudding heart, his own, to keep him warm and alive.

As soon as he had located it, he renounced all ownership, and gave it to Kate, forever and ever.

Pax, wrote Kate to Ruby, *is another word for peace.*

TWENTY-ONE

Erik and Hans

Germany, January–February 1940

It was the best news for a very long time. Erik and Hans were together again, flying their planes from the same air base. Perhaps it was good luck. Perhaps it was fate. Perhaps, perhaps, thought Erik, longing for a past world, it was Uncle Karl, murmuring a word to some old Luftwaffe friend from before the war, "Do what you can for the boys."

They flew little Messerschmitts, single-seater aircraft, and their task was nearly always the same: to escort the heavy bombers, to defend them from the fighter planes that rose up in fury from their invaded homelands.

Often in private, tired Erik rubbed his head, and tried to trace his journey from his *kleine Schwalben*, his little swallows, to being part of the planned attack on France. He could never quite manage it, and neither, when he consulted him, could Hans.

They were in the mess, drinking golden lager from tall glasses.

"It was probably because of the zoo that we ended up with wings," Hans decided, after thinking for a while. "Almost certainly, all our troubles began with your great need for elephants and monkeys and the like."

"All Berlin went to the zoo," said Erik. "They didn't end up flying Messerschmitts."

"True . . . Drink up! True, but we were different. Remember the time we swept the paths and met Herr Schmidt?"

"Your idea," said Erik, smiling at the memory. "We should have stuck to my expert and knowledgeable guided tours."

"'How I Spent My Sunday Morning and Why I Will Never Do It Again,'" said Hans. "That was the title he set us."

"I remember," said Erik. "A thousand words each, to be handed in the next day."

"Yes. And we wrote them in my room so your mother wouldn't know you were in trouble. And Uncle Karl came in."

"He did," agreed Erik. "And I told him about my swallows."

"Those swallows!" exclaimed Hans. "They were a bad lot! That Cumulus never stopped eating. By the time they flew away, you were so exhausted that if I hadn't been there, you would have toppled out of the window."

"Well," said Erik, clinking glasses. "You were there. So."

Now that they were together again, Erik and Hans often escaped into the old stories, the swallows and the zoo, and the pastry stall outside. Running out onto the airfield to climb into their cockpits, Erik would shout, "Have you got fresh gingerbread? Is the coffee hot?" and Hans would call back, "Of course, but are the bears all brushed and fed? Do the flamingos look pink enough, and is that elephant happy?" Then, for a minute or two, they were boys back in Berlin, with no worse troubles than lost mittens, and bossy sisters, and how to find the price of a ticket to the zoo. "Two Reichsmarks," remembered Erik. "Two Reichsmarks, to be happy all day."

‿ ℒ ∾

Uncle Karl had kept his word and their families had left Berlin. It had all been arranged very quickly, the goodbyes and the packing, and then, before anyone could think, Hans's parents and little Frieda were riding in a truck loaded with the furniture from both apartments, and Erik's mother was following by car with Uncle Karl.

"Ah!" Hans's mother had exclaimed, when she heard of this arrangement. "I have thought for a long time, you and Karl—"

"I know you have," said Erik's mother. "But no."

"No? It would have been nice for Erik when he was smaller."

"Erik was happy enough."

"He was," her friend agreed. "That smile! They were both happy boys, thank God. Hans was a rascal."

"There was never a better boy than Hans," said Erik's mother at once.

"All grown up now," Hans's mother sighed. "I miss Lisa. Boys leave, I know they do, but girls should stay near their mothers."

Lisa hadn't gone with them when they moved. She'd finished her national service and was back in Berlin, living in a hostel and working long shifts in an office. Hans heard that she was miserable.

"It's her work," he told Erik. "She detests being stuck in a dreary office, and she doesn't get on with the hostel people. She says she's lonely every day."

"Surely she could find something else?" Erik asked, hating to think of Lisa so unhappy.

"Not that easy," said Hans.

"Perhaps Uncle Karl . . . ," suggested Erik, as the families had said for years, *Perhaps Uncle Karl*, but this time Hans shook his head.

"No."

"No? Definitely no?"

"Definitely no. The family magician has disappeared."

"Since when?"

"Since Berlin. My mother says he moved them across half of Germany to work in Munich and then turned his back on them all. My father says he's up to no good."

"What does Frieda say?"

"He forgot her birthday."

"Disaster! How did they manage?"

"Luckily, a random kitten turned up and saved the day."

"A kitten?"

"Yes."

"On her actual birthday?"

"Just walked through the door, my mother said."

"A completely random kitten?"

"Must I continually repeat . . . ," began Hans, and then finished, in quite a different voice, "Oh, I see."

"At last."

"Perhaps, after all, the magician is not dead."

"Dead?" asked Erik, startled.

"I have wondered."

"What a terrible thought."

"He is a terrible meddler," said Hans. "A magician and a meddler. Are such people welcome these wonderful days?"

Erik said nothing.

"He magicked us here," said Hans. "Where would we be without him?"

Erik thought wistfully and briefly of his beloved Berlin Zoo. Hans read his mind and laughed. "No, you wouldn't," he said.

"You'd be conscripted into the infantry before you could say, 'Mind the tiger.'"

"So would you. Before you could say 'apple strudel.'"

"Certainly," agreed Hans. "He magicked us away from the fate of our fathers. Out of the mud. Into Luftwaffe pilots. So now, where shall we fall?"

"Stop it, Hans."

"How is your mother?"

Erik glanced at him. He had never forgotten the evening of the police raid. He'd come out of their apartment with his duffel bag on his back to find Hans stationed as if on guard at the top of the stairs. Later, when the police had gone, Hans had actually lifted his bag.

"Don't forget this," he had said. He must have felt the weight.

They had never spoken about it. Erik had never known what Hans guessed, what Hans knew.

"Your mother?" repeated Hans. "Does she miss Berlin?"

"She hasn't said so."

"Is she happy?"

"I wouldn't know."

"Be careful, Erik. Don't fall out of the window. I'll do what I can, but what if one day I'm not there to save you?"

"Hans. What is this?"

"I don't know. I don't know. I feel very mortal. Do you?"

"No. Not really."

"Not when the searchlights catch you? Not when the guns on the ground won't stop? Not when the fuel's on zero and you can't find the way back down? It may have been a completely random kitten, you know. The magician may be gone.

Then who will look after them? My complaining parents. Bossy Lisa? Little Frieda?"

"You shouldn't be thinking like this."

"But I am," said Hans. "Would you look after them, Erik?"

"I . . ."

"Frieda? Someone has to take care of Frieda. Would you do what you could?"

"Yes," said Erik. "I would. I promise. I'd do what I could."

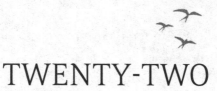

TWENTY-TWO

Ruby

Plymouth, Devon, May 1940

Germany invaded France, and Ruby's brother Will suddenly, shockingly, catastrophically, stopped being bored. Before the bewildered eyes of half the world, none more bewildered than those of Will, France fell in forty-six days. Denmark, Belgium, the Netherlands were also lost. In Paris, Rupert was soon behind enemy lines, with Hans and Erik in the air above. Day after day, the news grew worse.

The newsagent's shop in Plymouth had never been as popular. People might hear the latest happenings on their wirelesses, but they absorbed them best written down. Besides, they needed to talk. In the shop there was always someone to listen, even if it was only Ruby, with her atlas and her opinions.

Violet and Ruby were glad to be so busy. It helped to have people about, because in France the British Army was in retreat, moving backward to the coast as the German troops advanced. And for everyone in the newsagent's shop, the army had more or less become one particular soldier, and he was Will.

Will, who they had known since he was a screeching toddler, who played knock-down-ginger all along the street when he should have been in bed, who chalked rude remarks on walls, who started his gang carol singing in November and tried it on again in January, who left his bicycle chucked down on the pavement for anyone to fall over. Will, who had been such a pest, until the army took him in hand and about time somebody did.

But now he was their own heroic Will.

Day by day, with Sooty and Paddle weaving anxious circles round their feet, the visitors to the shop read of how Will and the rest of them were being forced toward the coast, abandoning gear, sheltering in ditches, tuning and retuning their field radios to catch the latest static-crackling instructions.

They saw the pictures, too. Dispatch riders, desperately trying to hold the lines of communication together. Frightened local people gathered in town squares. The refugee-filled roads that crossed the French countryside.

As the days passed, it became increasingly clear what would happen next. Will would be trapped. The army would be trapped. They would reach the coast, they would be herded onto the French beaches, and there would be nowhere left to go.

When Ruby heard this, she wrote a letter addressed to *Mr. Churchill, London.* She also wrote *URGENT* on the envelope. She felt very virtuous as she did this, because she wasn't that fond of Will.

During all those days, Ruby's mother couldn't rest. When everything else was done, she polished. She polished the insides of drawers and the undersides of cupboards and every plate and saucepan that they owned. She polished the pennies and shillings in the till. Also, since she was the mother of a hero and standards must be upheld, she buffed her nails with lemon peel, powdered away the shadows beneath her eyes, and nearly wore her precious scarlet lipstick to a stump.

"I thought you were saving it for special," said Ruby, at her bedroom door.

"And isn't Will special?" demanded Violet.

"They're sending boats," said Ruby. "That's what I came to tell you. Mrs. Cohen's just run down to say she heard it on her wireless. A special announcement. They're sending boats across to France. Big ones are waiting out where the water's deep. Little ones are going right up to the beaches to get the soldiers off and carry them out to the big ones. It was my idea."

"WHAT?" shouted Violet.

"It was my idea, and I think they should say thank you," said Ruby. "I wrote a letter to Mr. Churchill, and I think he could have written back. Even if they're keeping it top secret."

"What nonsense you do talk," cried Violet, nevertheless hugging her, and then she put on even more lipstick and rushed down to the shop to exclaim about the big boats and little boats and how Will had swum like a fish from five years old, because his dad had taken him to the pool every summer.

Such was the kindness of the shop's customers that they paused their discussion of the evacuation at Dunkirk to say that they well remembered what a swimmer Will was and how proud his dad had been of him, and would be now, more than ever.

But then someone spoiled it. They said, "It's going to take days to get them off."

"Days?" asked Violet, in a voice so shocked that it was clear she had been thinking in hours, not days.

"There's tens of thousands. Hundreds of thousands. There's three hundred thousand and more."

"Three hundred thousand and more?" exclaimed Violet.

"It's a lot to move, under fire."

"Under fire," repeated Violet. "Surely they wouldn't . . . not under fire . . . They're just boys, half of them. Our Will's hardly twenty. I'd have thought common decency . . ."

She looked helplessly around for someone to agree that of course no one would dream of firing at young boys, stranded on a beach. That they had driven them out of Europe, and what more could they want? It should be youngest rescued first and everybody home safe, the sooner the better, and after that talk about whatever should happen next.

Said Violet.

The shop had fallen silent, nobody having the heart to say, "Violet, there's a war on." Ruby scuffed her foot angrily behind the counter. Under fire hadn't occurred to her, either. Perhaps her wonderful plan to save the British Army was not so wonderful after all.

"They've got guns," she pointed out crossly. "They can fire back, can't they? Anyway, isn't it past closing time? What about tea?"

"Tea?" said her mother, like it was a word she'd forgotten, and then she said, "Yes," and flipped the OPEN sign to CLOSED and held the door for people in a meaningful kind of way. "Goodbye, goodbye, we'll see what the morning brings. Thank you . . . I'm sorry but we're just closing up. Ruby, get those cats off the counter and come into the scullery. I'm washing your hair."

"Now?" asked Ruby, dismayed. Hair washing was an ordeal,

involving green soap and vinegar rinsing and jugfuls of water poured over her head.

"Now," said Violet, her eyes too bright and her lipstick gallant.

Ruby saw these things, and because of them she didn't put up her usual fight, understanding that this was all part of the polishing that was keeping her mother from despair. With hardly a sigh she kneeled on the wooden stool, hung her head over the scullery sink, and clutched a face flannel to her soap-stinging eyes. In silence she endured the deluges of water, until she emerged to the buffeting towel and the steel-toothed comb in her tangles.

"OUCH," said Ruby, then.

Violet put down the comb, picked it up again, and said, "We've got to carry on."

"Yes," agreed Ruby. "But listen. Will always manages, you know he does. He'll be with his friends, lots of friends, all looking after each other. And I bet any day soon he'll come back and hug you and dump his stuff on the chairs and eat all the food in the cupboard and fuss the cats and say, 'What's an amaryllis, anyway?'"

"Oh, Ruby Amaryllis!"

"You could do a welcome-home party, with sausages and cider," said Ruby.

Violet laughed a small laugh.

"We could borrow Mrs. Cohen's gramophone and set it going in the shop! We'll get all the neighbors round!"

"We'll do that," said Violet, and she took Ruby's hand and spun her under her arm and danced her round the scullery, round and round, until they were both breathless and neither of them crying anymore.

On the beaches of Dunkirk, the soldiers waited on the sand. Now and then, German planes flew low, strafing the lines with machine-gun bullets. The tide rose and fell and Ruby's little boats scurried back and forth, all sorts of little boats from all along the south coast of England. They hauled on board men waist-deep in water, ferried them over to the bigger ships, and then scurried back again for more. It took three days and at the end of it, more than three-quarters of the army were rescued.

It was a miracle so great that it was hardly to be believed.

But not all of them made it.

Will did not come back.

TWENTY-THREE

Kate

Oxford, June 1940

K ate's diary, begun in peacetime in a pink notebook with white kittens on the front, had next moved to a purple journal with scented pages that her mother said she could do without, and then into a series of paper-covered school exercise books provided by Clarry. They were so ancient that their pages had buckled with damp, but the soft yellowed paper was perfect for both writing and drawing. Clarry had donated a boxful, and Kate was working through them at a rate of about one a week.

The Christmas that hadn't worked was recorded; the one with neither Janey nor Bea at home, Clarry in Plymouth, and even Charlie's voice now too unreliable for the choir. The long January and February of cold and snow that followed were there too, with coal suddenly much harder to get and Bea freezing on a Lincolnshire farm with not a lamb in sight. Bea wrote that her glasses steamed up every time she breathed and she had chilblains on her fingers as well as her toes. They posted a rescue package, with bed socks and a hot-water bottle, a knitted patchwork blanket, double-thickness mittens and an ancient sheepskin hat. Kate noted all this, together with Bea's opinions of winter greens, turnips, and sorting seed potatoes in a drafty open shed. When Bea said in her next letter that she wore everything they sent in bed, Kate immediately drew the picture. She also drew the snow in Oxford: the city's bicycles flung down and abandoned by college walls. They had turned overnight into great bumpy snowdrifts.

"Mine's there somewhere," Clarry had said, and Kate helped her search, scooping pillows of snow from saddles and banging their shins on hidden pedals. "It's black," Clarry had added, but all colors were faded to black and gray that day. They abandoned their search when the cold got too much. Later that week the snow half melted and then froze in the night. Kate drew the bicycles all locked in ice, like tangled scaffolding, with every tire flat.

Only Pax enjoyed that winter. His oily doormat coat was perfect for snow, and nobody had the stamina to bathe him. As Charlie said, it was a waste of time, anyway. No soap in the world smelled as strong as Pax. Once he was finally housetrained (an ordeal that took up many pages), he was allowed upstairs, where he slept across Kate's bedroom door and was an excellent draft excluder.

Spring filled more exercise books, and then in June, Janey came to visit. An unfamiliar-looking Janey with new short hair, rushing around Oxford, meeting up with old friends. Nevertheless, she still found time to check Charlie's stilt-walking ("Fantastic, just what the country needs!") and Kate's homework books ("Kate, I swear your math is going backward"). Kate knew that perfectly well, so she didn't argue, and it was nice having Janey again. Together they walked with Pax across Port Meadow, marveling that there were chestnuts in flower, and chiffchaffs and white butterflies, just like any other year.

"I sort of expected it to stay always winter," said Kate, and then, in a completely different voice, "Quick! Ducks! Catch Pax!"

She was too late, and Pax was gone. He wasn't a dog with much self-control at the best of times, but what little he had, he lost with ducks. Ducks dismayed him. He hadn't minded them at all when he thought they could only swim, but the day he discovered they could fly, he was absolutely horrified. Since then, whenever he encountered them, he went careering after them in yapping, outraged pursuit.

"Dreadful!" Janey scolded, when they finally caught up with him. Pax rolled humbly on his back and came up green with goose poo and Kate put that in her diary too.

"Does everything go in?" asked Janey, and Kate let her look at the latest exercise book, which, as well as Pax and ducks and Janey herself, had the news that had come from Ruby about her brother and Dunkirk.

"Poor Ruby," commented Janey.

"I had to write it down."

"Of course you did. It matters. Did you put in about the bells?"

"What bells?"

"They announced it last week. They're not to be rung, except for air raids. Imagine Oxford without bells."

"Grandfather would be pleased," observed Kate, thinking of how grumpily he had complained about the clamoring Christmas bells.

Janey laughed, because she also remembered how Grandfather had grumbled that visit, but then she said, "Will you write about it in your diary, Kate? I know it's just a little thing. . . ."

"I'll write it down," said Kate, hugging Janey's arm. She was getting more and more requests like that. "Tell Kate to put it in her diary" or "Don't forget, will you, Kate?" Simon and Tod's turning sixteen and Mother's voice going ragged in the middle of "Happy Birthday." Pax's fear of the washing on the washing line. Mr. Churchill's "We shall fight on the beaches," Clarry's sudden, tearful, "What happened to my old pink beret?"

All these things Kate recorded, writing steadily evening after evening in the faded paper-covered notebooks, so they shouldn't be forgotten.

TWENTY-FOUR

Erik and Hans

Germany, Summer 1940

"The aim," Erik had said to Hans, "is to destroy the French Air Force. Not the French. The planes."

"And the airfields and hangars and landing strips and factories where more planes might still be built," said Hans. "And the supply lines to the factories. The rail tracks and the roads."

Erik said unhappily that he supposed it had to be done, and that if only the French would surrender instead of fighting back, it would be much less difficult for all of them.

"You talk like an old woman," said Hans brutally. "Or as if you were made of wood and rags. A stuffed puppet of the Third Reich."

"Do I?" asked Erik. "Is that how I sound?"

"I saw a plane hit from really close today," said Hans. "The first shots caught the wing, tipped it over. And the next bullets went through the fuel tank and it sprayed into the cockpit. Those French planes have no armoring round their tanks, like we all do. Still, the pilot could have bailed. Well, I admit, he tried. I saw him reach to try. But the fuel caught. It was strange the way the fuel caught fire before the tank exploded. I swear I was so close I heard him scream. Maybe I didn't. Maybe I just heard the machine guns. They fired for a long time after it was over. I don't know why. Don't touch me."

Erik, who had reached out a hand, stopped. He said, "I'm sorry, Hans."

"Who for?" asked Hans. "Why do you think the machine guns kept on going?"

"Maybe something jammed."

"No, it didn't," shouted Hans. "I just couldn't seem to stop. I must go! You come as well."

"Where to?"

"To celebrate, of course," cried Hans, his eyes full of horror.

One night, Erik dreamed of the Berlin Zoo. It was a summer dream; the linden trees were in flower and he could smell them as he hurried toward the entrance. It was perfect, no queues, no kiosk selling paper flags. It was as it had been long ago and it was still early morning, so he had all day to spend exploring. When he'd come as a small boy, he'd been so eager to reach the animals that he had hardly looked at the architecture. Remembering this, Erik paused at the Elephant Gate, the entrance he had scampered through so many times before. The carved elephants were magnificent, the bright arch full of welcome, but it was just like the old days: he couldn't wait to look properly, so he hurried through, half laughing at himself.

Inside, the baboons were hooting at some joke, and a patterned giraffe was reaching for a bundle of green leaves. In the past, he and Hans had made mental maps of all the different ways around to take. The slow trail. The tiger trail. The wet-weather circuit and the rush-round. Erik set off on the rush-round for old times' sake, and then the slow trail, pausing as often as he liked. He wished his familiar zoo-wish for a camera.

To wake up and find himself a Luftwaffe officer was a sort of grief. He couldn't believe it at first. All day he was haunted by the smell of linden trees and all day he thought, *I'll go back. I'll go back. At the first chance I'll go back.* And he comforted himself thinking, *I could write to Herr Schmidt at school and ask for news of the zoo. I could do that,* thought Erik, *for an hour or two,* and then thought, *No, I couldn't.*

He had to be a stuffed puppet of the Third Reich, not in any way interesting enough to cause the briefest raised eyebrow. Nor could he renew any link with anyone who might suffer if it was discovered that he wasn't a stuffed puppet after all. That, far from being a stuffed puppet, he was Erik, who together with other people had saved Fräulein Trisk; now, he hoped, safely with his mother. He wished he knew, but he couldn't write and ask, and of course, they couldn't tell him.

Erik's mother wrote him letters that said nothing at all. She would mention her factory work, or that she had bought a "good loaf" and given half to Frieda to take back to her parents, or that the sun was welcome after the long, cold winter, things like that. Once she told him she had washed three towels and they'd dried very nicely. Erik would search her letters for the slightest hint that she and Fräulein Trisk were safe, but there was never a word. Nor did she ever mention the old life in Berlin. She wrote to him as if he were someone she hardly knew.

The letters Hans received were no more helpful. They were all grumbles, mostly about illnesses and Frieda. His mother's aches. His father's sore stomach. Frieda wasn't ill, but she wouldn't have her hair combed. She had cut it off herself with Hans's mother's scissors and now it was too short to plait and she would undoubtedly pick up *Kopfläuse* at kindergarten, but what was anyone to do? She was growing into a very stubborn girl, just like her sister. True, she was bright, but what was the use of that? Lisa had been bright, and where was she now? Not writing letters home, that was certain. Never mind, wrote Hans's mother glumly, the war was going well and the sooner it was over the better. It was all very tiring for someone of her age to deal with, and she hadn't been able to buy either butter or a piece of good cheese for weeks.

Erik and Hans often shared their letters. Hans passed this letter to Erik with a shrug that said, *There's nothing here.*

It was Frieda who sent the news. Hans had a birthday and she drew him a picture. *For Hans*, she wrote on the top.

It was a picture of her world, with every person labeled. Frieda in the center, the tallest of them all, standing beside an equally tall animal, probably a cat.

Frieda, it said underneath, and *Mitzi*.

On either side of Frieda stood a woman. They looked very much alike, except one had a heart shape over her head with the word *Erik* written in it, and the other had another, larger heart, with *Hans + Lisa*. Underneath the first woman it said *Tante Anna*, which was what Frieda had always called Erik's mother, and under the second it said *Mutti*.

Mutti was propping up Vati, who was shown clearly with one leg. Tante Anna also had a companion. A small, small woman, half the height of the rest. *Kleine Oma*, it said underneath.

Little Grandma.

All the people that Frieda had drawn were smiling large smiles.

Hans showed the picture to Erik and asked, "Happy now?"

"Yes, thank you, Hans," said Erik. "Yes. Much better."

TWENTY-FIVE

Ruby

Plymouth, Devon, July 1940

It took a while for Violet to admit that Will wasn't coming back. During that time no one, not even Ruby or Clarry or Mrs. Cohen, could say a word that would help. This went on until Ruby could bear it no longer and went into Will's bedroom at two in the morning, where her mother was busy polishing a pair of old shoes he'd left under his bed.

"Stop it!" she said. "Stop it, Mum! He hates having his stuff messed about with."

Violet became quite still.

"You'll have to unpolish them in the morning," continued Ruby. "Or else he'll moan he can't leave anything safe. You know he always does."

Her mother looked uncertainly down at the shoes in her lap.

"Don't worry, I'll help," said Ruby. "I'll scuff them round the yard."

"I don't think . . ."

"But now you should go to sleep." Ruby took the shoes and put them down on the floor. "I've checked the blackout and I've set the alarm clock for a quarter to six. I'm taking it up to the attic with me, so I can wake up when they bring the papers in the morning."

Violet gave a great weary sigh.

"Stand up," ordered Ruby, heaving on her mother's arms. "Come on, this way. Here's your room. Here's the bed. Give me your skirt and I'll sort it out. There . . ."

By the time the skirt was folded and laid on the bedroom chair, her mother was asleep.

Ruby crept away. She thought, *He's alive. I'm sure he's alive because he's still being a pest.* Then she tumbled so deeply asleep herself that it was like falling into the sky.

Five seconds later, or so it seemed to Ruby, the alarm clock was ringing and it was dawn. Any minute now the morning bundles of papers would be dumped on the doorstep. Unless the shop was open, the deliveryman would ring the doorbell to let them know they'd arrived, and that would wake her mother. Ruby rolled out of bed and tiptoed sleepily downstairs.

The postman must already have been.

On the doormat—the worn, so-old-it-had-become-invisible doormat—there was a postcard, lying like an unexploded heart.

Ruby froze, halfway across the floor.

Will. It was Will: she knew before she saw the printed heading, the unfamiliar stamp. It was Will, back in their lives again, and for one shameful moment, she was swept with dismay.

Then she shrieked.

"It's Will, it's Will!" she shrieked, and Violet came flying down the stairs, grabbed her, hugged her, grabbed the card, stared, hugged it too, and cried, "Oh, Will! Oh, Will!" hid her face in her hands and re-emerged, shining eyed and radiant. Then, together, they bent over the card and read:

Kriegsgefangenenlager
Glad to say that this place is fine, great,
etc. I hope you don't go worrying about me.
Love from Will.
Address to follow. For parcels. If poss.

It was Will's handwriting, very carefully printed, every let-ter separate. Violet read it twice, then ran out to the street and cried, "Look! Look!" Early-rising neighbors collected around her. Mrs. Cohen came hurrying, her face alight with joy. Everyone asked over and over, "Is that your Will?" and each time Violet would reply, "Yes, yes, it is. It's Will." But she couldn't let go of the card so they could read for themselves. She just held it out so they could see, and laughed with relief, drew a finger under an eye to slide away a tear, blinked, and laughed again.

All that day was bliss.

To go from Will, very possibly dead, to Will in a prisoner-of-war camp, hoping for parcels, all in a few hours.

Just before they went to bed, Ruby was allowed to hold the card at last. She looked carefully at the penciled words. Very carefully. Ruby knew Will much better than their mother did. She knew his sharpness, and his subtle means of getting his own way, and she took the card and looked at how Will had written it:

Glad tO say ThAt this PLAce is fiNe,
GrEaT, eTc. I hope you doN't Go wOrrying
aboUT me. Love from Will.
Address to follow. For parcels. If poss.

"He's got a plan. He's getting out," she told Violet, and pointed to the letters where Will had written his message. "It's the capitals," she explained, and her mother suddenly saw the words, hidden in plain sight. Then it was all Violet could do not to run down the road in her dressing gown and slippers and wake up Mrs. Cohen to tell her.

He wasn't just alive, and hoping for parcels. He was writing secret messages under the noses of the enemy. He was scheming to escape.

"Is your brother clever," demanded his proud mother, "or what?"

He was clever. He was remarkable. He could come walking through the door anytime. The whole street agreed.

"And we'll be here waiting," said Violet, with shining eyes.

The photograph of him in uniform was now in a silver frame. Mrs. Cohen had brought it. "Not new," she'd said, when she handed it to Violet. "Old stock, but still, nice silver plate. Mr. Cohen polished it for you."

"Oh, I couldn't!" Violet had exclaimed. "I couldn't take it, not silver!"

"For Will, of course you could," said Mrs. Cohen. "Handsome frame for a handsome boy."

Now the photograph seemed to be the most precious thing in the house. It moved around, to the windowsill, or the kitchen table, and Violet's bedside shelf at night. Ruby was always encountering it. Will's skin was satin smooth, not even a freckle, and his smile was very pleased. Ruby wondered how long it would be before he managed to escape.

An address had arrived, and they'd packed their first parcel. Playing cards, toffees, cigarettes, a toothbrush, and two white cotton handkerchiefs.

"In case he wants to surrender?" asked Ruby, not entirely as a joke, and was walloped on her behind with a copy of the *Devon and Exeter Gazette*. "That's no way to talk!" said her mother. "You heard Mr. Churchill. You know what he said."

Ruby knew. All the newspapers had reported that speech, and she and Violet had agreed with every word. Ruby herself had snipped out the last few lines, glued them onto cardboard, and propped them up beside the cash register:

> We shall fight on the beaches, we shall fight on the
> landing grounds, we shall fight in the fields and in
> the streets, we shall fight in the hills. . . .

"And, in case you've forgotten, my fine lady," said Violet severely, "we shan't ever surrender."

"I never said I would," said Ruby indignantly.

"No, and nor will none of us," said Violet. "Least of all our Will!"

So Will was a war hero now, plotting behind enemy lines, and Ruby knew she should be pleased about it, if only because it gave such courage to her mother, now putting on her air-raid warden helmet, ready for her evening patrol.

"It's about time we had a uniform," said Violet.

"Perhaps you soon will," said Ruby. "If it goes on a bit."

"It'll go on a bit," said Violet.

It was July of 1940. All along the south coast, the Battle of Britain, in all its murderous beauty, was splintering the skies. Plymouth had had its first bomb. It had landed on a street of ordinary houses. People had been killed.

"There wasn't anything exciting to see, though," said Ruby, who had been to have a look and was a little disappointed. "There was just some tape around, and a lot of bricks and rubble. Why d'you think they picked that house to bomb?"

"It would have been a mistake," said Violet. "They'd be aiming for the dockyards."

"Well then, they're rubbish shots," said Ruby. "That street is ages from the docks."

"Hmm," said Violet, and gave her a look. It was a swift, appraising look, the sort that might precede a green-soap-and-hair-washing session.

"What?" asked Ruby.

"The thing is, Ruby, nowhere in Plymouth is ages from the dockyards. Not to a bomber. Don't give that sausage to the cats!"

They were eating their supper, a lot of mash and gravy and one sausage each, because sausages, although not rationed yet, had become much more expensive. Ruby was feeding Sooty and Paddle. They loved sausage. They wound in silky spirals, fluid with desire.

"They have to eat something," said Ruby.

"There's no shortage of mice," said her mother absentmindedly. "Mrs. Morgan's overrun with them, out there in the country. I spoke to her yesterday. They've eaten her peas."

"What peas?"

"Peas that she planted. She said what's the use of digging for victory if the mice get the peas. Now Ruby, listen, I've got something to tell you, and I want none of your arguments, because it's just common sense."

"I know what you're going to say already," said Ruby.

"Oh, you do, do you?"

"You want to let Sooty and Paddle go and live with Mrs. Morgan so as to catch her mice."

"I had thought of that, yes."

"Well then, let them go," said Ruby bravely. "It would be better. I can see it would. There might be more bombs here."

"With a great naval shipyard on our doorstep, there'll be bombs for sure," said Violet, and once again she gave Ruby the green-soap look.

Ruby didn't see it because she had scooped up Sooty and buried her face in his furry shoulders. "It'll be all right," she said from that warm place, with hardly a wobble in her voice. "Mrs. Morgan is kind, and anyway, it will only be a lend, until after the war. We can go on the bus to visit them, can't we?"

Violet said, "Ruby, it's not just the cats that'll have to go away. It's you as well. This time we've got to face it. Mrs. Morgan's got a spare room. She said she'll have you to stay any day we choose."

"Me go to Mrs. Morgan's?"

"For a few weeks, yes. I've lost your dad. Will's where he is. I'm not risking you."

"But—"

"And after that," continued Violet, "it's time you were back at school."

"BUT—" exploded Ruby, so loudly that Sooty leaped to the floor.

"I said no arguing, remember?"

"But it's the holidays!" exclaimed Ruby. "The school holidays! Anyway, there's no school except a village school where Mrs. Morgan lives, and I'm too old for that."

"There's Clarry's school in Oxford."

"OXFORD!"

"Clarry tells me Kate will be starting there when the new term opens, sometime in September, and when it does, you'll be leaving Mrs. Morgan's, staying at Kate's house, and going there too."

"I can't, I can't," screeched Ruby. "You know I can't! What about my face?"

Violet said, as she had said so many times before, "You have a lovely face, Ruby."

"You have to say that because you're my mother."

"No, I don't," replied Violet, rather sharply. "I have to keep you healthy and make sure you're not hungry and see you have clothes and are learning the right things and growing up proper because I'm your mother. But I don't have to tell you you've got a nice face. Although you have. Very nice indeed. Lovely. Bright."

"No," said Ruby.

"And," said Violet, going one stage further than she ever had before, "those marks, they add to the brightness. I can't explain how, but they do."

"You can't explain how because they don't," shouted Ruby, and jumped to her feet and stormed out of the door and down the stairs and away along the street, slap-bang into Mrs. Cohen, who was putting up her shutters.

"Ruby," said Mrs. Cohen's gentle voice, and Ruby's panicking madness ran away from her, like water pouring into sand, and she turned round and went back home.

"Except for that one bad night, it's been quiet so far here in Plymouth," said Violet, carrying on the conversation as if nothing had happened to interrupt it, as she always did at these times. "It won't be for much longer, though. I'd like to know you were safe."

"*I'd* like to know *you* were safe," said Ruby. "You come to Oxford too. We'll find somewhere to live together."

"And what about the shop?" asked Violet, but as she spoke, she glanced at Will's photograph, and Ruby knew she really meant, *And what about if Will comes back and finds that I'm not here?*

"Someone else could do the shop," said Ruby, and shrugged. The shrug meant, *You're thinking about Will. You are always, always thinking about Will.*

There was a pause, full of unspeakable blackness.

"When can I come back?" asked Ruby eventually.

"When we've won this war."

"I wish I could fight."

"Oh, Ruby Amaryllis!" said Violet. "I expect you'll find a way."

TWENTY-SIX

Kate

Oxford, July 1940

Mrs. Morgan wrote Kate's parents a long letter all in one sentence that said:

> To let you know I have told old Mr. P that what with the journey from the cottage into Plymouth and the blackout and me being the age I am (71) not to mention that when young Ruby comes to you for school as has been arranged there may be my Christopher's two little ones here come the autumn since word is it will be bad in Plymouth when they start aiming for the shipyards this is to give notice that after this summer I will not be able to do for Mr. P as I have all these years and he has taken it very badly.

"She deserves a medal for putting up with him for so long," said Kate's father. "I'd better get to Plymouth and see what can be done."

He went on his next free day and came back in the evening to tell them that Grandfather had taken Mrs. Morgan's perfectly reasonable announcement not just badly, but disgracefully, saying that he supposed he'd have to starve.

Mrs. Morgan had been, as she ever was, more than a match for Grandfather.

"Of course you won't starve, you silly old man," she'd replied. "You can either take yourself off to your family as you've been asked a dozen times before . . ."

"That madhouse in Oxford," Grandfather had commented.

". . . or find yourself someone nearer to home to cook your blessed dinners and put up with your shocking ways."

Then Mrs. Morgan had left with, as was her habit, a good slam of the door.

"OH, YOUR GRANDFATHER!" wailed Vanessa to Charlie and Kate, and they understood, because how could Grandfather be left to take care of himself when the bombing raids began? And yet how could he be made to come to Oxford if he refused? Peter said that if the worse came to the worst, he'd drive down and kidnap him, and Vanessa said she'd help. Also, said Vanessa, when Grandfather came, kidnapped or of his own free will, he'd need a comfortable room.

This was the start of the great bedroom reshuffle, not only because of Grandfather, but to make space for Ruby, too. It was decided that all the boys could go together in the attic, Ruby and Kate would share Janey and Bea's old room, Grandfather would have Kate's room, and the little closet left over could be used for whoever might turn up. A great many cobwebs and grimy corners appeared during this reorganizing. Scrubbing was done, and painting begun, all directed by Vanessa. "War effort!" she cried when people rebelled or tried to slope off to be sailors and stilt-walkers.

"Very kind. No, thank you," said Grandfather, when he was told of all this hard work.

"Kate's making you new curtains," Vanessa told him. "Lovely warm red ones, all by herself on the sewing machine. I'm only helping a bit."

"Thoughtful, but I have curtains," said Grandfather, and added that the sensible thing would be to have Clarry come and live with him for the duration of the war. It was no use explaining that this was impossible as Clarry had a job, since Grandfather thought it was all nonsense, women working, when they should really be at home. If Clarry wouldn't help him, he said, what about Janey or Bea?

"Or Kate?" asked Peter sarcastically, taking the telephone from Vanessa and causing Kate, too alarmed to realize he was joking, to whisper urgently, "Dad!"

"Hold on a minute," said Peter to Grandfather, and he looked solemnly down at Kate and asked, "Problem?"

Kate nodded, speechless for a moment while she summoned the extraordinary bravery that had once seemed such a simple plan. Could she manage? Could she? She thought of Grandfather all alone, and remembered the silver flask in church.

They were waiting for her to speak.

"I could probably do the cooking," she said at last, "if he liked to eat the sort of things I cooked for Clarry. . . ."

Peter nodded.

"And I'd have to take Pax."

"Ah!" said Peter. "Yes, of course you would. Kate's worrying about the dog," he relayed to his father. "Says she can manage the cooking, but she'd have to bring her dog. . . ."

Grandfather said he couldn't see Kate being much use, what with the damage she'd done to that Christmas tree and the way she never stopped coughing, but he supposed he could put up with the dog.

"There'd be school, too, after the holidays," said Kate. "And bombs."

"She says school, too, and bombs," said Peter to Grandfather.

"Obstacle after obstacle," said Grandfather peevishly, but there was something in his voice that made Kate quite suddenly remember his wink to her as he left the room, another world ago. It made her abandon bravery in favor of common sense. She reached for the telephone herself and said breathlessly, "Grandfather, by the end of summer the red curtains will be finished and the painting, too, and we'll have enough petrol saved up to drive and fetch you in the car and it really would be *much* better if you were here."

There was a very long silence from Grandfather.

"Well," he said at last. "If you say so . . . er . . ."

"Kate."

"Kate. I suppose I shall have to be resigned."

Then the beeps that meant the telephone call was over, and Kate and her father were left staring at each other and laughing with relief.

TWENTY-SEVEN

Erik and Hans

French coast, August–September 1940

Erik's first-ever sight of the sea was the English Channel, early one gray August morning. France was now under German occupation and so the squadron had been moved again. Now they were encamped in an apple orchard, very close to the French coast. The airstrips were newly made and spongy, they'd been told they could expect mail once a month at best, and the farmer who owned the land hated them. All the local people hated them. In the town they took their money, cheated them, and hated them. There was a story told around the camp to new arrivals about another Luftwaffe base, farther up the coast. The guard at the entrance there, although prudently armed with a machine gun, had been discovered in the morning with his throat cut from ear to ear.

"And not a sound was heard nor bullet fired," finished the story. "And on the ground beside him, an open cut-throat razor."

Erik and Hans glanced at each other with raised eyebrows. What might have alarmed them a year ago couldn't disturb them now. They were used to how quickly stories grew in camps, and the people who liked to tell them.

"Shaving in the dark is bound to be risky," said Erik.

"What happened to his machine gun?" asked Hans.

"What d'you mean, what happened? Nothing happened."

"It was still there in the morning?"

"Certainly it was. Clutched in his hands."

"Nothing to worry about then," said Hans. "Machine guns are expensive. Any sensible assassin would never have left it behind. It was, as my friend Erik realized from the start, a self-inflicted accident that could easily be avoided in the future by the allowance of shaving mirrors."

"Or safety razors," said Erik.

"Shaving mirrors and safety razors," agreed Hans. "Or simply encouraging a fashion in beards."

"It's not so easy to grow a beard," remarked Erik. "They say to rub the chin with a raw onion."

"Hard to find a raw onion," said Hans. "The poor things are relentlessly roasted."

"Boiled," said Erik.

"Battered."

"Fried."

"I had an onion omelet, last time I was in Berlin," said Erik. "It was very good."

"I had potato pancakes," said Hans. "They were excellent."

"My favorite," said Erik, nodding, and Hans nodded too, and the cut-throat storyteller exploded with indignation.

"You find this funny?" he demanded. "If so, you have entirely misunderstood the situation here in France."

"Yes, you could be right," said Erik. "I speak very little French. Well, none, except *joie de vivre.*"

"You probably won't need that," remarked Hans.

"And *je ne sais pas.*"

"You probably will need that," said Hans. "Quite a lot."

"Hans is a linguist," Erik explained. "Not only French, but English, too, for when we invade."

"I am hoping for a kind and peaceful invasion," said Hans. "And so I have learned some useful phrases such as: This is a pleasant place. I am sorry. I didn't mean to frighten you. Do not forget me. You are very beautiful. Please tell me your name. I admire your dogs and cats."

"The English are very fond of animals," explained Erik. "As am I, of course."

"Erik has hopes to work in a zoo," said Hans.

"Hans has hopes to sell pastries at the gate," said Erik.

"Jokers," growled the storyteller. "And you can forget 'You are very beautiful.' My brother spent a year in England just before the war. He said all the girls were terrible. Gray skin. Green hair. Scarlet lipstick. Bad teeth."

"I'm sorry to hear that," said Hans gravely.

"And don't try flattery anyway, because my brother did that, too, and had his head chewed off."

"Serves him right," said Erik, at once. "After all, there are other pleasant things one might say. Such as about the dogs and cats."

"True," agreed Hans. "But I won't forget 'You are very beautiful.' I may meet the only girl in England your brother didn't see, and imagine not having the right words."

The storyteller sighed with annoyance. He had the Iron Cross for shooting down four enemy planes. He also had a constant stomachache, which he told them about. They were immediately very sympathetic and said he had done his share to contribute to the Third Reich's *joie de vivre* and should now be allowed to rest and take care of his health.

The Iron Cross hero grew more friendly and told them that when he was a boy, he had dreamed of studying music. The great German composers. "What am I doing here?" he asked, now entirely their friend. "In this sodden tent. Beside this terrible sea."

"Je ne sais pas," said Erik. He was feeling quite melancholy himself. His first sight of the sea had depressed him very much. Sunless, steel-colored water, littered with ships, churning and slapping and giving the complete appearance of being entirely on the side of the British. Among all the deaths he had been forced to consider since he became a Luftwaffe pilot, he had never included drowning. It now seemed to him much more likely than having his throat cut in silence while carrying a machine gun. He said so to Hans.

"You must be very careful," said Hans, "not to fall out of the window."

It was in this camp that Erik and Hans met their first British pilot, face-to-face. Not only face-to-face, but also able to speak to them. In a mixture of German and English they were able to understand each other perfectly. His plane had been shot down, but he had managed, with great good luck, to parachute right onto their new bumpy airstrip. Everyone liked him very much; he became, for a few hours, the camp hero and comrade. They gave him cigarettes and chocolate and proper German beer. He spoke of Mr. Churchill and Herr bloody Hitler and of how the British would never surrender.

"If only you would," they told him, "our countries could work together as friends."

"Yes, but we won't," said the British pilot, shaking his head. "So there it is." He was as stubborn as the rest of his nation.

After a few hours, with many handshakes and good wishes, he was taken away to become a prisoner of war.

"A pity," said Erik. "Poor fellow."

"He went off with a certain *joie de vivre*, don't you think?" asked Hans.

"*Je ne sais pas,*" said Erik.

Now the Luftwaffe were targeting the Royal Air Force, the RAF, aiming at the airfields of the south of England. It was the job of the Messerschmitts to engage the Hurricanes and Spitfires that scrambled in defense. Dogfighting, they called it, when little plane sought to destroy little plane, spattering bullets, tangling and hunting in the blue summer skies. Sometimes a pilot would unravel the tangle and flee to safety. Other times, the loops would break, the sky would lurch, and there might be black smoke and orange fire where no fire should be. Often a parachute would appear, drifting down like a dandelion clock, its breathless slow motion stilling the watchers on the ground into silence. There was a chivalry between enemies about that: the man with the parachute was never a target. For those minutes, between sky and earth, he was safe.

The casualty lists at the camp in the apple orchard grew longer and longer, even though they were assured that very soon, in a matter of weeks, if not days, the RAF would be so utterly obliterated that the next stage, the invasion by land, could begin.

"About time the army did some work," said the exhausted Luftwaffe pilots, flying day after day across the Channel, and coming back again with so little fuel that the only way to make it was to fly low, out of the strong upper winds, wave-hopping with the fuel gauge on red.

"How's the *joie de vivre*?" Hans asked Erik, late one night when the antiaircraft guns, firing at the stubborn British fighters pestering overhead, put an end to all hope of sleep.

"Je ne sais pas," said Erik.

TWENTY-EIGHT

Ruby

Mrs. Morgan's cottage, Devon, July–September 1940

Two years before, in 1938, the British government had begun making preparations for war, and so had Mrs. Morgan. By the time Ruby came to stay, her cottage garden was stuffed with herbs and fruit and vegetables, she had eight hens and two ducks, and was contemplating bees.

"We had bees at the forge when I was a girl," she told Violet and Ruby. "Growing up, we had bees and often a goat as well. I shouldn't mind a goat now."

"For milk?" asked Ruby.

"Well, of course for milk. They don't lay eggs. I've thought of a pig, too. A pig or a goat. One or the other."

"But," began Ruby in alarm, "you can't milk a . . . I've never heard of . . . What would you *do* with a pig, Mrs. Morgan?"

Mrs. Morgan gave a big noisy exasperated sigh and said, "It's about time you spent a few weeks in the country. Sausages and bacon is what I would do with a pig, but perhaps I'll start with a goat."

A week later this happened. A spotted goat, grandly named Victoria, appeared, and with her, to Ruby's entrancement, a snow-white kid that they immediately christened Plum. Plum was very pretty, but Victoria had horns, which she did not hesitate to deploy. Milking time became a lively occasion.

"She'll quieten," said Mrs. Morgan, and as the days went by, she did. Also little Plum grew, and Sooty and Paddle hunted mice in the pea rows and rats in the henhouse, and Violet came on the bus now and then, and spent the night. Three times every week Mrs. Morgan went into town to cook and clean for old Mr. Penrose, and Ruby was left in charge of the hens and the goats and the garden.

"Will you be all right?" asked Mrs. Morgan the first time.

"I'm thirteen," said Ruby indignantly, and Mrs. Morgan came back to find the kitchen scrubbed, hot scones just out of the oven, the eggs collected, the henhouse swept clean, and Ruby herself just setting off on a valiant mission to attempt to milk the goat.

"Your mum said you were handy," said Mrs. Morgan. "And I see she was right."

"Did she really?"

"She did, and more."

"What more?"

"Never you mind or we'll have you bigheaded. You need to wash Victoria down nicely before you try milking. Warm water and soap."

"I know."

"And have you the milk pail scalded and ready?"

"Yes. I just did it."

"Don't forget, you'll need to have Plum tied up where her mother can see she's not lost."

"She already is," said Ruby, nodding.

"Smart as paint, Violet told me," said Mrs. Morgan approvingly, and Ruby glowed and learned to milk the goat well enough to show Violet the next time she came.

"You're getting to know all sorts," said Violet, laughing, and it was true, Ruby was.

Clarry sent a pile of books and a message. *You might like to read these before term begins.*

Between her ransacking of the library, and the newspapers in the shop, reading had become as natural to Ruby as breathing in and out. However, for Mrs. Morgan it was not the same at all. For her, reading was a labor, like shifting furniture or heavy digging, and she looked distrustfully at Ruby, flat on her stomach with the book in front of her, turning the pages with no apparent effort.

"Are you sure you're taking it in?" she asked.

"Mmm," said Ruby. "I skip the boring bits."

"I should think so too. Leave off and come and help me brush the goats."

"In a minute. He's met Betsey Trotwood again."

"And who is she? And who is he?"

"David Copperfield. She's a sort of aunt."

Ruby absorbed *David Copperfield*, puzzled her way through a French storybook, and shared with Mrs. Morgan a textbook called *The Microscope*. It fascinated Ruby, but it had color illustrations of things Mrs. Morgan could hardly bear to contemplate. A math book arrived as well, questions in the front and answers in the back. *Times tables are useful,* wrote Clarry on a postcard. *Everyone stops at twelve times, but when I was little my brother made me learn up to twenty. I used to write them out and look for the patterns in the numbers.*

Ruby chanted as she weeded the onion bed, ". . . Seventeen

seventeens are two hundred and eighty-nine. Seventeen eigh-teens are three hundred and six. . . ." All her life, afterward, the murmured chant of tables took her back to the sunlit, almost perfect summer of Mrs. Morgan's garden.

Almost perfect, but not quite. August was passing, vanish-ing in a blink of bean rows and books and meeting the bus. September came blowing in and Ruby wrote to Kate:

> I thought I was coming to your house by train,
> Mum and me together, and Mum staying a few
> days afterward.

That was what they'd planned, but now Clarry had written that she'd be borrowing her brother's car and driving to Plym-outh early in September to collect Kate's grandfather. She could stop at Mrs. Morgan's on her way back to Oxford and pick up Ruby, too.

We'll be staying the night with Mrs. M, she wrote to Violet, *because I don't think I could get my father packed and loaded and out of his house in time to reach Oxford before the blackout. It's such a long drive. At least six hours, plus stops. So instead of rushing him, we'll set off from Mrs. Morgan's early the next day, with plenty of room for Ruby, if that would suit you too?*

Violet was delighted. She wouldn't have to find the train fares, nor leave the shop for days with Mrs. Cohen. However, Ruby heard the news in absolute dismay, all her fear of staring strangers suddenly once again alive.

"I don't know Kate's grandfather," she wailed to Mrs. Morgan. "Will he look at my face?"

"Ruby Amaryllis, this has gone on too long!" Mrs. Morgan

declared. "Will *you* look at your face?" She'd unhooked the kitchen mirror and handed it to Ruby, but Ruby hadn't looked.

Instead she wrote to Kate.

> Now they've changed everything. Mum is glad but I'm not glad. The only thing I'm looking forward to is Pax.

TWENTY-NINE

Kate

Oxford, September 1940

K ate read her message from Ruby and had an idea.

"Could I come with you when you go and fetch Grandfather?" she asked Clarry.

"I should have thought of it myself," said Clarry. "You can map-read for me on the way there and be company for Ruby on the way back. If you're allowed, of course you can. Is Ruby worrying?"

"Yes."

"I know it'll be hard for her. She ran back home when they tried to evacuate her before. That's why Violet was coming with her on the train."

"She says the only thing she's looking forward to is Pax. So, do you think we could take him?"

"Take Pax?" asked Clarry, startled. "Gosh, Kate, I don't know. What if he's sick? He was awful on the journey from London."

"I think that was just because he was frightened."

"He was *dreadfully* sick," said Clarry. "I didn't know there was so much space inside a dog for so much stuff. It was like a terrible magic trick. Don't laugh!"

"Perhaps we could take him for a little drive and see if he's all right?"

Clarry shook her head. "Since they started rationing petrol, there's not a teaspoonful to spare. Your dad's been saving it for weeks for this trip."

"Well, there's buses," suggested Kate. "There's one that goes right past our house. I could take him for rides to see how he manages. Very short rides first, one stop. And then a bit longer."

"What if he's sick on the bus?"

"I could take some newspapers and my old seaside bucket."

"Kate, you're wonderful," said Clarry solemnly. "The bucket is heroic. Give it a try, and if it works, we'll take him with us."

For several days Kate did this, very short rides, and then longer ones, and then all across the city. At the end of the week she reported to Clarry that there had been much tail wagging and tongue hanging and cheerfulness and no need of the bucket at all.

"Excellent," said Clarry. "Shall you tell Ruby you're coming, or keep it a secret?"

"I'll tell her that I'm coming, but I'll save Pax for a surprise," said Kate, and wrote,

> Dear Ruby,
> When Clarry comes for you, I'm coming too. We can sit in the back of the car together. As well, I am bringing a secret surprise.
> You needn't worry about Grandfather. He's only fierce because he's shy.

Even as she wrote it, Kate was startled. Grandfather? Shy? But it was true. Noticing him, thinking about him, writing about him, she'd discovered it.

He's quite a lot like Pax, wrote Kate.

Even more startling, and also true.

Another discovery.

THIRTY

Erik and Hans

Sky, September 1940

It was the best sort of morning. Clear, bright September. In Berlin there would be the first hint of autumn in the air. The swallow flocks would be gathering, limbering up for their great journey south. Under the trees there would be a primrose light, and the first yellow leaves coming down. It was soccer weather, new book weather, back to school weather.

It was no use being homesick. Erik said, "This time five years ago . . . ," and Hans said, "Oh, shut up."

Everyone was jittery. The destruction of the RAF that in early summer had seemed close enough to touch, now seemed more impossible every day. Losses were much higher than they'd ever expected, the English Channel a bigger obstacle, the opposition better armed than anyone had guessed.

That day they were trying yet again. Erik, Hans, and eight planes had flown out in formation over the Channel. They were aiming for the west of England, and the new airfields there. Six bombers, four fighters. Not enough.

They'd been waylaid by Hurricanes, diving in to attack with the sun behind them. They'd been outnumbered and outgunned. Planes had tumbled from the sky, commands had been fragmented, the static so bad that their radios were all but useless. Finally the squadron had split, each pilot turning to find their own way back. Fuel was getting low.

Erik's plane was staggering, bullet-bitten. The Perspex cover was holed and a pain like fire scorched down his back and into his left shoulder. The shock of it was brain-dazzling. His Messerschmitt flew heavily now, as if the air was thick and tangled. He thought he was alone, and then suddenly knew he wasn't. Hans came bursting through the radio static:

"BEHIND! BEHIND! BEHIND!"

THIRTY-ONE

Ruby and Kate

Mrs. Morgan's cottage, Devon, September 1940

The day before Ruby was to leave for Oxford, Violet came to stay at the cottage. As always in times of stress, she had comforted herself with present-buying. Cherry brandy for Mrs. Morgan and a real leather satchel for Ruby with surprises inside. Ruby found a pencil case, a box of writing paper and stamps, and a bag of lemon drops.

"It's like being Will," she said, very pleased indeed.

There was also a fountain pen, silver and crimson, with her name in curving letters on the side: *Ruby Amaryllis*.

"Mrs. Cohen bought it for you, and Mr. Cohen engraved it," Violet told her.

Ruby was overwhelmed; she'd never owned anything like it. She borrowed Mrs. Morgan's bottle of ink and tried to write her thanks.

> Dear Mrs. Cohen and Mr. Cohen: I didn't know there were pens like this, shining like a jewel. I didn't know Mr. Cohen could write like that either. It is very beautiful and I will keep it forever and I hope it didn't cost too much. I miss you, and I

> miss the street where everyone is used to me. I
> will write to you as often as I can . . .

Ruby looked up at her mother. "I can put letters in for Mrs. Cohen when I write to you, can't I?" she asked. "To save stamps?"

"Of course you can."

"And you won't read them?"

"The cheek," said Violet. "Did I ever read your letters to Kate?"

"No," said Ruby, and she wrote,

> Mrs. Cohen, please, please look after Mum. Until
> I come back. Love, Ruby

She had hardly finished when Clarry drove up, together with not only her father and Kate, but also, to the absolute horror of Mrs. Morgan, Pax.

"What is that animal?" exclaimed Mrs. Morgan. "Clarry Penrose, are you crazy?"

"He's mine," said Kate bravely. "I thought he'd be a surprise."

"And did we need a surprise?" demanded Mrs. Morgan. "And would you look at those cats!"

Sooty and Paddle, spitting their outraged feelings, were up on the cottage roof with ears laid flat and every hair on end. However, Violet was laughing, and Clarry too, and Mrs. Morgan's face was not half as cross as her words.

"You should be warned, as I was not," Kate's grandfather remarked, "that the animal isn't house-trained." He was clearly enjoying the situation, his mouth turned down in a secret, smiling smirk.

"He's house-trained at home," said Kate loyally. "Mostly, anyway."

"Mostly?" repeated Mrs. Morgan indignantly. "Mostly!"

"You never said one word," said Ruby, almost accusingly, to Kate.

"No, I know," admitted Kate. "Only I read your letter and I thought you . . . I thought he . . . I thought it might be more cheerful if I brought him. Do you mind?"

Ruby shook her head. She'd sent out a plea for help and Kate had answered. How could she mind?

"Tie him by the doormat while you come and see my arrangements," said Mrs. Morgan resignedly. It had taken some planning to find a place for everyone to sleep, but she and Ruby had managed. Clarry and Violet were to have Ruby's room, with Ruby moved downstairs to share the sofa with Kate. "Head to toe, you'll fit," Mrs. Morgan had said to Ruby. "It's only one night. And I'm putting old Mr. P in the storeroom, along where I keep the hen food, because it's nice and dry."

The hen food smelled strong, nutty and earthy.

"I hope he likes it," Ruby had said doubtfully.

"He can like it or lump it," Mrs. Morgan had replied cheerfully. "I doubt he'll notice with that pipe."

All the same, Ruby had pushed open the window as wide as it would go, and by the time the visitors arrived, the smell was so much fresher that all Kate's grandfather said was, "Ah, melons. Am I right?"

"I daresay you might smell melons," said Mrs. Morgan diplomatically. "I've all sorts tucked away up here. Come and look at this."

The landing was almost filled with an enormous dark oak

wardrobe. Mrs. Morgan opened the doors to show rows and rows of stores. Stewed beef in cans, sardines in oil, raisins, blue paper packets of sugar, tins of tea and cocoa, and on a high shelf at the top, bars and bars of bright yellow Sunlight Soap.

"The government can call it hoarding if they want," she said. "But I call it common sense. I remember the last war, not a bit of soap or a sausage to be bought without you stood in a queue for hours."

"Really?" asked Kate's grandfather from the back of her audience. "I don't recall that at all."

"No, because me and Clarry did the queuing for you," said Mrs. Morgan. "While you drifted around thinking lamb chops and socks floated down with the autumn leaves. Now just you come outside and see the rest."

She led them past the overflowing vegetable beds, the flower patches, the chickens, the bees, and the ever inquisitive goats, talking as she went.

"I've got paraffin and petrol in the old henhouse that we never got round to pulling down, and a new padlock on the outside convenience at the end of the garden."

"Hardly a convenience," remarked Kate's grandfather sardonically. "At the end of the garden."

"It'll be very convenient indeed should anyone unwanted turn up," said Mrs. Morgan. "Spies, or whatever. They're sending them over from Germany disguised as nuns and peddlers selling onions and I don't know what, but you can tell them in a minute because they can't say their *W*s. It's all in the papers about them."

"It is," agreed Violet.

"So my thought is, once I have them inside our convenience,

I shall snap on the padlock and telephone the police."

"Admirable," exclaimed Kate's grandfather, nodding.

"Not very comfortable," observed Clarry, laughing.

"Comfortable!" said Mrs. Morgan. "I wasn't planning on making them comfortable. Not that they couldn't perfectly well sit down if they lowered the lid. I was thinking of keeping them fast! They couldn't burrow out because we ratproofed it two summers ago, and I think it couldn't be better."

"But how," broke in Kate, terribly bothered by this whole conversation, "how would you get them in there in the beginning, Mrs. Morgan?"

"I should prod 'em in with the potato fork," said Mrs. Morgan triumphantly. "I've got it sharpened up by the back door ready."

"Very well thought out indeed," said Kate's grandfather approvingly, and went off at once to test the sharpness of the prongs. Clarry and Violet headed inside with Mrs. Morgan to get ready a picnic lunch, but when Ruby and Kate followed to help, they were immediately shooed away.

"They want to talk without us," said Kate.

"I know, they always do," agreed Ruby, flopping down on the tiny, hearthrug-sized patch of grass. "I hope Mrs. Morgan catches someone. She'll be disappointed if she doesn't. And she's going to have an awful time, eating up all that stew."

"I thought that too," agreed Kate, stretching out beside her with Pax for a pillow.

"If I was hoarding food," said Ruby, "which I wouldn't because everyone knows, whatever Mrs. M says, that it's not patriotic, I'd hoard golden syrup and peaches and Mars bars. What would you?"

Kate pondered. A great sleepiness was overwhelming her,

partly sunshine, partly getting up before dawn to help pack.

"Peppermint cremes," she said at last.

"They wouldn't be much use," said Ruby critically. "Not in a war."

"It is a war."

"I know."

It didn't feel like a war, out in the warm garden, walled in by flowers and runner beans, with Mrs. Morgan's hens crooning in their dust baths under the apple tree. From the cottage came sounds of laughter, and from toward the road another sound: the car engine firing and stopping.

"That's your grandad," observed Ruby.

"Yes, don't tell on him."

"Can he drive?"

"No. He'd like to, though. He tried to make Clarry let him, coming here."

"Kate?"

"Mmm?"

"Is it posh at your house?"

"No. The landing carpet's worn right through and the plates never match because they get broken so often."

"What else?"

"Shoes everywhere, and Pax."

"That school we've got to go to?"

"It's posh," admitted Kate. "It's got ivy."

"Ivy's not so special," said Ruby, comforted, and they became quiet again.

THIRTY-TWO

Erik and Hans

Sky, September 1940

It was a Spitfire, fresh in the sky, newly fueled, and hunting. Hans dipped his wings in mock salute, rolled, deliberately taunting it, and then, already much higher than Erik, went into a spiral climb.

"Get out of here!" bawled Erik into his radio, but if Hans heard, he took no notice. He wheeled round again, firing now, and suddenly the Spitfire left Erik and turned after Hans. Bullets spat between them, high up in the shining blue.

Two minutes later there was no Hans, only a spurt of fire and a plunging black smoke trail. The Spitfire wheeled away and vanished into the sun. Then the pain in Erik's ruined arm overwhelmed him, and he slumped into a numbing blackness as his plane careered out of the sky.

THIRTY-THREE

Kate and Ruby

Mrs. Morgan's cottage, Devon, September 1940

From the cottage came the sound of the wireless, mixed with the voices and laughter of Violet, Clarry, and Mrs. Morgan, three good friends making the most of their time together. Close by, the chickens murmured and squabbled. The loudest sound was the bees. There were many bees, fumbling through scarlet poppy flowers so freshly unfolded that their petals still showed creases. The bees moved between poppies, potatoes, and a sowing of late summer peas, which thanks to Sooty and Paddle, were doing very well indeed.

"If Mrs. Morgan is digging for victory," observed Kate, "I think she's going to win."

"I do too," said Ruby. "If I was Hitler and saw Mrs. Morgan's garden, I'd be frightened."

They laughed together, but wedged between them, Pax suddenly stirred and growled.

"Don't, Pax," said Kate, and put her hand on him. "Shush."

Pax wouldn't shush because coming from high in the sky above his head, his least favorite place in the world, there was sound. It was a new sound, far away.

A mosquito, perhaps.

"Kate," said Ruby, squinting into the brightness. "There's

something way up in the sky. Moving. I can see it, then I can't."

Kate turned on her back to look as well. The blueness seemed immense and empty, except for a high dappling of small white clouds, the sort that never rain.

Ruby spoke again. "A plane. Two planes. Flying round each other. You're looking in the wrong place."

Kate sat up to see better.

"I see one."

"There's two."

"Oh, yes! Pax . . ." Kate held him by his collar. "No, Pax! Be quiet. Yes, I see them now."

"What's the matter with Pax?"

"He always hates things in the sky. Anything, even the moon."

The mosquito sounds came and went, as the hardly visible little planes left faint white trails like chalk dust, looping and spiraling in the clear September sky. There were other sounds too, like the tiny puffs of a very small fast piston. Pax was tense with awareness.

"I think they're fighting," said Ruby suddenly.

"Fighting?"

"That's one of our Spitfires. See the little rounded wings?"

"I can't . . . Pax, keep still. . . . Oh, I do see! Oh, Ruby!"

"It's firing."

Kate wrestled with Pax.

"There's bits coming off the other one!" exclaimed Ruby, now on her feet with excitement. "Gosh, how brilliant to see them! How lucky! Wow . . ."

"Ruby!" protested Kate.

"It's breaking up . . . there's a whole wing gone. . . ."

"It's horrible!" said Kate. "Oh no, oh no!"

The spurt of fire, clearly visible, halted Ruby's gloating.

"It's burning," whispered Kate, and Ruby, suddenly quelled, said, "Yes. But look . . . ," and then, "KATE! *KATE!*"

They had been so engrossed with the two little planes that the third, much closer one took them completely by surprise. It was suddenly roaring toward them, dreadfully big, dreadfully low. . . .

"Lie FLAT!" screamed Kate, and as Pax wrestled free from her grip, Ruby flung herself down.

Overhead, so close it seemed it must take off the top of the apple tree, roared a German Messerschmitt fighter, gray-green, with a bright yellow nose cone, and black crosses on the underside of its wings.

Pax, barking madly, tore after it in frantic pursuit. Kate and Ruby raced after him, out of the garden and to the front of the cottage, where Grandfather, most luckily, had just managed to start the car.

"Drive! Drive! Drive!" screeched Kate and Ruby, tumbling in, and Grandfather hurried away for a moment, came back with the potato fork, said, "I absolutely will," and did.

THIRTY-FOUR

Erik and Hans

Sky to Earth, September 1940

"*Wake up, you fool!*"

Two miles away, where Hans's plane had fallen, an ancient oak tree split and roared, briefly blossomed into crackling gold, ripened hot live bullets and flung them all around, and later dwindled into tangled blackness. Twisted shapes smoldered quietly under a reeking shroud of smoke.

Yet, in the cockpit of Erik's damaged Messerschmitt, very clearly, Erik heard Hans speak:

"*Erik! Wake up!*"

The voice came not from the radio, but from behind, as if Hans were standing just out of sight, at his shoulder.

With a great effort, Erik lifted his head. His swimming, floating, bubbling head, and found that he seemed to be ricocheting down an invisible giant stone staircase in an unfriendly sky.

"*Open your eyes,*" Hans told him calmly.

Erik blinked.

"*The rudder, if it still works.*"

It did still work, more or less. The plane regained some balance, his descent on the giant staircase slowed, but not enough. There was a village, a church spire, scattered houses.

"You must get higher," said Hans.

Molten pain flowed down from Erik's shoulder. His left arm was as immovable as a sodden sandbag.

"Lift. LIFT NOW," ordered Hans.

Erik couldn't move the joystick with his right hand alone, so he unstrapped himself and used his stomach muscles and his chest and the weight of his dead arm. He took control, and the plane lifted. From behind he heard Hans sigh, like someone who had held their breath too long.

Now he was flying much too fast and much too low over green countryside. He took the top off a haystack, leaving a trail of burning wisps.

"Circle round again," said Hans. *"Get some height. Use some fuel."*

It was true. The less fuel they hit the ground with, the less of it there was to explode into flame, and the better their chances would be. Erik hauled his wounded, flailing wings round another circuit, a little higher. The vibrations were so bad that he bit through his tongue. He was awash with pain and fear.

Hans said urgently at his shoulder, *"Try not to kill anyone. Miss that house."*

Oh, God, he couldn't miss the house. He gasped, "Help me, Hans," and the house flew beneath them.

"Still right behind you," said Hans calmly. *"Nearly down. Nearly over."*

How much fuel was left? Oh, for the long wings of a glider. Hans again.

"Miss . . ."

Too late. The haystack.

"MISS THE GIRLS!" roared Hans.

There was no way to miss the girls. They were racing across a meadow. They cowered beneath him as he lurched overhead.

"Miss the dog," said Hans.

It was easy to miss the dog. The dog dodged.

"Down," said Hans. *"And get the top off!"*

Since the French plane, Hans had been terrified of fire, but at that moment moving the heavy cockpit cover seemed impossible.

"No time," gasped Erik, and hit the ground so hard that the propeller plowed a trench. Torn soil rained down in clods, but he was landed and, miraculously, the Perspex cover was flung back.

The strong raw smell of soil and the fumes of aviation fuel. The wave surge of returning pain. Hysterical barking. Sunlight.

"Now, don't," said Hans, suddenly very far away, *"fall out of the window . . . Erik . . . Erik?"*

THIRTY-FIVE

Kate, Ruby, Pax, Erik

Sky to Earth, September 1940

Pax was out of sight, although not out of hearing, barking frantically in a hay meadow. Grandfather had driven grandly and quite slowly into a hawthorn hedge. Kate and Ruby left him there, safe, but swearing, to fling themselves over the gate and rush after Pax. As they ran, they realized that the plane must have veered away and was circling to return. Once again it was behind them, even louder, even slower, so low that for a second time they instinctively dropped flat.

It lurched and shuddered. The wheels looked enormous, the weight impossible.

It was on them. They lay braced in fear.

It passed.

"Pax!" screamed Kate, because it couldn't miss Pax.

It did.

It missed him.

It was down.

Unsteadily, they got to their feet and stared. Churned earth and the three propeller blades twisted like ribbons. The wings somehow pitiful, splayed out like a fallen bird. The Perspex cover open and the pilot clearly visible, his goggles gone and his helmet half off.

"We have to get him out," shouted Kate, and ran stumbling over the tussocky grass with Ruby and Pax behind.

"There's a step on the wing," called Ruby, catching up. "Look, there."

It was the step that the pilots used to vault in. Kate climbed up and made room for Ruby, and together they looked down into the cockpit, and at the body of the airman slumped inside.

"He's dead," said Ruby, but he groaned.

"His arm's all wrong," said Kate. "There's blood . . . there's a lot of blood, still coming out. . . . Help me, Ruby, quick!"

"He'll be strapped in," said Ruby, but he wasn't. By hauling on the collar of his heavy flying jacket, they got him over the edge and then, using his own weight, they rolled him onto the wing and down. He moaned as he hit the grass, and his eyes stayed closed.

His jacket was so drenched in blood that they dragged him by his feet.

"Leave him now," begged Ruby. "Let's get help."

"We have to stop the bleeding first."

"How can we without bandages?" wailed Ruby. She was hating the whole thing, the blood, the touching, the weight of this alien stranger.

"Simon and Tod showed me," panted Kate. She was peeling off the flying jacket, one sleeve at a time, first the good arm, then the bad. "Compression, that's what they did. . . . I think it's his shoulder. . . . It is. . . .There!"

Underneath the jacket was a shirt, soaked and torn.

Any bones broken? Simon had asked.

Yes.

And then there was the bullet hole. Ruby saw it first and ran away in horror. When she came back, Kate had pulled off her cardigan, folded it into a pad, and was pressing down hard.

"Take off his helmet and turn his face sideways," ordered Kate. "Then if he's sick, he won't choke."

"I can't."

"Hold this then, and I will."

"No. It's all right, I'll do it. . . . There . . . Oh . . ."

"What?"

"I thought he'd be a grown-up."

"He is."

"He looks younger than Will. My brother, Will."

"He's getting cold. There's a rug in the car. Could you fetch it, and maybe Grandfather's jacket?"

"How do you suddenly know what to do?"

"Hurry, Ruby."

"All right," said Ruby, and left. She came back very soon, bringing the rug, but also the news that the car was stuck and Grandfather in it and his jacket with him.

"He said you're to come away at once and leave the dog on guard. And he made me bring the potato fork just in case."

Kate groaned. She was still pressing hard against the pilot's shoulder, but she managed, one-handed, to tuck the car rug around the rest of him. "I wish you'd put your sweater under his face," she said. "It would be a bit more comfortable than grass."

"He's the enemy, Kate!"

"Not anymore. He's not fighting now."

"Oh, I wish someone would come," moaned Ruby. "What are we going to do?"

"If you come here and press where I tell you, I'll go and get the car out of the hedge and send Grandfather for help."

"How could you get the car out of the hedge?"

"It's just reversing. I've seen them do it often. I could climb in from the back and make Grandfather move over."

"I'll come with you."

"Ruby, I can't let go here even for a second. I tried."

"I hate blood," said Ruby, who, with all her approval of war, had never considered actual bloodshed as one of the side effects.

"Shut your eyes, then. I won't take five minutes. Please, Ruby. Pax will stay with you. Look, press here."

"All right."

They changed places, Kate guiding Ruby's hands, Ruby's eyes tight shut. "Pax, stay!" ordered Kate, and ran. Commanding Grandfather into letting her reverse the car was difficult, but no harder than anything else she'd done that afternoon. She let him bark instructions, and although she ignored them, when the car was on the road, they were both breathlessly triumphant.

"Now," said Kate. "It's pointing the right way. Could you drive it back to Mrs. Morgan's and telephone for help?"

"Naturally. The steering went the first time. Nothing to do with me."

"Yes. Could you drive very slowly, in case the steering goes again?"

"Only sensible. Of course."

"I'm not quite sure which pedal is the brake," said Kate, and Grandfather admitted that neither was he, so they worked it out together, and then Kate waved him off, calling untruthfully, "No hurry . . ."

Back in the hay field, Ruby pressed on Kate's folded cardigan, with her eyes firmly closed. She told herself that she didn't care if he died, as long as it didn't happen while she was alone with him. Unscrewing her eyes to see how he was managing, she found he'd turned his head and his own eyes were now open. They were very young and frightened. When he saw that she was watching, he whispered, *"Danke."*

Then he gasped and continued to gasp. Blood seeped up around Ruby's fingers. She'd forgotten to press. There was nothing else for it. She tugged off her sweater, folded it into a fresh dressing, and started again. Despite Pax, whose worried eyes had never left the gate over which Kate had vanished, she felt so lonely that she started to talk.

"You'd better not die now you've ruined my sweater."

He was silent.

"It's much worse for me than it is for you."

A big lie.

"I don't mean to hurt you."

That was true, anyway, and oh, thank goodness, here was Kate coming back to take her place.

Kate had not only got the car out of the hedge, taught Grand-father the rudiments of driving, issued him with instructions as to what to say when he arrived, but she had also grabbed his jacket. She draped it round the pilot and he opened his eyes again, whispered another *"Danke,"* noticed Pax, and smiled.

"Pax," said Kate, seeing where he was looking. "It's another word for peace."

Ruby burst into tears and said, "I hate this war, I hate it. He's going to die. Look at him," and she scrambled to her feet and ran away, weeping. She ran in a big circle, and when she came back, she said, "I can hear a car."

It was help at last. Clarry and Violet, Mrs. Morgan and Grandfather. Very quickly after them, an ambulance arrived.

"At last," said Kate thankfully. "People who know properly what to do."

"If anyone knew properly what to do, I'd say it was you two girls," said the ambulance driver.

"Not me," said Ruby. "It was Kate."

"Who looked after him while Kate went off for help?" asked her mother, hugging her. "And what's Mrs. Morgan's potato fork doing up here?"

"It was for in case, but we didn't need it."

"I should think not, poor young chap," said Mrs. Morgan, seeming to entirely forget that she had sharpened the prongs herself. "You lift him in careful," she told the ambulance people. "He's been through enough for one day. And is anyone traveling with him?"

"I will," said Clarry. "I can manage a bit of German. It might help. And maybe Kate could come too so she can explain exactly what happened. But only if the ambulance can wait while I drive the rest of you back to the cottage."

"I will drive back to the cottage," said Grandfather firmly. "As I did only an hour ago. And if anyone doesn't like it, they can walk."

So Erik was taken away with Kate and Clarry, while the rest traveled back to the cottage with Grandfather driving and Mrs. Morgan beside him, making helpful remarks like, "You've not hit anything so far," and "Go past the tree before you turn," and "Get ready with that brake."

Despite this, they arrived safely, and found that the day had somehow vanished. They were all suddenly exhausted. Ruby realized that she was splattered with blood. Violet thought how young the airman had looked, and how out of reach was Will, and that soon Ruby would be far away in Oxford, and these thoughts made her sad. Sadness for Violet always turned to briskness and crossness, and so she ordered Ruby into a not very warm bath with Mrs. Morgan's yellow soap, told her off for dripping on the floor, gave her boiled eggs and stewed gooseberries for supper, said she should be thankful, reminded her that there was a war on, bundled her off to the sofa in the front room, and commanded her to sleep.

"Kids," she said irritably, flumping down at the kitchen table with Grandfather and Mrs. Morgan. Grandfather said, yes, vastly overrated, and Mrs. Morgan agreed.

After a while they opened a bottle of last year's rhubarb and barley wine, and although Grandfather said it was raw poison, most of it got drunk. They staggered off to bed at last and were not impressed when Ruby woke them up with shrieks in the middle of the night.

"For goodness' SAKE, Ruby!" said Violet.

"Night terror," said Mrs. Morgan. "Those gooseberries were too much."

"Child," said Grandfather, "we cannot help if you will not control yourself."

Ruby made no attempt to control herself. She blubbered that they must go and save the airman. She jumped out of bed and ran panicking to the door, and would have tugged it open and raced into the night if they hadn't held her back.

"Quickly, before he burns," sobbed Ruby.

Then they thought they understood and gathered around to comfort her.

"Ruby, Ruby," they said, all of them, even Grandfather. "Ruby. Listen. Clarry telephoned from the hospital, not an hour ago, just before we went to bed. He's safe. He's being cared for. Kate's asleep, like you should be, but Clarry's sitting up with him. You did it. You and Kate. He's going to be all right."

Ruby became furious at this stupidity, but it did no good. When they wouldn't let her out of the door, she rushed to the window and tugged at the blackout.

"Ruby!" they said sternly, and pulled her away, and sat her down and told her all over again about the hospital and how wonderful she and Kate had been, and that this was only a nightmare, and that everyone was very, very tired and must now go back to bed.

"You don't understand," said Ruby, blubbering, and they said she was in shock.

"Sugar for shock," said Mrs. Morgan. "I'll go and put the kettle on and make something hot and sweet. And Violet, you telephone the hospital. You won't be popular, this time of night, but maybe it'll put her mind at rest."

With this, they both went off and left Ruby with Grandfather.

"You've got to help," she said to him, hiccuping with misery, and it was at this point that Grandfather produced his magic flask.

"Drink this," he said to Ruby, pouring the silver cup half full, and Ruby, now very thirsty with all her shouting, drank it in one frightful burning swallow, gazed at Grandfather with astonished eyes, and became very woozy indeed.

"Drop more," said Grandfather, administering another dose, and by the time Mrs. Morgan and Violet came back, Ruby was fast asleep on the sofa, perfectly quiet and good.

"Did the trick!" said Grandfather smugly. He was feeling very happy altogether, what with his heroic driving, and ambulance calling, and his own celebratory doses of whisky. "Did the trick. It'll be all right in the morning, and now I'm going to bed."

THIRTY-SIX

Kate

Plymouth, Devon, September 1940

While Ruby was keeping people awake at Mrs. Morgan's cottage, in the hospital in Plymouth there were also dramas. Erik had been x-rayed, and very quickly it had been decided that his arm was so badly hurt, and putting so much strain not only on his heart, but also on his equally damaged shoulder, that it couldn't possibly be saved. The news was told to Clarry at two o'clock in the morning by the elderly doctor who was on duty that night. He spoke as if he couldn't care less about his diagnosis, and was turning to go when Kate, who for hours had been dozing and waking and dozing again in the little, bare, green-painted waiting room, woke instantly and completely.

Kate jumped up, got to the door, leaned against it, and said, "I won't let you cut off his arm."

"I'm sorry. I'm afraid I must ask you not to make a nuisance of yourself," said the doctor, staring. "I need to return to my patient. I really don't know why you're here."

"You've got to ask my dad," said Kate, taking hold of the door handle in both hands. "He's a . . . he's . . ." Her breath caught suddenly, and Clarry took over.

"It would be a good idea to speak to Kate's father," she said, now also on her feet and standing in solidarity with Kate. "He's a surgeon in Oxford. He specializes in reconstructive surgery. If you would give permission for him to come and see your patient, I could telephone right now."

"I very much doubt that he would be able—"

"He would," said Kate, wheezing furiously. "And the airman's not just your patient; he's mine as well. I got him out of the plane."

Something changed in the doctor's face then. Perhaps, as Clarry said afterward, he hadn't understood that Kate had been the one who'd pulled the German pilot from the plane. Perhaps it was Kate's sudden desperate coughing. Whatever it was, he transformed before their eyes from an elderly, impatient doctor into a tired but helpful friend.

"You're quite right," he said, speaking directly to Kate. "If you're the person who rescued him, then the young man is your patient too. I would be very glad of your father's advice. Shall we wake him now, or wait till morning?"

"Now," said Kate. "Thank you. Not in the morning. Now."

THIRTY-SEVEN

Ruby

Mrs. Morgan's cottage, Devon, September 1940

"Snoring," said Ruby, in disgust.

It was dawn, pink dawn over the gray-green fields outside Mrs. Morgan's cottage window. The whole house was snoring, and Ruby had woken in a state of rage. At first she couldn't remember why, and then she did.

Pax was looking at her.

"Come on," she told him. "We're going out."

She found her shoes in the kitchen, and looked around for her clothes, but the only ones she could see were soaking in a bucket. The water was rusty red. Ruby shuddered and turned away. Mrs. Morgan's old garden coat was hanging from a hook in the porch, so she took that instead, pulled it on over her pajamas, and opened the door.

Pax streaked out at once, and then stood watching her, asking where to go.

"Back to where we saw them first," said Ruby.

The garden was very silent, the chickens still shut up, the bees not yet awake. Every leaf was heavy with dew, and the flowers hung like wet laundry. Ruby's feet left dark footprints on the hearthrug lawn.

"We were standing here," she told Pax. "There were two little planes. One turned away and the other fell into the wood. There was a line of black smoke. Then the big plane came over. But before that, there was something else. . . ."

Ruby tried to picture again that split-second moment, between the little plane falling and the big plane so low overhead it had seemed they might reach up and touch it.

"There was something white," she said, and began to run.

The whole of Ruby wanted to believe *parachute*, but she had seen parachutes on a cinema newsreel. They floated. They slid in airy zigzags down the sky. Whatever she had seen hadn't done that: it had tumbled and lurched.

Nevertheless, she carried on, leaving the road to climb gates and cross meadows. Skirting round a field of red-and-white cows. Paddling carefully across the slippery hidden stones of a shallow stream, with Pax behind her, just as cautious.

Arriving at the wood.

The early light hadn't reached it yet. It crouched in its own shadows, greenish and thick with hidden shapes. There was no breeze, but from somewhere seeped a bitter smell, the smell of wet and recent burning. It frightened Ruby, and it frightened Pax, too. He pressed against her legs.

There was no clear way into the wood. It was ringed with tangled brambles.

"We'll go round the edge," said Ruby, leading the way, "until we find an opening."

Pax followed very slowly, pausing often to look mutinously over his shoulder, back the way that they'd come. He'd had enough of wet fields and briars and ice-cold streams. He wasn't a country dog and this girl wasn't Kate. However, a few minutes later, when Ruby suddenly stopped and whispered,

"Pax, oh, Pax," he nudged into her hand for comfort.

Even Pax, city dog that he was, could see that they had arrived at no ordinary tree.

It was enormous, standing right on the edge of the wood. A ravaged oak, laced in torn green ivy, decked with broken branches and garlanded with loops and swags of scorched white silk.

Nothing moved. No birds sang. But the tree spoke.

"You are very beautiful," said the tree, and Ruby jumped and spun round in shock, her hands raised to cover her cheeks.

"There's only me here," she said.

"I am sorry," said the tree apologetically. "I did not mean to frighten you."

Slowly, Ruby lowered her hands. The leaves rustled, a green-and-silver sigh. "You are very, *very* beautiful."

"Where are you?" asked Ruby, trembling, and she clutched Pax hard as she spoke.

The tree didn't seem to notice Pax. It took some time to reply.

"This is a pleasant place," it said eventually.

Ruby peered and peered into the great kaleidoscope pattern of greenness and ivy and oak and twisted silk. She retreated back into the field, hoping to see better from a distance.

"Do not forget me," called the tree hoarsely.

"I was trying to work out where you were."

"Please tell me your name."

"Ruby Amaryllis. Wave your hand or something."

"Pardon?" said the tree.

"Are you hurt?"

"Yes."

"You're German," said Ruby.

"Yes. From Berlin."

"Kristallnacht," said Ruby.

The tree became very quiet.

THIRTY-EIGHT

Erik, Kate, Ruby

England, November 1940

Erik's arm stopped being a weight in a sling and he could move it, lift a cup, turn his hand. His shoulder (explored, cleaned, stitched, and pinned by Peter) became a useful thing again. His fever cooled and his wounds closed and enough new blood flowed in his veins to keep him standing on his feet. He was lucky. He was well.

Well enough to be sent, along with nearly a hundred other German prisoners, on a late Atlantic sea crossing to a camp in Canada.

"Canada?" Kate had repeated, when the news arrived.

"A lot of captured airmen are being sent to camps over there," her father told her, and his words startled Kate. Until that moment, she had thought of Erik as rescued, not captured.

But of course, he was both.

"Why Canada?" she asked, at last.

"I suppose it's so far away there's less chance of people escaping back to Germany and joining up again. It won't be that bad. He should be pretty safe. Safer than flying a fighter plane, anyway."

"Will his arm be all right?"

"It was a straightforward enough mend, once I got every-thing back in place. I did a nice job on his shoulder."

"Good."

Kate hadn't seen Erik since the day she and Ruby pulled him out of his plane. She knew nothing of him except the way he had whispered *danke*, that his eyes had followed Pax. Her father hadn't seen him since the final of the surgeries that had fixed him back together. Yet both of them felt that he was still, somehow, in their care.

"He had a lot of damage in that shoulder," said Peter. "He'll need to build back his movement very carefully. I'm going to write him out a table of exercises to do."

"In English?"

"I'll draw diagrams. You can help."

"All right."

Before Erik was sent away, Peter was able to get a parcel to him. He had to put in a special request to send it, and it had been passed as *Medical Advice and Supplies*. As well as Peter's exercises, they managed to add a German-English dictionary from Clarry, barley sugar from Kate, and yellow soap from Mrs. Morgan, another person who felt that Erik was somehow in her care.

"Could we put in a letter?" asked Kate.

Peter shook his head. "We did well to get permission for the parcel. Barley sugar and soap can count as medical supplies, and the dictionary to help with understanding his exercises, but I think a letter would be pushing our luck too far. I'm pretty certain it would count as fraternizing with the enemy."

"I keep forgetting Erik is supposed to be an enemy," said Kate to Ruby, much later that day. "And we're not meant to know he's going to Canada, either."

It was night, pitch dark in the room they shared, the blackouts down, the school day over, the streets of Oxford running like rivers under yet another deluge of ice-cold November rain. It was the time when they talked.

"Canada?" asked Ruby, who had not heard this before. "Well, I hope he likes bears."

"Why?"

"There's thousands of bears in Canada. I remember reading about them in that book you gave me, and afterward I looked them up. Grizzly bears, eight feet tall with paws as big as dinner plates. Black bears as well, and mountain lions."

"Nowadays?"

"Think so. Packs of wolves, too."

"He'll be all right then," said Kate, with such certainty that Ruby laughed in the darkness.

"I think he likes animals," said Kate. "He liked Pax. I could tell. Isn't it cold? It feels like it might snow."

"Haven't you got warm yet?" asked Ruby. They'd both gone to bed in woolly socks, with old cardigans over their pajamas, but for the first time that winter, it didn't feel like enough.

"Not properly." Kate began tugging the cover from her hot-water bottle in case there was any heat left to be had from its bare rubber inside.

"You can have mine if you like," offered Ruby. Her hot-water bottle was new, and it definitely lasted longer. Sometimes it was still warm in the morning. "I was going to dump it on the floor soon, anyway," she told Kate.

"No, you weren't," said Kate. "You're not that crazy. Besides, I'm having Pax." She slid out from under her blankets, groped across the floor for Pax, snoring in front of the door, lugged him up onto her bed, crawled into the narrow space he left for her, and covered them both with her eiderdown. The effects were immediate and wonderful, worth the venture into the cold. Pax radiated a fuggy warmth more enveloping than half a dozen hot-water bottles.

"I don't know how you bear it," commented Ruby.

"I've got a lavender bag," said Kate. She loved Pax, but she was under no illusions. In bed it was best to have your back to him, and your nose in a lavender bag.

"Oh, let me have a sniff of lavender," begged Ruby, and Kate passed it over in the dark.

"Hmmm," said Ruby, inhaling deeply. "Mrs. Morgan's."

"Yes, she sent it."

"Remember that last day we were there?"

"Yes. Oh, yes," said Kate.

"I wish . . . ," began Ruby, and then paused.

Kate waited, as she had waited so many nights already that winter, understanding that Ruby had memories not easy to shape into words.

"No, it's nothing," said Ruby at last, and then, in a completely different voice, "I wrote to Will today."

Kate nodded invisibly in the dark to show that she was listening.

"I asked Mum to post me Will's chocolate bar and she did and I sent it with my letter."

Kate knew all about that chocolate bar. She knew about Sooty and the arrival of Paddle. She knew about the scrubbing brush and the white water, Mrs. Cohen and the silver photo frame. She knew about the early morning postcard from the German prison camp. Little by little, night by night, Ruby had told her all these things, but she had never ever told her the story of exactly what had happened on that last day at Mrs. Morgan's.

Kate remembered how she and Clarry had come back from the hospital in Plymouth to find Mrs. Morgan making sand-wiches in the kitchen, Grandfather snoring on the sofa, and Ruby nowhere to be seen.

"The German boy . . . the pilot . . . Erik . . . is conscious and talking," Clarry had announced, rushing in. "Kate's had a good sleep in the car. . . ." Then she'd paused, noticing what was going on for the first time. "Goodness, Mrs. Morgan, what's all this?"

"Now, you stop with your questions, and I'll tell you every-thing," Mrs. Morgan had replied, shuffling great heaps of food around the kitchen table as she spoke. "The egg and lettuce are for you to have in the car on your way, and there's half a sponge cake cut in slices and some gooseberries that want eating. So that's that. Those are sardine paste, and them's mar-row and ginger and they're for the teams with the fire engines. There's two of them there now, and a police car as well, and they're sending up a lad to collect—"

"FIRE ENGINES?" burst out Clarry.

"There's no fire," said Mrs. Morgan. "You'll hear if you listen! I've some apples for them too, and yesterday's scones that got forgotten—"

"PLEASE—"

"Stop!" Mrs. Morgan raised a majestic hand, just like

Britannia on the back of a penny only with a bread knife instead of a trident, and when Clarry had closed her mouth, continued, "They're working over by Miller's Wood, past the stream through the bullocks' field, and how Ruby knew it we haven't got out of her. . . ."

"Knew what? Knew what?" asked Kate.

"There's one of them parachutists caught tangled in a tree," announced Mrs. Morgan solemnly. "Been there all night and his plane burned out and goodness knows the state of him—"

"OH NO!" exclaimed both Clarry and Kate.

Mrs. Morgan pointed the bread knife very fiercely indeed at this latest interruption, and then shook her head and whispered hoarsely, "Don't say nothing about that to Ruby, either of you. He was still alive when she came running back, and there's fair hope he'll stay that way. That's all we know for now."

"BUT WHERE . . . ?"

"Violet's had to go. She's said her goodbyes to Ruby and caught the bus back to Plymouth. She couldn't wait, she's on duty tonight. She said to tell you she would write."

"I thought she might have to leave before we got back," admitted Clarry mournfully.

"Now," continued Mrs. Morgan, counting off news items on her fingers. "What else? Your dad's had that flask out, Clarry, I'm sorry to say, but he's caused no trouble and it might be worse. The goat's milked and the hens fed. That dog came back in such a state I've tied him up by the bin. Plastered in mud. He's had two buckets of water over him, but I have to say it's not made a blind bit of difference."

"SO . . . ?"

"So now you know all." Mrs. Morgan had finished, putting

down the bread knife and crossing her hands on her apron. "And where are you off to, young Kate?"

"Ruby," said Kate.

She'd discovered Ruby deep in the greenness of the garden, hunkered down behind the runner beans. Ruby had a very small mirror in her hand, and she was tilting her face from side to side. When Kate arrived, she'd looked up.

"I've seen them now," she'd said.

"Good."

"I don't look awful."

"The opposite of awful," Kate had told her, and had hunched down beside her, hugging her knees.

"Kate, if you didn't see me for ages, and then you did, would you remember who I was?"

"Yes."

"For a long time, years maybe?"

"Probably forever," said Kate.

"Oh," said Ruby, "they're useful then." And she'd looked in the mirror again and laughed, and jumped up and pulled Kate to her feet and hugged her.

"Guess what?" she said.

"What?"

"Nothing."

"Oh, Ruby, what?"

"Tell you one day."

Was it one day yet? wondered Kate, months later, in bed in the dark, with Pax behind her, twitching and snuffling in one of his enormous, animated dreams.

Across the room, Ruby was still silent. Presently she sighed and Kate guessed she was asleep. She still had the lavender bag; she'd forgotten to give it back. The smell of it drifted faintly across the room to Kate, clean and sweet, garden-scented.

Kate wriggled backward into Pax's doggy warmth and remembered once more that September day.

Ruby's face had been shining. Dark-splattered, sun-dappled, bright as light on rippled water.

Very, very beautiful.

Shining.

THIRTY-NINE

Erik

Canada, December 1940–1945/6

Canada, thought Erik.

As Kate's father had guessed, it wasn't that bad. If Erik's flying days were over, then so were his fighting days. Every time he remembered that, he was thankful.

"I was always on the point of falling out of the window," he told an imaginary Hans.

Conversations in his head with Hans were a habit that had begun the September afternoon when he had been shot down over England, and his friend's voice had taken control of his shattered thoughts and talked him down to landing without killing anyone. That time it had happened unconsciously, but now Erik did it quite often. He laughed at himself, but he did it.

Before many months in camp, Erik had picked up English, as nearly everybody had. Soon he found that there were books he could read and courses he could study. In the Luftwaffe he had learned a good deal of engineering, and starting that first winter in Canada, he went on learning more. It quickly came in useful. When spring arrived, prisoners who could be trusted were sent out to work on the local farms. Erik was one of them, and his reputation soon grew. He had always liked mending things, and now he found himself fixing bikes and milking machines, generators and hay binders. He laughed out loud when a small girl arrived in the tractor shed, one hand clutching her father's jacket, a doll held tight in the other.

"Katy-Ann," she said, presenting the doll to Erik like a baton in a relay race. "Her eyes won't open."

"Long ago I had a dolls' hospital," Erik told her, in his new, careful English. "Look away while I operate. I will tell you when it is done."

She looked away, Erik removed Katy-Ann's head, reattached the mechanism that opened and closed her eyes, put her together again, and said, "There you are. I think she's well. If she has a little headache, give her tea with chamomile flowers."

This spectacular repair raised Erik's reputation even higher than fixing the milking machine had done. He was invited to a dolls' tea party.

"You do know everybody is talking about you, don't you?" said Hans the next day, and not for the first time, either.

Erik nodded, and continued working on an ancient seized-up tractor engine that hadn't run for years.

"The great thing about tractors," he explained to Hans, "is that they don't drop twenty thousand feet out of the sky if you happen to get something wrong."

"Clearly we should have flown tractors all along," said Hans.

"It might have been wise."

"You think that thing will ever run again?"

"Sure it will," said Erik, and cranked the engine, and the old tractor rattled and coughed and steadied into a regular *chud-chud-chud* of life. It was harvest time by then, nearly a year since the crash, and they were getting in the wheat and carting it by trailer down to the depot. Now that the farm had an extra tractor, it could be sifted twice as fast.

"We're sending it overseas," said the farmer, when Erik came to tell him the news of his success. "Like to drive a few loads down for me? I'll go ahead, show you the route. You follow on behind."

The old tractor blew out blue smoke and went at a top speed of about ten miles an hour. Its seat was bare steel, and its original color lost in time, but Erik, bumping along the country roads, thought how much better he felt about feeding people than fighting them. A sudden jubilant happiness made him shout out, over the racketing of the engine, "Look at this, Hans!"

"You be careful. Miss that bear!" the voice in his thoughts called back.

Sometimes, in the dusty harvests of summer, the giant snowfalls of winter, war seemed another world away. But then a rare letter would arrive, or a scrap of news would be heard in camp: London was burning, Berlin was a battleground. Rumors would spin the globe of war: Norway, North Africa, Japan, India, Greece, and Malta. Pacts were broken. New weapons invented. Russia became a terror.

America was in.

It was a world war.

FORTY

Will

Germany, 1940–1946

British prisoners of war in Germany nearly all made plans to escape, and some of them managed it, and most of them didn't. The first time Will escaped was easy; he ran away from a work party sent out to help with timber felling. It all went very well. Will made his furtive, hurrying way across three or four miles of farmland at dusk, and was pleased to come across an open barn with a stack of clean hay at the back. He was discovered the next morning by two very small girls, who found him fast asleep there and woke him with their giggles. They were holding hands, standing just inside the open doorway, with the dusty sunbeams flooding in around them. They looked like twins, with their brown boots and stubby brown plaits and identical blue-striped dresses. When they saw Will's eyes open, they asked him very politely if he had slept well, and if he liked their grandfather's barn.

"*Ja, ja,*" said Will, the only word of German he knew. "*Ja, ja,*" he repeated, as if he had understood everything they said, when in fact he had grasped nothing at all.

"*Ja, ja,*" and he nodded his head and smiled.

The little girls smiled back, and one of them held out a small bread roll and asked if he would like it.

"Ja, ja," said Will gratefully, and ate it in three bites.

Nudging each other with anticipation as they spoke, the little girls next asked if he was an escaped prisoner from the camp beside the forest.

Will didn't disappoint them. *"Ja, ja,"* he said enthusiastically.

The little girls smiled more than ever and said something else, which Will guessed was an offer to fetch more bread rolls.

"Ja, ja, ja," he agreed, and they whirled around, and vanished into the morning sunlight, and Will stretched and thought how well he was getting on, happily unaware that what the little girls had actually told him was that they would now go and fetch their grandfather, who had a big gun.

Afterward, in his horrible, much more secure new camp, Will thought about that welcoming open barn with its tempting pile of hay, and he knew what a fool he'd been. It was more than a year before he tried escaping again. This time he had taken the precaution of learning a fair amount of German and, with the help of the camp escape committee, had some much less prisoner-like clothes. Also he had a copy of a map that had arrived in the camp in very small patchwork pieces rolled up in cigarettes. With its help, he headed south toward the border with neutral Switzerland, and he was two weeks into his journey, when early one damp morning he came across a bicycle. It had been discarded at the side of a road, with not a soul in sight.

Will was very tired of walking and eating raw potatoes and sleeping under hedges and hiding in ditches and trudging, trudging, trudging with nothing on his feet but the remains of his soccer shoes and blisters. He wanted the journey finished.

It was the barn and the hay bed all over again.

The owner of the bike chased after him on a better, faster one and caught up with him at his first flat tire. He was a much less pleasant captor than the little girls had been, and Will had a couple of very bad days until, once again, they took him prisoner and put him into a camp. Just as before, it was far tougher than the last, and he had to make new friends again, and wait even longer for his parcels to arrive. He gave up all hope of escaping for a third time. He didn't want to risk it; he was afraid of being shot. He wanted to get home. In his bunk at night, he walked the streets of Plymouth and he thought if he ever got there he would earn his living as a postman because he had got so fond of parcels. Even more than that, above all things, he wanted to get back and hug his mum and make it up to Ruby. The first winter that he had been a prisoner she had sent him the chocolate bar from behind the kitchen clock. The paper wrapper was faded to grayness and the chocolate had turned pale and crumbly, but the message that came with it had read:

> Peace, pax, friends.
> Love from Ruby Amaryllis
> Come home soon and say, What's an amaryllis anyway?

In Will's latest prison camp, there were experts on lots of things. To help pass the time and keep the grinding hunger and boredom at bay, they used to do sports and concerts and plays, and quite often they would take it in turn to give lectures. Bird-Watching, War Poets, Scottish Mountains, The Ten

Best Pubs in Plymouth with route maps in between them and illustrations of their signs (that was Will's). One evening, someone spoke about growing flowers and was pleased to answer questions. That was why, years later when the war finally ended, and Will was on his way home at last, he lingered for a while in the Netherlands. The hungry Netherlands, where the winter before had been a famine, and the people had eaten grass and tulip bulbs. Although food had arrived at last, the children were still white-faced and thin, and you could trade chocolate or tinned army rations for almost anything. Will had traveled from his camp in a US army truck, and he had both chocolate and tinned beef in his pack. He went about the streets and markets with one request that he repeated over and over, and at last somebody offered what he sought. It was a swollen, bruised-looking thing, wrapped in ancient newspaper. Acquiring it bankrupted Will of both chocolate and tins, and he was sure he'd been cheated, but he took it home anyway and gave it to Ruby.

It grew long leaves and a tall green spike, and then great, glowing, ruby-red trumpets, speckled inside with gold and chocolate. It lit the room like a flame. It shone for weeks, and Will and Ruby and Violet never stopped dragging people in to admire it.

"That's an amaryllis," Will would tell them with pride. "It's a flower like a lily, but better."

FORTY-ONE

Kate

Oxford, February 1946

Pax still looked like an animal raised in a scrapyard, but it was a long time since he had worn the rope collar and the leather luggage label. For six years he had owned the respectable brass tag of a dog with a home. Kate had kept the leather label, however, and now she threaded it back onto his collar. She put it there because she guessed it had come from somebody who loved him, before she had, before Rupert had, in his unknown past before the war.

This night, Kate thought, Pax needed love. After the last goodbyes on the doorstep he had sunk into a shabby heap. They'd carried him in and the vet had come and said, "Slowing down now. Not surprising with that heart, and he's fifteen years, or more, I would guess. What do you want me to do?"

"Nothing if you don't have to," said Kate, and the vet said, no, he didn't have to, Pax was probably just slipping away in his own time. Not in pain.

They had laid him on the hearthrug, because that was his favorite place, and he hadn't moved since. All the house was asleep now, except for Kate, and in the old red armchair across from the fire, Grandfather, in much the same state as Pax.

Kate was, as so often, writing. Catching the moment before it was gone.

This is now, she thought as she wrote. *Now Pax. Now Grandfather. Now the fire glow, the flames finished, the ashes whitening. Now the rain in the street.*

Too precious to be wasted.

That day family had gathered and gone. Charlie and Tod to the station together, Janey to her college, Bea and her little daughter, Barley, back to their Lincolnshire lambs. *Goodbye, good dog, best dog,* they had whispered at the door. Barley said, "Kiss him better," and stooped with a kiss, but he hadn't got better. He was deep, deep asleep, blanketed and layered and heavy with time.

"Pax," murmured Kate, with a hand on his shoulder, and, with infinite effort, he raised very slightly one gray wispy eyebrow.

"He heard you then," commented Grandfather. "Done well. Done very well." He was sitting the night out with Kate, with his glass of whisky and the firelight and no particular thought except that the girl might need company. He'd done well too, he considered. Kept them steady. Voice of reason. Found the words for Charlie when Simon's ship was lost. Torpedoed in the North Atlantic, and the boy had been bent with grief, speechless, until he had unlocked a memory.

"That night, that Christmas Eve he sang in church. Your doing, wasn't it?"

Charlie had looked up, surprised.

"I knew! Saw your face. What was it?"

"Once In," said Charlie.

"Watched him," Grandfather had continued. "He had a look

not often seen." Grandfather had paused. He had no easy access to the words of happiness: *radiant, glowing, luminous.*

Yet he found the right one. "Joyful."

He and Charlie had become friends. It was Charlie who'd got him to his feet that afternoon, to make his wedding speech for Clarry and Rupert. *Charlie and Kate,* Grandfather thought. *Pick of the bunch. No brains, unfortunately.*

He looked across at the girl.

"Still writing?"

"Finished now."

"Astonishing how you keep it up."

It was true, Kate thought. She had kept it up. More or less. Simon had silenced her for a while, but eventually she'd picked up her pencil again. The stack of exercise books had grown. As the war went on, paper had been hard to come by, but in a way, that had helped. She'd learned to ration words, to tell a happening in a few lines. Untangling Ruby's story: following the threads, she'd learned to listen.

"Dog still with us?" asked Grandfather, breaking the silence.

"Fast asleep. Nice and warm. I was thinking about Ruby."

Grandfather snorted. "That one. Girl who fell in love with a tree. Don't look like that! Fact. Charlie told me."

Kate laughed.

"Asked me to dance this afternoon," he said. "At my age!"

"But you did. I saw you."

"Totter. Gave it a totter. She in your book?"

"Of course. And you."

"I'm in there?"

"Lots of times."

"Good. I did my bit, didn't I?"

"Every single night," said Kate. *Give me a job,* he'd said, and Vanessa had given him the blackout to manage. He'd relished it; no glimmer of light had escaped the house through all the years of the war.

"That German lad you got out the plane. What about him? In there too?"

"I wrote as much as I know, but I wish it was more."

"Hun!"

"He wasn't."

"How'd he end up flying a Messerschmitt then? I was ready with that fork, you know. One bad move and I'd have been there."

Kate kindly didn't say, *You were stuck in a hedge,* but she did remark, "You'd never have used it."

"Wouldn't I? Think I'm soft?"

"Yes."

Grandfather grunted and sank back in his chair. Pax sighed and Kate rubbed his ears. His tail lifted a fraction. *See that?* Grandfather wanted to ask, but hadn't the energy.

For an hour he slept, his breathing irregular, crackling like scrunched-up paper crackles. Shallow. When he woke, Kate was half asleep herself, curled on the hearthrug, her cheek against the ancient dog. She opened her eyes to find him gazing at her.

"You'd better find out."

"Find out?" she repeated, bewildered with sleep.

Grandfather spoke slowly, between breaths. "The boy . . . in the plane . . . How he got there."

"I could try."

"Do it. Could make a real book. All the tales."

"Perhaps."

"Put me in. Don't forget."

"Never."

"Promise? Be . . . a task."

"I'll do it. I really will. I promise."

"Left you my money. When I'm dead."

"Don't talk like that!"

"What there is. What I didn't . . . drink."

"Grandfather! You're not going to die."

"Oh, yes I am," he said, suddenly vigorous. "Oh, yes. Dog will see another day, though. Look!"

Kate turned to Pax and saw his head raised, eyes now open, brightness there. Thump went his tail. Another day.

"Oh Pax, oh Pax," she murmured.

"Odd choice," said Grandfather. "Odd"—he stopped, started again—"name."

"It's another word for . . . Grandfather . . . Grandfather?"

He smiled at her, and the years fell away from him. It was Charlie's smile, wistful, merry, endearingly kind. He said, "Peace," and closed his eyes.

FORTY-TWO

Erik

On the way home, June 1947

When the war ended, all over the world there were millions of people in places where they had never planned to be. It took months and often years to get them on their way back home again. It was nearly two years for Erik. He traveled by lorries and trains and ships, by America and England and France, and the nearer he got to home, the more he feared what he would find. He'd read the newspapers and heard the broadcasts, seen the sickening newsreels of the concentration camps.

His mother was back in Berlin. *For good or bad, nowhere else is home,* she'd written. She had found some rooms in a building on the outskirts of the shattered city.

Even smaller than the last, she wrote, *but there is a school for Frieda where I have cleaning work and also serve the hot meals that the Americans supply. Good soup, a whole mug each, with peas or meat in it. The children drink it thankfully and we see the difference it makes.*

If one mug of soup could make a difference, thought Erik, what had it been like before? He remembered the meals of his own childhood, the winter broths, the sausages and pancakes, apples and Christmas gingerbread, Hans's mother's homemade plum cake with whipped cream on top. Lisa would wrinkle her nose and spoon her cream onto Erik's slice.

Lisa, lost in the bombings of Berlin, but always, always when Erik thought of her, turning her defiant cartwheels in the snow.

Hans's father and mother were gone too. *They just gave up, after Lisa,* his mother had written. Frieda was well, a bright lovely girl of twelve. Uncle Karl, condemned as a traitor, had stood blindfolded in front of a Nazi firing squad, having done what he could once too often.

Armer Mann, Erik's mother wrote, and he could hear her voice in the words. *Poor man.*

The journey home had seemed endless. Nights sitting upright, dozing into days of weary boredom. Snatched meals of bread and cooling, chicory-flavored coffee. Wariness of strangers, sleeping always with your belongings hugged tight in your arms. All the people hungry, all the landscapes war-broken, and all of them alien. Erik lost track of time. He had written that he was on the way, but he hadn't been able to guess the day he would arrive.

So, of course, there'd been no one at the station to meet him. There were no familiar faces in the bomb-shattered streets. The address his mother had sent was hard to find, away from the center of the city.

Yet he got there at last, pushed open the heavy door that led from the street, and paused.

Someone had swept the stairs very clean, and as he climbed them, Erik could smell cooking. Potato pancakes, the sort he had eaten as a little boy, with applesauce or a sausage or a dollop of sour cream. Hans, if he could get it, used to like them best with cheese.

"Hans, I'm back," said Erik.

As he climbed past each floor, there were quiet, closed doors. At one he heard a baby cry, and from another there was the sound of a static-bothered radio. Then he was on the fourth flight, the last flight, and there were voices.

Familiar voices, that chattered, and then paused.

They'd heard his footsteps on the stairs.

"It's me," called Erik, setting down his armload of packages, and then, with a catch in his throat because the silence on the other side of the door had grown so long, "It's only me. It's Erik."

The door was flung open and they hauled him into a room filled with light. There was a large gray cat, a table set for supper, and an album of fairy-tale cigarette cards lying open on a chair. There was Frieda's screech of delight, his mother's joyful, "Come here! Come here!" and an explosion of miniature firecracker sounds, "Tck! Tck! Tck!"

"Kleine Oma, see, it's Erik!" shouted Frieda, prancing with excitement. "Tante Anna, did you know? Erik, Erik, you came back!"

"Frieda!" said Erik, turning to hug thin, long-legged Frieda. "Fräulein Trisk. Oh, Fräulein Trisk, I thought of you so often. Wait, I'll fetch what I brought you!"

"Presents!" exclaimed Frieda, and Erik, returning with his packages, really had managed presents. Tinned meat and a bag of rice, a box of dried egg. Chocolate for Frieda, a package of coffee for his mother, and something he'd bought at a stall by the train station in Paris, and clutched to his chest all the way to Berlin.

"Oh," said Fräulein Trisk. "Oh," and she looked up at Erik's mother. "Oh," she said to her. "Look, a new fern, green as a forest."

The new apartment was very small. A room with two narrow beds for Fräulein Trisk and Erik's mother. A curtained alcove for Frieda that opened from the kitchen, which was also the living room. Erik, Frieda observed, would have to sleep under the kitchen table.

"That will be no trouble," said Erik. "I slept on a luggage trolley in Paris."

"No, you didn't!"

"Yes, I did. There it was, all flat and empty. There I was, in need of a bed. In England I slept in a bus."

"All night?"

"No, but all one afternoon. I didn't mean to. I just closed my eyes for a little minute and the next thing I knew, I was at the bus depot and there was a whole crowd of people looking down at me."

"What did they say?"

"They asked, 'What are you doing here?'"

"What *were* you doing there?"

"It's such a long story, Frieda. Before I was sent to Canada, I had a parcel from the people who had helped me when my plane came down. The ones who were there at the time, and the surgeon who saved my arm . . ." Erik paused and laughed. "And an old lady who lived nearby. She was a friend of theirs. She put in a big bar of yellow soap. . . ."

"Useful," said his mother, nodding. Two years after the war

had ended, a bar of soap was still a thing of value in Berlin.

"Yes," agreed Erik. "And she wrote a message on it too. Here . . ."

From the breast pocket of his jacket, Erik pulled a bundle of papers. Letters. An ancient ticket to the Berlin Zoo. Battered photographs in black and white. Frieda flicked through them and said, "No picture of me. Tante Anna and I sent you one, I remember, two Christmases ago. Both of us together. Did you lose it?"

"Sorry, Frieda. I gave it away."

"Erik!"

"You'll not mind when I explain. Look, this is what I wanted to show you. The message from the soap."

Erik held out a scrap of yellow soap wrapper, with careful letters in old-fashioned handwriting.

"I kept it because it was so kind," he said. "It made me smile. It's in English, of course, but I'll translate. It says: 'One fine day you come back and see us properly, young man!'"

"In Canada, I often wondered if I could really do that," he continued, "find the people who had helped me, I mean. Then I heard that to get back to Germany I had to travel by England, so I thought perhaps I could make a detour. If I could find the hospital where they took me, I hoped it would be a start. In the end it was easier than that. When I reached the city, I caught a bus and fell asleep, like I told you. . . ."

"And when you woke up, there were all the people," prompted Frieda. "Saying 'What are you doing?'"

"Exactly. And as soon as I started to explain, one of them stepped forward and said, 'You're German, aren't you?'"

"Oh no!" said Frieda, clutching her hands to her mouth.

"I know. But it was all right. He said, 'From Berlin.' So I said, 'Yes, from Berlin. How did you guess?' and he laughed and said, 'I know someone who talks just like you.'"

His mother suddenly gasped.

"And that's how I found . . ."

Erik's face gave him away, so alight was his smile.

"HANS!" shrieked Frieda.

"Hans!" said Erik's mother. "Oh, my dear heart! Oh, Erik! Is he safe? Is he well?"

It was nearly eight years since they'd last seen Hans, more than six since they had heard any word of him.

"Yes, yes," said Erik. "He's safe and well. He was badly hurt, but he got better."

"And you met him? You spoke to him?"

"Just for an hour at the end of the day. He's based in a camp, still waiting to be repatriated. They send work teams into the city, clearing the bomb sites, and that's where I met him."

"How did you know the way?"

"He took me. Will. The person from the bus. He was very kind."

"And did Hans know you straightaway?" asked his mother.

"Yes. I said, 'Hello, Hans,' and he looked at me and said, very slowly, 'Erik? Erik? Well.'"

Erik paused, remembering what had come next. It had been oddly awkward. He'd wanted to grab Hans, fling his arms round his shoulders like they'd done when they were boys. But instead he'd just nodded and said, "Yes. Well, Hans."

"They're all lost," Hans had said blankly. "At home. All lost."

"No!" he'd exclaimed. "No, Hans. Not Frieda."

"Not Frieda?" Hans had repeated.

"Frieda is with my mother."

"Frieda is with your mother? Safe with your mother?"

"Yes."

"You're sure of that?"

"Yes. Yes." Suddenly Erik had remembered, fumbled in his pocket, found the photograph they'd sent him two Christmases ago. Hans took it and stared, and then he cried out to everyone around, the people he was working with, the people in the street:

"My little sister is with his mother! *Meine kleine Schwester ist bei seiner Mutter!*" He'd seized Erik and hugged him then, held him tight and shouted again, "My little sister is with his mother! *Meine kleine Schwester ist bei seiner Mutter!*" louder each time, tears rolling down his cheeks.

"He was overjoyed to hear you were here with Tante Anna and Kleine Oma," Erik told Frieda. "He didn't believe it until I gave him your photograph."

"Will he come back to Berlin?"

"Yes, as soon as he possibly can."

"We had one letter years ago," said Erik's mother. "I wrote when his parents died, but we had no reply. Of course, we moved around after we left Berlin. . . . He knows about his parents?"

"Yes. And Lisa." Erik was quiet for a moment. Lisa, always arguing, always hoping. Lisa in the snow. "Yes, he knew," he continued. "He had your letter. But he could find out no more. With help from the Red Cross, he managed to contact our old teacher, you remember Herr Schmidt? But Herr Schmidt could give no news of any of you."

"Poor, poor Hans," said Erik's mother.

"Not too poor anymore," said Erik. "Not now he has Frieda, and also"—Erik paused—"and also Ruby."

"And *who*?" asked Frieda, instantly suspicious.

"Ruby. Ruby is the girl who saw his parachute open, and went to look for him."

"And did she help rescue you, too?"

"Yes, she and Kate together."

"You met the girl Kate as well?" asked his mother.

"Yes. She's learning to be a nurse now. She said I was her first patient. She drove down with her father when they heard I was in England. He was the doctor who fixed my shoulder."

"Of course, of course," said his mother. "But first, tell us about Hans."

"Yes. Hans comes first. Ruby never lost contact with him. Hans visits their home sometimes, since it's been allowed."

Frieda was watching him.

"Frieda, I have to tell you something very important about Ruby. Hans said I must."

"Why did he?"

"Because he's going to marry her."

"MARRY HER?" shouted Frieda, and fell flat on the floor.

"Tck, tck," said Fräulein Trisk. "You are a very noisy girl, Frieda. How can you be so surprised at a happy ending, after all those fairy tales you read?"

"Is she nice?" demanded Frieda from the floor.

"Yes."

"Pretty?"

"Very."

"Does she like cats?"

"Yes."

"How do you know?"

"She invited me to visit. Her family were very good to me. They have two cats named Sooty and Paddle."

"English names," said Frieda.

"Very nice cats," said Erik.

"Oh, well," said Frieda. "I suppose he'd better marry her then."

The lovely laughter of home.

"And you, Erik," said his mother at last. "What are your plans now?"

"We have to start again," said Erik, stretching and running his hands through his curly brown hair. "We have to fix so many things."

"The zoo?" asked Frieda. "They say at school one day they will rebuild the zoo. Please fix the zoo, Erik. Then you can work there, and take care of all the animals, and Hans can help."

"No, no," said Erik, smiling down at her. "Hans always had other plans. I was to work at the zoo, but he was going to have a pastry stall outside the gates and sell apple strudel and almond cake and hot chocolate and lemonade. We arranged it years ago."

"Dreamers," said his mother lovingly.

"Tck, tck, who knows?" said Fräulein Trisk. "Some dreams come true. You were a good boy, Erik, except that time you lost those mittens. You were our little sugar rose."

"Erik," exclaimed Frieda, "a little sugar rose!"

"And Hans was Dumpling Boy," remembered Erik's mother.

"And what am I?" asked Frieda.

"You are our shining girl," said Erik's mother, hugging her.

But for Erik, so long away, they were all shining at that moment. It was June, and the evening light was apricot gold, streaming in through the high window. He pushed it open to look out over the city.

"Long ago, I had three small birds," he told Frieda. "They'd fallen from their nest, and I kept them safe in my winter hat, which was never the same again. When they were big enough, they flew away. But . . . do you see?"

All over the rooftops of Berlin, the broken rooftops and the whole, there were swallows weaving sky trails.

"They're back again," said Erik.

"Do they always come back?" asked Frieda, leaning over the windowsill to look.

"Careful," said Erik. "Don't fall out! Yes, always, every spring."

THE WORLD
BEHIND
THE STORY

Kate and Ruby, Erik and Hans, were of the generation of young people born between two wars. That is, World War I (1914–1918) and World War II (1939–1945).

In the days when Kate and Ruby grew up, there were fewer cars in England. Money was different: pennies and shillings, half crowns and sixpences and threepenny bits. After primary age, girls went to girls' schools, and boys went to boys' schools. There were no antibiotics, so if you were like Kate, always catching things, you were probably fussed over with umbrellas and advice and extra-warm vests. World War I was over, but not forgotten. What everyone wanted was for there never to be another war. My own grandfather fought in World War I and he survived it, and came home, and he could just about bear it (as long as he never had to talk about it), but what he could not bear was the thought of his own two sons having to go through the same.

Probably everyone felt pretty much like that.

In Germany at this time, the shock of losing World War I was still affecting every part of society. There was great poverty, and a feeling that justice had not been done. People wanted change: national pride to be restored, and stronger leadership.

Adolf Hitler promised these things, and he was the leader of the Nazi Party, which became more and more powerful, year after year.

At first Hitler and his party gave people hope. There were more jobs, and less poverty. There was money for education, and industry. There were things to be proud of: a healthier population, investments in arts and science (which included Erik's beloved Berlin Zoo). But at the same time, growing just as quickly, was the terrible darkness of the persecution of the Jewish people. It's really not my story to write, because I am not Jewish, but also it's not my story to ignore, because while one part of society can say of another part, "They are not like us and we don't want them," no one, none of us, should forget what happened before when that was said, and what must never happen again.

FAMILY TREES

(with thanks to Venetia)

🌿 PENROSE FAMILY 🌿

This family also includes Rupert, as honorary uncle to Janey, Bea, Simon and Todd, Charlie, and Kate, although he was in fact no relation at all and, as Grandfather often gracelessly remarked, a cuckoo in the nest.

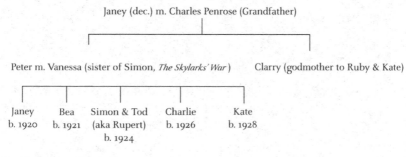

Janey (dec.) m. Charles Penrose (Grandfather)

Peter m. Vanessa (sister of Simon, *The Skylarks' War*)   Clarry (godmother to Ruby & Kate)

Janey	Bea	Simon & Tod	Charlie	Kate
b. 1920	b. 1921	(aka Rupert)	b. 1926	b. 1928
		b. 1924		

🌿 RUBY'S FAMILY 🌿

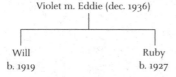

Violet m. Eddie (dec. 1936)

Will	Ruby
b. 1919	b. 1927

🌿 ERIK'S FAMILY 🌿

Anna m. Otto (dec.)

Erik
b. 1921

🌿 HANS'S FAMILY 🌿

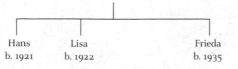

Hans's mother m. Hans's father (elder brother of Uncle Karl)

Hans	Lisa	Frieda
b. 1921	b. 1922	b. 1935

✴

ACKNOWLEDGMENTS

There would be no books without editors, and I have the best. Thank you, Sam and the lovely publishing team at Macmillan, who have been unfailingly supportive. Thank you, Karen Wojtyla at Simon & Schuster in New York, especially for loving Pax.

Thanks also to Fraser Crichton, for the most helpful copy edit I've had in thirty-plus years of writing.

Molly, my brilliant agent, Hans made it because of you.

British Library in St. Pancras, I salute you. Your staff were magnificent before lockdown, but after that time, when I thought, *Now I'm on my own,* I wasn't. Thank you for the shipping lists from Plymouth, and the maps of Berlin streets, and the articles discussing the historic price of rubies.

I wrote this book through grim pandemic days. I couldn't have done it without my lovely kids, working far harder than I, in hospitals and single-bedrooms-turned-into-call-centers, locked down in London and Manchester. Thank you, Jim and Bella, for keeping me going.

Venetia, who did the editing, suggested and put together a set of family trees for each main character. They are on the previous page.

HILARY McKAY is the award-winning author of *The Time of Green Magic* (which received five starred reviews), *The Skylarks' War* (which was a Boston Globe Best Book and received three starred reviews), *Binny Bewitched* (which was a Kirkus Reviews Best Book of the Year and received two starred reviews), *Binny in Secret* (which received three starred reviews), *Binny for Short* (which received four starred reviews), and six novels about the Casson family: *Saffy's Angel, Indigo's Star, Permanent Rose, Caddy Ever After, Forever Rose*, and *Caddy's World*. She is also the author of *Wishing for Tomorrow*, the sequel to Frances Hodgson Burnett's *A Little Princess*, and *Straw into Gold*. Hilary lives with her family in Derbyshire, England. Visit her at HilaryMcKay.co.uk.